Hotel Oriente

To Billy,
With all my love.
Welcome home!
Jennifer Hallou

Hotel Oriente

Jennifer Hallock

Book design by Stephen Wallace

Cover photograph used under license from Shutterstock.com

Printed in the United States of America

First Printing, February 2016

ISBN-13: 978-1530176090

ISBN-10: 1530176093

Little Brick Books
PO Box 498
Weare, NH 03281

www.LittleBrickBooks.com

Suppose you were an idiot. And suppose you were a member of Congress. But I repeat myself.

Mark Twain

CHAPTER ONE

Pawn

Della Berget lashed her steamer chair to the bow rail and wrapped herself snugly in a rubber poncho. Wave after wave of sea spray beat against her face as the *Kilpatrick* tumbled through the mouth of Manila Bay. She laughed as the ship bucked the waves—laughed or squealed or shrieked or whooped, she did not know. It hardly mattered since her grandfather, Hughes Holt, Representative of the Second District of West Virginia, was not there to be embarrassed by the sound. He had shut himself away in the first-class lavatory to keep his seasickness a state secret. Great men did not like to be brought low by their stomachs.

Too bad for him, Della thought. He could not see their approach to Manila, a city of red Spanish-tiled roofs set against distant green mountains. He could not see the charming mismatch of Intramuros, an old Spanish walled enclave in the style of Gibraltar, plunked down in the middle of the tropics. He could not see how close both he and Della were to their individual-but-intertwined destinies.

In the calmer waters close to the city, a steam launch approached from starboard. It carried men with tanned, rested, and salubrious faces. These were men confident in the working order of their digestive systems, Della noticed. They were the men who would inspect the *Kilpatrick* to determine if the smallpox outbreak in Singapore had made it aboard ship.

How the Bureau of Health distinguished between the early stages of smallpox and ordinary seasickness was a mystery, especially when the decks were so crowded with soldiers that those who could not force their way to the railing had to vomit in buckets, in their shoes, or on the deck. These boys had enlisted to prove their manliness through the forge of battle, but instead they spent their last day of peace in white-knuckled, unmanly terror. Of course, had they possessed any sort of readiness for ocean travel, they would have joined the Navy instead of the Army. Sadly, a number of them would not live to prove themselves more seaworthy on a transport home. The guerrilla insurrection of the Filipinos was proving a costly one.

Fortunately, the transport passed inspection, thanks to the timely appearance on deck of Congressman Holt. A progressive in favor of new American markets in the East, her grandfather had been a loyal friend to every Philippine appropriations bill that came his way, and local officials would do nothing to impede his disembarkation.

New boats clustered around the *Kilpatrick*: clumsy native craft about seven feet wide and fifty feet long, each with an arched hood of dried grass. The pilots maneuvered their floating houses against the white hull of the enormous transport. If one miscalculated, his boat would either be sucked under the *Kilpatrick* or tossed up against its side. The Filipinos jockeyed to get the best position in front of the line, where escape was easiest if the water got rough; and the American crew tried in vain to direct the chaos from the steps above the water. All the seamen gestured frenetically, trying to make themselves understood in different languages above a furious wind.

Della smiled. She felt right at home.

Once the lighters were stacked three or four deep along the length of the *Kilpatrick*, she and her grandfather scrambled over the inner boats to get to one at the head of the line. Holt dragged Della into the darkness under the musty hood, sat her down, and turned back to look after their luggage.

She smelled her new neighbor before she saw him. The rooster was tucked under a bench in a nifty bamboo cage, and—if his flared neck feathers were any indication—he did not appreciate sharing accommodations. Piled on top of the cage was a thick, scratchy hemp cover, but Della would not yank it down—doing so would engulf the bird in darkness, and losing a sense against one's will was never calming.

Their boat was under way. Holt, still the biggest cock on board, dealt with stress in his usual way: self-important tirades. At first, Della paid attention to his tantrum because it amused her. Her grandfather could work himself up over anything—he even blamed the swelling around his eyes on the climate, instead of on the time he had spent bent over the toilet in his stateroom. When Della tired of his complaints she shut her eyes.

But she soon realized her mistake—there was much to see outside—and poked her head around the edge of the matted roof to watch their approach into the bowels of the city. They pulled past a large fort flying the American flag and headed into the mouth of the Pasig, a river as wide as the Potomac but ten times as crowded. Bossy American steamers, lighters heavy with food and livestock, outrigger fishing boats, and single-man canoes fought upstream for a space at the north-side dock. Her boat won a place and tied up in front of a huge warehouse marked *Produce Depot*.

The place swarmed with natives, all eager to sell trinkets to the new arrivals. Della was the first to be hauled to shore, and since she was used to being a curiosity, the open stares did not bother her. People pawed her arms to get her attention, but that was okay too. She was starved for touch. And no one here assumed she could understand their strange words—a freeing lack of expectations.

Her grandfather did not know what to make of all the chattering brown people hawking everything from pineapple sticks to jasmine flower necklaces. It was not the welcome he had been expecting.

Della closed her eyes again and let her feet feel the activity of the city surrounding them: the quick strike of horse hooves, the plodding thud of huge horned carabao, and the irregular beat of cart wheels moving across uneven stones. The air was spiced with sweat, humidity, and a dash of excrement.

She opened her eyes just in time to see an escort approach. This man, indistinguishable from the other Americans in his white pants and white jacket, introduced himself to her grandfather. His eyes darted past Della as he gave a quick, awkward smile. Obviously he had been told about her in advance.

He extricated his charges from the disappointed crowd and led the guests to a line of two-wheeled carriages. Della carefully watched the driver's hands secure the horses before she climbed in.

The entourage rode in a line through the beautiful, crowded streets. There was a strange jumble to the buildings, as if all the architects had been given instructions in a foreign tongue and each had interpreted the plan a little differently. One thing they all had in common were the large, colorful signs that advertised the wares kept inside:

Adolfo Richter, Fabrica de Sombreros.
The Central Studio, Photographers.
Singer, Máquinas para Coser.

Above the merchants' shingles were rows and rows of windows, each a checkerboard of wood and ivory shell. All were slid shut against the heat of the day. The crowds, the colors, the textures—it was a silent symphony.

The line of carriages pulled into a traffic circle—or, rather, a traffic oval—and passed an ornately appointed cigar factory. It was a three-story building with balustrades, carved arches, and five-ball lamps on the balcony. The carriage stopped next door, in front of a building just as grand. Also three stories, it was a little less Morocco and a little more Madrid. Three large arches decorated both sides of the grand entrance. This was the Hotel de Oriente, the Waldorf Astoria of Manila.

Della watched her grandfather disembark into the small crowd gathered near the door of the hotel. Waiting there were a few obsequious bureaucrats eager to keep their funding; one or two local elites seeking favor; and a few reporters whom Holt himself had summoned with cable updates from each major port of call: Malta, Port Said, and Colombo. The newsmen were unconcerned about their shabbily-tied bows, non-existent jackets, and soiled armpits. Their words would be dressed up just fine under the mastheads of the important papers of Washington and New York. It was her grandfather's job to woo them, not the other way around.

Holt turned to Della, his wrinkled face aping concern for his precious ward. It was an act, one that she was prepared to play out with him. She walked obediently to his side.

There were too many people talking at once. She wanted to ask them to take turns, but this was his show, not hers.

"Congressman," one of the reporters said, pushing forward impatiently. Della concentrated on the man's mouth as he spoke. "You must have heard by now of the proclamation of martial law, but you still felt it safe to come to the Philippines. Do you disagree with the necessity of the general's order?"

Della turned to watch her grandfather. She knew he had expected this question, practiced for it. "The Army's final blow must be the hardest. It is because of General Arthur MacArthur's order that we are closer to civil government in the Philippines."

The reporter asked the inevitable follow-up: "You think the guerrillas are finished? The war is won?"

Her grandfather smiled, ready for his moment. Della carefully watched his words.

"I ask you," he said, "if I had any less faith in the future of peace, would I have brought my granddaughter here with me? Surely, if these islands are safe enough for a vulnerable woman like my Della here, they are safe for any American. Not only is she young and naive—the girl is deaf."

Della glanced back at the reporter, anxious to see what he would make of this. He looked to be struck as dumb as he probably assumed she was. The bureaucrats and hangers-on nodded their heads but looked bewildered. The other reporters gave her piteous looks, as if she were blind to their condescension, not deaf to it.

Della shaped her features to show timidity, fear, and just the right touch of vacancy. The guise was a small price to pay for her passage. The next step would be harder.

CHAPTER TWO

Eggs and Floods

Moss North stood by the entrance to the Hotel de Oriente and watched Congressman Holt and his granddaughter descend from their *calesa*. Moss wondered what he had gotten himself into.

"The girl doesn't look deaf," his assistant, Seb, said.

Moss watched the young woman in question. "What does that mean?"

"I have no idea," the Filipino admitted. "She is handsome enough, I suppose."

The woman appeared to be in her early twenties. She had brown hair, a pointed chin, and a fine nose, but there was something odd about her. Maybe it was in the eyes? "She doesn't look all that bright," Moss decided.

"Good. Dumb is easy to please."

Moss sighed. "The Congressman is going to be trouble, isn't he?"

"Of course. He is an American."

"I'm American," Moss pointed out.

"You cannot help it."

Had Moss been in a better mood, he would have laughed. He had known Eusebio Lopa almost three years, which was forever by

American colonial standards. Moss had been one of the first Americans to land on Philippine soil, back when the 13th Minnesota Volunteers seized the city from the Spanish. After the glory of victory faded, Company E was relegated to police duty. That was when Moss met Seb, a lieutenant at the David Street Station in Binondo. They remained friends after Moss left the Army, and now Seb had joined Moss in hotel work.

"Do you think we're ready for this?" Moss did not admit his worries often, but right now he could use some reassurance. The two men had only taken over management of the Oriente the previous week.

"We are the best in Manila."

That was not saying much. Manila was almost as untamed as the American West. Four days before, the rest of the world had rung in the twentieth century, but everyone here was still cleaning up a nineteenth century mess.

In 1898 the first American battle with Spain had been won not in the Caribbean, but in the Pacific. President William McKinley had been so thrilled with Commodore—now Admiral—Dewey's victory at the Battle of Manila Bay that he ordered the Army to take the Spanish guns, then the city, and then finally the whole island chain, for which he later paid Madrid twenty million dollars. Just like that, the United States of America had an overseas empire.

But no one had asked the Filipinos for their opinions on self-government, and rebel leader Emilio Aguinaldo harassed the American newcomers with his guerrilla army. Three years on, the stateside jubilation that had greeted war with Spain had left America with a mighty Philippine hangover. Aguinaldo escaped every trap set by the pursuing American Army, and his escapades encouraged rebellion throughout the islands. General Arthur MacArthur placed the entire country under martial law and pursued the *insurrectos* without restraint. Though the capital was outwardly calm, fierce battles were still being fought only fifty miles from Manila.

None of this drama made it easy for an honest hotelier to obtain regular, reasonably priced staples for his kitchen. Most managers stockpiled supplies to guard against lean times, but the previous ownership of the Oriente had cleaned out the storeroom. Since Moss was left with nothing but bare shelves, it was a miracle he had kept the dining room running at all—albeit with a painfully limited menu. As if the shortages were not bad enough, Moss now had to cater to a spoiled American politician.

If it weren't for American politicians, though, he would not have the job at the Oriente. The new Australian, Scottish, and Filipino owners wanted an American out front to curry favor with the new regime. Since Moss had grown up in his uncle's White Elephant Hotel—the finest establishment in St. Paul, Minnesota—he was the perfect choice. He had never risen higher than assistant clerk at the White, but no one in Asia knew that. In classic carpetbagger fashion, he parlayed his limited Minnesota experience into a job managing an undistinguished hotel in Manila for a year and a half, before being plucked by the Oriente owners for this new assignment.

Now the careers of Moss and Seb hinged on one man's opinion: if Congressman Holt liked the hotel, other prestigious clients would follow, and the investors would be happy. Moss told his staff that he would personally handle any problem, no matter how small—because no problem was ever small to a guest.

Thirty minutes later, when Moss answered the call of the frazzled clerk, Congressman Hughes Holt was already drumming his fingers loudly on the front desk. Annoyance bred annoyance, and Moss was good at being annoyed. Nevertheless, he smoothed his face over with a look of patient goodwill. It beat wearing a big, false smile. Customers are not stupid, his Uncle Carl had taught him. Nor do they want the staff to be happy in their work, just efficient at it. Moss had been taught this since age six. Service was in his blood.

"Congressman," Moss said, keeping his shoulders confident and relaxed. He offered his full name and a handshake. "I'm Moses North, the manager. How may I help you?"

The congressman pretended not to see the hand, so Moss let it drop. Holt's granddaughter stood beside him. She was unnervingly attentive, not blinking as she watched Moss's mouth move. Unsure of the polite way to acknowledge her, he ignored her altogether.

"Look here, North," the congressman said. "You gave us unmade rooms!"

Moss had checked the rooms himself. "What are you missing, sir?"

"Most of my bed!" Holt huffed. "Why, there isn't a stitch of bedclothes on the blooming thing. Not even a mattress! I raised the mosquito-netting and found nothing but a bamboo mat."

Moss tried to ignore Della's eyes flickering back and forth between him and her grandfather. If she pulled back Moss's lips and examined his gums, she could not have been more intrusive.

"Are you listening to me, North? This may be a joke to you—"

"No, sir, I assure you—"

"—but I'm paying ten dollars a night for more than fancy woodwork and a clay roof."

"Sir—"

"Forty dollars, actually, including my staff and family, and I expect fully furnished rooms. Do you treat the Army like this?"

The Army was the Oriente's best customer. Despite several ownership changes, they continued to rent an entire block of rooms on the third floor, many of which were used for the wives of high-ranking officers. It was a good account, one the hotel could not afford to lose. Of course the congressman knew that, which is why he had issued the vague threat.

"What may I bring for you, sir?"

"A real mattress for starters," Holt said, still glaring. "Two sheets. A quilt and pillow."

If the man used all that bedding, he would boil. Where did he think he was? Sure, January was the coolest month in Manila, but no American would ever think so until they lived through a tropical April. And, in Moss's admittedly limited experience, the rooms of the Oriente never got cold. For one thing, the mosquito netting blocked any real air circulation. For another, most guests insisted on shutting the windows at night; while this ensured privacy, it also trapped in the day's heat. None of the "civilized" Americans he served seemed to notice that Manileños shut the windows in the day and opened them wide at night.

"I will have my man bring you another set of sheets right away, a set for each room." Actually, he would send a man out to buy some. The few linens left by the previous owners still needed to be laundered with heavy bleach.

"And the rest?"

"A quilt, sir?" Moss did not mean to be impertinent, but he had to check. It was probably still 85 degrees at seven in the evening.

"Are you deaf, man?"

Moss could have heard the congressman's roar even if he had been deaf. But what a thing to say, Moss thought, right in front of his own—

Wait. Was the deaf woman laughing—and at Moss? Did the deaf laugh, even if they could not hear themselves do it? Or was this evidence of the woman being not right in the head?

"The bed is appropriate for this country," Moss explained, far more patiently than the congressman deserved. "The perforated cane bottom is designed for this climate, to keep you cool. If you need more support, you can add the bamboo mat."

"That sounds deuced uncomfortable!"

"It takes a little getting used to, sir, but I assure you that it is the universal practice here." Nevertheless, Moss made a mental note to commission a mattress to be made—immediately.

The congressman agreed to try the Philippine sleeping machine, as is, for a night, but he left the desk with an extra huff for good measure. Better, he took his granddaughter with him. Before she climbed the first stair, she looked back at Moss and shook her head slowly, almost sadly. Not anxious for anyone's pity, especially hers, Moss busied himself checking off imaginary items in his sparse guest register.

Moss did not hear a complaint from the congressman for the rest of the night, and the young hotelier congratulated himself on his early hospitality victory. He did so far too soon. Any illusion of contentment—either Holt's or Moss's—was dispelled first thing in the morning. Moss walked into the dining room to find the congressman screaming at one of the Chinese waiters.

"There are six different kinds of eggs on this menu, boy. Six. Boiled eggs, scrambled eggs, poached eggs, ham and eggs, eggs and bacon, omelets. I know you may be confused on that last one, but I assure you that omelets are eggs. Catchee me, boy? Understand? This menu is all eggs." Holt took a breath. "So how can you tell me you don't have any eggs?"

Tan Cheng-sien, known in the hotel as "Ko" because he was the eldest of the Chinese waiters, repeated his simple message. "No eggs."

The other customers in the dining room listened as the congressman's diatribe carried effortlessly across the large, airy room. A few laughed.

Moss rushed to the table. "Ko, it's okay, I've got it." He passed the waiter some coins and, as quietly as possible, commanded him: "Buy eggs."

Ko left immediately.

Moss turned back and smiled as if they were all in on the joke together. "You may avail yourself of anything on the menu, ladies and gentlemen."

Everyone except the deaf girl gave egg preferences, and then Holt ordered for his granddaughter.

Inside, Moss raged—an entirely unproductive emotion, he knew. The White Elephant's cook would have had eggs to order, hashed brown potatoes, lamb cutlets, codfish cakes, and milk toast. The pastry chef would have whipped up buckwheat griddle cakes and buttermilk biscuits on the fly. Not to mention, someone would have made sure to double the egg delivery the day before an important party arrived. Moss still had much to learn.

Once breakfast was served, Moss had a day's worth of peace before the next interruption. It was late in the evening when the deaf woman rushed up to his desk in her robe. "Mr. North!" she cried.

She could talk? Moss had no idea that was a possibility. He stared at her, too stunned to speak.

"Mr. North!"

He composed himself, but in the scrambled eggs of his brain, he forgot her last name. "Miss Della," he said. "How can I help you?"

"Berget," she corrected him. Her voice a little nasally and distorted, like she had been swimming too long and was waterlogged.

Actually, he noticed, she was a little wet. She hadn't been swimming in an estuary, had she?

"Miss Berget, what is the matter?"

"There's water in my room!"

She occupied a suite with private bath. "Of course there's—"

"It is pouring in," she explained, a small lisp distorting her "r" and "s" sounds. It sounded a little like: "It ith poi-wing in."

"The pipes must have burst," she continued. "You need to come up right away."

The plumbing was perfectly sound. It had been fully fitted and updated by the previous owners of the hotel. Maybe this woman did not know how to work the knobs? "Should I ask your grandfather to help you with the controls?"

"Help me?" She sighed at him, like he was the stupid one. "I know how to work indoor plumbing, Mr. North. My family may be from West Virginia, but we had bathrooms, I assure you. I was raised in conditions a damn sight better than this shabby hotel."

He had no idea what to say to that.

"There is a difference between water coming out of a tap—which I like—and water pouring down from my ceiling—which I do not. Or maybe you would rather wait until your lobby is flooded, too?"

When she put it like that, what else could he do? He nodded, chastened, and followed Miss Berget up the stairs. He apologized to the back of her head before realizing that wouldn't work, and then he was too embarrassed to repeat himself face to face.

She led him to the room, where water indeed streamed down the seam of the bathroom wall. He was doubly unhappy: first about the leak, and second because the woman had been right.

Moss turned, ran out of room 27, and jogged up the stairs to number 37. This was the room of Mrs. Helen Cooper—the wife of Captain Maurice Cooper, currently stationed in Batangas.

Moss knocked furiously. No answer. He put his ear to the door and heard unrecognizable sounds. A laugh, maybe? A series of squeaks, definitely. He pounded the door. "Mrs. Cooper!"

Still no answer.

He was reaching for his master key when the door cracked open to reveal Mrs. Cooper in a soaking wet robe that clung improperly to her body.

"There's water downstairs," he said, peaking around the woman to spy a flustered man trying to vanish under the water line of an overflowing bathtub. His vain efforts only sent more water onto the floor.

Moss saw two problems here. The first was that the couple's vigorous aquatic lovemaking was flooding his hotel. The second was that the man in question was not Captain Cooper.

Moss turned to Mrs. Cooper. "That"—he motioned to the inch of standing water on her floor—"has to disappear."

"But—"

"It is leaking into the room below."

"But you can't expect us, I mean me, to—"

"You have two minutes before my staff will be up here with mops and towels." Two minutes would give Mrs. Cooper's friend time to clear out—barely. Moss could see her doing the calculations.

"I was not here," he assured her. "But my staff will be soon."

Mrs. Cooper's bit lip gave way to a grateful smile before she hastily shut the door.

Moss sighed. This was an aggravation he did not need.

He turned and nearly ran into Miss Berget. She appeared to have been hiding—badly—behind a potted plant. How did she get behind him? Were deaf people naturally silent? That made no sense.

There was no way that this woman could have overheard any of his conversation with Helen Cooper, nor could she have added up what was happening in room 37. But when Moss saw her face, he knew that Della Berget had understood everything.

This could be a problem.

CHAPTER THREE

Clarke's

D ella felt no compunction about commandeering her grandfather's carriage, a rickety contraption known as a *calesa*. She learned the word after a frustrated assistant manager of the hotel wrote it down for her. Getting the actual driver of the *calesa* to understand her was far easier; everyone in the city knew Clarke's Confectionery.

Located at the entrance to Escolta, Manila's Fifth Avenue, the establishment proudly proclaimed its name on both the roof and on a half dozen oversized awnings facing every direction. Even without the signage, the place was clearly marked by a large crowd. The spacious wood-paneled room was full of businessmen and civil servants from all over the islands, officers of the army and navy, and tourists from half the world. Della would not have been surprised to run into her grandfather inside—he seemed to be the only white man of consequence not present.

Even though she could not hear it, the place felt loud, especially the heavy treads of the wait staff pounding a path from the kitchen. But Della's strongest impression was of the fragrance of fresh bread— yes, bread in Manila! After three days of the atrocious food at the Hotel Oriente, her stomach almost jumped out of her throat to lay claim to a loaf.

As if the smell of fresh bread wasn't enough, an advertisement proudly proclaimed: *CLARKE'S MAYON COFFEE. Fresh Roasted, Steel-Cut, Prepared with the Most Modern Machinery at Our Own Manila Plant from Handpicked, Carefully Selected Berries, Roasted to Meet the Demands. No Old Stock. Never Rancid!*

Della chose a wicker chair in the corner of the room, underneath a sign touting imported phosphate sodas. A bored soda jerker wiped down glasses and piled them high on the dark wooden bar. Save for the sweat making its way down her meager cleavage, Della would be hard-pressed to remember that she was in Manila at all.

She was savoring the delicious gingerbread cookies that accompanied her coffee when a jolly party of colonials entered. Della did not trust happy people. The Oriente's manager—Mr. North—he was one. He had let her grandfather rant and rave for three days straight, and none of it seemed to bother North. He did not exactly smile in response, but his attitude was so frustratingly good-natured that she felt sorry for the man. He could not be very bright.

A boisterous gang of new customers pushed together a few tables and sat next to Della. Included in their number was the woman who had nearly flooded Della out of her room two nights before. Today Mrs. Room 37 was paying particular attention to a new man, not the one Della had spied from her leafy camouflage in the hall.

Della settled into her usual pastime—which she refused to call spying, even though that was closest to the truth.

"…he's missed too many boats, you reckon?" The speaker, an Army officer, enunciated well, probably to catch the attention of the women at the table. "Stashed away some sweetheart in town," he finished, waggling his eyebrows.

"A squaw man," another said. "One bambino here; one on the way in the barrio." The group bemoaned the moral turpitude of their friend, who had "Philippinitis."

A waiter interrupted the gossip. The Navy officer turned away from his party—and, fortunately, toward Della—to order his coffee, pastry, and fruit for fifty cents "Mex," or half a silver dollar. Della had worked out the jumbled money system after her grandfather overpaid for a *calesa* with four silver pesetas. The congressman had been the most sought-after customer in the Oriente's stables ever since.

"No got," the officer said, shaking his head. "Jaw-bone?"

In her head, Della replayed the visual of the man's mouth but divined no better interpretation than jaw-bone. Shaman? Shoreboat? Chore moat? Nothing made sense.

"Put it on your account?" the waiter confirmed. "Of course, sir."

Della wondered about the strange place she had landed, where the Filipinos were easier to understand than the Americans.

It didn't take long for the sailor's food to arrive.

"They say that Clarke has been in Manila as long as Dewey," he said. He sipped his fresh coffee and sighed. "Both men are heroes in my book."

The Army man would not let Navy ego go unchecked. "What does your admiral know of war? I mean real 'shit-on-your-boots-because-you-have-just-marched-a-bunch-of-goo-goos-through-a-reeking-mangrove-swamp' kind of war? He carries a $10,000 Tiffany sword cast in 24 karat gold, for God's sake."

"At least Dewey wouldn't have encouraged the Filipinos with talk of pulling out."

"Democrats." The Army man scowled. "Now the bush is filled with *insurrectos* every night."

Della knew that this was not too much of an exaggeration. General Arthur MacArthur had just requested a force of 150,000 men to help pacify the islands—and the duties of these soldiers would be more strenuous than sipping coffee with pretty women in Clarke's. She felt sorry for them all.

"What do you think of that congressman?" Mrs. Room 37 asked. "The one staying at the Oriente with me and Susan."

"I think it's sweet that he's brought his granddaughter here," said the other woman, presumably Susan.

Mrs. Room 37 nodded. "Poor girl."

No one seemed to notice that the poor girl was sitting close, watching them intently. Della generally attracted little notice because of her plain looks. She didn't mind. The only thing she objected to was being labeled a "girl"—she would turn twenty-four later this month.

One of the Army officers made it clear that he did not think it was a good idea to bring a "deaf and dumb" woman to the Philippines. "We need 20,000 men in and around Manila to make the city safe for you able-bodied ladies. Now we're supposed to worry about a Capitol Hill cripple?"

"If something happens to her, the Democrats will run with the story, just wait and see." The Navy officer shook his head. "They'll call on us to abandon the whole Asiatic project."

Della spent a lot of her time reading the papers at home, and she agreed that the press could undo the war just as quickly as they had made it. She respected the power of the Fourth Estate, which is why she wanted to be a part of it.

She always had. It was why Della had stayed at boarding school, despite desperately wanting to go home and reestablish a connection with her parents in West Virginia. She left them when she was seven, two years after spinal meningitis took most of her hearing and nearly her life. Her grandfather gallantly offered to pay her tuition at the Kendall School for the Deaf in Washington, D.C., so she went. There was no better school in the region, and the congressman could afford the $250 annual tuition. Della's father, an accountant at the West Fairmont Coal & Coke Company, could not. Moreover, her grandfather had promised to keep an eye on Della during the half year that Congress was in session. No one thought to ask what would happen during the other half.

From Kendall, Della matriculated into Gallaudet College, which really meant moving across the sidewalk to Old Fowler Hall. Her life there teetered between opportunity and frustration. She had been permitted to take courses in English literature and composition, but extracurricular activities—like the school newspaper—required a chaperone. She wrote half of the articles that made up the *Buff and Blue*, but her male counterparts earned all the editorial positions because they needed no chaperone, so could be counted on to show up for all meetings.

Della made several close friends at Gallaudet—almost sisters really—but none shared her ambition. Too many aspired to be faculty wives, as if that would be the pinnacle of a deaf woman's achievements. One friend had married a professor on the same day she graduated. No one had thought the wedding odd, let alone distasteful.

At least the new bride had completed her degree. Della was one of many women who failed to graduate. When her grandfather had insisted that she come with him to Manila, she obediently packed and left school. But she was glad that she had—she would find her story here. She was sure of it. What would a degree matter?

Motion at the door caught her eye. Della watched in surprise as Mr. North walked in. Actually, it would be more accurate to say that he slid inside Clarke's. Instead of taking a table, he made straight for the kitchen door but was stopped by a quick-moving Mrs. Room 37. She caught his elbow before he noticed her. North gave her that generic half-smile, the same one that so infuriated Della. Mrs. Room 37 was not infuriated, though. She ran her hand slowly down North's arm, lingering at the cuff just long enough to brush his wrist with her fingertips. If she stood any closer, her red lipstick would rub off on his clean white lapel. The seductive tilt of her head—slightly up and to the side—promised surrender.

Whatever the woman said to North seemed to take him by surprise. He stepped back and ran a hand through his disheveled hair. How could he maintain such a nicely pressed suit but still never comb his hair? Despite this—and despite her own better judgment—Della found the man handsome. His short sideburns, bold eyebrows, and blue eyes were hard to overlook, no matter how simple he seemed.

"There's nothing to thank me for, Helen." North's lips were the only ones in the conversation Della could see. Since they were full and clean-shaven, they were easy to read. "There was a leak, so I sent my men upstairs to fix it. Nothing more."

Mrs. Room 37—Helen—used her hand to tame the runaway curls that had escaped her Gibson girl up-do. Della could appreciate the subtlety of that gesture. The woman had dark, silky hair with just the right amount of swing. It would certainly draw a man's attention—and it did, briefly. But Mr. North seemed distracted by something other than the beautiful woman. His eyes searched the restaurant for curious onlookers, but he made the mistake of only considering those within actual hearing distance. Della was halfway across the room and went undetected.

"I wish you would believe me," he said. "I am not your husband's agent, nor the Army's."

Della processed these clues. An Army wife? Cheating on her husband in a room paid for with taxpayer funds? That story had potential.

Helen's hand brushed something off North's shoulder. Most likely it was nothing, just a pretext to let her nails graze the skin of his neck above the collar.

"That's, uh, nice, Mrs. Cooper." Mr. North looked uncomfortable, like his tie was too tight around his neck. "Thank you."

Della noted that his words did not constitute a refusal. She would have to pay closer attention to the traffic upstairs from now on. If she could catch the manager himself in a dalliance with Mrs. Army Officer, it would make an even better story.

The kitchen door opened and a Filipina woman rushed toward North. Another amorous appointment? Mr. North seemed to be Manila's Don Juan.

North excused himself from the American woman only to be immediately chastised by the Filipina. Della could not see her face, but her hands kept pointing him back to the main entrance.

"I had to come here," he said. "This is the only place where I can find you. You have not given me an answer."

The Filipina peered back at the kitchen and then shook her head.

North's frown was stubborn. "What do you mean, he knows?"

North took a hold of the woman's arm and guided her to the calmest corner of the restaurant, even closer to Della's prying eyes. Too close, Della thought. She hid her face behind her hand and peeked through spread fingers. The only words she could parse were about ovens, yeast, and kitchens.

Unless Don Juan used these euphemisms for sexual congress, this was no torrid affair.

"You can start today if that makes a difference," North said.

Since the Oriente needed all the skilled cooks it could get, Della silently cheered North's efforts. The hotel could use the perfume of fresh bread. For that matter, so could the rest of Manila.

A balding fellow erupted from the kitchen. "North!" he cried. "I told you what would happen if you poached my people."

Judging from the way the female baker fled back to the kitchen, this man had to be Clarke himself.

"No one else has ever trained Filipinos to run a sanitary bakery," Clarke said. "And nobody is going to steal them away now that I have. I demand that you leave now."

Della looked around the room and confirmed that she was not the only one paying attention to the scene. Unfortunately, she was too close to the action to feign nonchalance. North scanned his audience again, and this time it was Della he found first. He stared at her for a moment, icy eyes wide and unblinking. Then he stalked out.

On principle, Della did not believe she needed to apologize for lip reading a public conversation, but she almost followed him out to do exactly that. She held back—it would do no good to act like his friend now. If she could come up with a real story about him for the papers, the result would be far more public and devastating to North than a small scene at Clarke's. If she got lucky, she would gut him in front of the whole city.

CHAPTER FOUR

Dinner

As if the day had not gone badly enough, Moss returned to the Oriente to find that the dining room had not been cleaned for dinner. Or, more precisely, only pieces of it had. One corner of the room had not had its floor waxed, but chairs and tables were carefully polished; another corner had dusty chairs on a freshly scrubbed floor; and two tables in the middle of the room were not yet cleared. No matter where a customer chose to sit, something would be filthy.

He called Seb over to explain what he needed done, and his assistant shrugged. "It is the new boys."

After the incident with Congressman Holt, Moss had told Seb to hire Filipinos to supplement the mostly Chinese cleaners and wait staff. "Surely you could have found better than this."

The assistant said something about fairness and saving face. Whatever he meant, his English was not up to the task, which did not happen often. Of course, he was not used to explaining himself to anyone, either.

Seb had been the warden at Bilibid Prison until the Americans took over and demoted him to ordinary officer with the native police, supervised by a lowly Yankee corporal, Moss North. As a middle class

Chinese *ilustrado*, Seb had a better education than Moss and, outside the colonial system, higher status. So it was Seb who taught the American how to police the locals. He knew the neighborhood: which water girl to trust, whom to hire to cook in the house, and how much to pay both. He entertained Moss into the small hours of the morning, playing music on his new gramophone, sharing his whisky, and teaching the American *panguingue*, a local high stakes card game.

Seb had made Manila bearable enough that Moss never considered going back to Minnesota when his Army term was up. Instead, Moss took a job at the English Hotel, the self-proclaimed "Bachelor Resort of the City" on the Escolta. "Resort" was a generous description. The floors were bare, the towels dirty, and the tea weak—the latter an unforgivable sin with the English guests. Moss worked hard to pull the establishment into presentable form, or at least good enough so that when the electric lights were installed inside, the guests did not curse the name of Edison for all the wretchedness now revealed to their eyes.

When the spot at the Oriente opened up, Moss needed a right-hand-man, and Seb was happy to be stolen away from the colonial police. He had no experience at hospitality but was willing to learn, even if he had to do so from a know-nothing American.

Moss would have to handle this lesson carefully. "Call the boys in," he directed. "I want them to explain this in front of me."

Three Filipinos were retrieved from the storeroom, where they had been organizing the new supplies Seb had ordered. None of the boys looked older than sixteen, but they all probably supported extended families. A job at the Oriente would be prized. No doubt at least one of these boys was related to Seb, maybe his wife's distant nephew from the provinces.

Seb drew a finger across the table and showed his dirty digit to Anastasio, the tallest. Anastasio stuttered a defense in simple English, claiming that he had cleaned most of the tables but left a few so that José could do his share. José quickly protested that he had done his share—he had wiped down all the chairs! But when Seb showed the group over to the dirty chairs, a forlorn José explained that he had to leave something for Fernando to do. With great indignation, Fernando pointed to the floor, which he had polished—mostly.

This whole conversation was accompanied with enough flailing of arms to have cleaned the room twice over.

Before Moss could jump in, Seb gave his own orders. "Three parts," he said. He held up three fingers to punctuate his English.

Pulling Fernando with him, Seb walked over to the left third of the room said in Tagalog: "This is your area. You clean the tables, chairs, and floors. Everything that sits on these boards. Understand?"

Fernando nodded, and Seb showed José and Anastasio their center and right thirds, as well.

"The boy with the cleanest area for the week will earn one extra Mex." Seb turned to Moss, realizing too late that maybe he needed to clear a raise with Moss in advance. But Moss nodded—a half-dollar was a cheap price for preserving Seb's authority.

By dinnertime, the boys were busy seating new customers. Then things got interesting. Moss watched Fernando seat one large party after another in the middle of the room. Anastasio followed his lead. When the two boys ran out of chairs, they plucked some from their own sections and squeezed them into the middle swath. The Oriente's dining room was beginning to look like ants over a line of jelly—a line smack-dab in José's section. Poor José was not able to defend his territory, stuck as he was pulling the rope to the huge *punkah* on the ceiling.

Moss had often heard imperious Americans decry the indolence of their "little brown brothers," but Moss thought these boys more mischievous than lazy. They were, after all, boys.

Moss would have to handle this intrigue himself, before it got out of control. He rotated Fernando to *punkah* duty, but not before informing him that responsibility for the floor sections had been changed. Fernando now had the crowded middle section.

The boy argued in quick Tagalog. Predictably it started with, "Señor Lopa said—"

"I don't care," Moss said, in English. Sometimes that was enough.

When Fernando cursed under his breath, Moss was certain that he had been understood. Anastasio had the same reaction when he learned that he was now responsible for either side of the middle—his original section and one more.

"*Hindi,*" Anastasio chirped up. No.

"*Oo,*" Moss said with authority. Yes.

Unwilling to lose his job, Anastasio nodded reluctantly.

Then there was the last boy, José, whose arms probably felt like taffy after pulling the *punkah* rope all night. "You are finished tonight," Moss told him. "*Sa buhay.*" Go home.

But José did not go. Instead, he stayed to toy with the others, laughing over his surprising "victory" in this improvised game. Eventually, though, with nothing else to do, he chipped in and helped the others clean the room.

At the end of the night, Moss gave them a stern warning: "Tomorrow—*bukas*—the chairs stay where they are. Same number chairs, same number tables. Same, same, *sige?*"

They all agreed, and Moss hoped they meant it. He liked the boys' spirit and did not want to have to replace them. In a country of eight million Filipinos, it seemed crazy to rely on imported labor.

Moss walked through the back door into the kitchen to check on preparations—more specifically, his stock of eggs—for breakfast. By the time he returned to the dining room, the late night drinking crowd had arrived. Mrs. Helen Cooper and friends had just ordered two bottles of Moet & Chandon, which meant they would be here a while. So much for sleep, Moss thought.

Miss Berget sat at the table next to them. A young woman her age should be enjoying the sunset social scene at Luneta Park, but he knew that Congressman Holt had not taken her there, not even once. The only place Moss had seen her outside the hotel was at Clarke's, and there, too, she had been alone.

It was not his problem, he reminded himself. But as he watched from across the room, he thought it a great injustice. What kept Mrs. Cooper from inviting Della to join her party? The women were not so far off in age. Usually, Americans clumped together in this city like iron filings on a magnet, even if they belonged to entirely different poles at home.

Before Moss had decided on an action, his feet were already moving. "Hello, Miss Berget," he called out as he approached. Of course, she did not hear him.

He tapped on Della's shoulder. She jumped and spun at the same time. Her hands fell immediately to her lap.

"Mr. North," she said flatly. He was not sure whether the way she softened her r words was more typical of a deaf person or a West Virginian.

"I thought I would check on you, since you seem to be alone," he said.

Something close to resentment flashed in her light brown eyes. "What of it? Is a woman not allowed to dine by herself?"

She was not dining, he wanted to say, but that wouldn't be polite. He was here to be nice. He pulled out a chair and sat down.

"Please, stay," she said, after the fact.

Moss thought he heard sarcasm, but she had a flat affect to all her speech, so he could not tell for sure. "I thought that you might want some company."

"Thank you for taking pity on me," she said, as monotone as before. "Or maybe it is something more?"

"Excuse me?"

She glanced at Mrs. Cooper, who looked up at Moss right at that moment.

"I may have already served my purpose," Della said.

"What?"

"Or are you looking for something novel? You suppose that a lack of faculties in one area might enhance my abilities in another?"

"Are you suggesting—?"

"Many hearing men make such assumptions," she said, a little too loudly. "They think it a singular experience, I am told."

There could not have been a worse time for the woman to lose control of her volume. Moss heard open snickers from the next table.

He would normally excuse himself from such a gross misunderstanding, but if he left now it would prove her—and their eavesdropping neighbors—right. "I don't know why you have such a poor impression of me," he said quietly. "But I wish you would be more discreet about it."

As usual, she misunderstood.

"I won't tell my grandfather anything unfavorable about the hotel, don't worry. The Oriente is a miracle beyond words. I have found my Garden of Eden."

For sure, that was sarcasm. He wasn't a total idiot.

Something slipped from her lap and fell onto the floor. Moss and Della bent at the same time to pick it up, knocking heads, but Moss reached the small red journal first.

Her wide-eyed-open-mouthed alarm was real. Did she think he would look in her precious book?

He held it out to her without a second thought. "How have I offended you?" he asked.

"You haven't," she said, but she grabbed the book quickly, as if he might yank it back any second. She looked down at it and then back at him—the bully made good. "I don't offend easily. If I did, I'd be perpetually offended."

He knew that she was aiming that remark partly at him. "I'm sorry."

"I know what people say about me, you know."

Moss believed it. He was starting to realize that this woman was shockingly perceptive, which made her bad opinion of him that much more worrying. She had him all wrong.

"You think I'm"—he lowered his voice to less than a whisper since she only needed to read it on his lips—"sleeping with my guests?"

"And would you like to comment on that?"

"No!" Now he was the one almost shouting. He looked over, but fortunately the other table had lost interest. "Because it's not true."

She shrugged—a universal sign for "so you say."

"Why would I?" He shook his head. "Never mind. I don't know what story you've concocted in your head," he said, before lowering his voice to a whisper again. "And please don't tell anyone about Mrs. Cooper's 'plumbing accident,' either."

Della's silence most definitely did not signal assent.

Moss leaned forward. He was feeling a little desperate, truth be told. "Half of my occupancy is paid for by the Army—"

"So you look the other way, no matter what these women do?"

It would hardly be good for morale if it came out that wives were entertaining men in a luxury hotel while their husbands were roughing it in the barrios. The enlisted men might get a good chuckle out of it—Moss knew because he used to be one of them—but in the end they could not respect a cuckolded man as a commander. And, worse, Moss would lose half his business and, therefore, his job.

"I am not their keeper, Miss Berget. And neither are you."

She actually started to write that down.

"What are you doing?" he asked. He had to tap her shoulder and ask it again. Della smiled, but she did not stop writing. He put his hand over hers. "Stop."

She did, but maybe only because she was finished. Then again, she didn't pull her hands away, either. "Why did you come over to chat with me, Mr. North?"

God only knew. "Where is your grandfather?"

"He did not return for dinner."

"You've been waiting for him all this time?" He wondered if she was loyal, obedient, or lying. He looked into her eyes so that he could read her, and with their hands still touching it seemed a very intimate interrogation.

When he removed his hands, she closed her notebook and sighed. "I have served his purpose on this trip already, so I think I will probably be stuck in your hotel for the remainder of our visit."

Surprisingly, that idea no longer sounded so bad to Moss, which was the strangest turn of the night.

"He was not happy about me going to Clarke's," she continued. "Maybe because I went without him."

"It's one of the few respectable places around—though you don't seem like the type to care what you should or should not be doing."

She smiled as if he had complimented her, and it was to her great advantage. Della had a symmetrical face—oval in shape—that formed a soft point at the chin. Her combination of brown hair and brown eyes had seemed common at first, but now Moss saw that both were speckled with gold.

"Grandfather is going to leave me here," she said. "Meanwhile, he will travel to the southern islands." She fluttered her eyes theatrically. "I suppose that soon enough I'll be entertaining the local officers, too."

"That's all I need," Moss said with a sigh. "I can give you the name of a few other lodgings that I'd prefer to see scandalized by the wayward granddaughter of a congressman."

"Are you asking me to take my business elsewhere?" She laughed a little—an airy, ringing sound—and something in Moss uncoiled a little.

He exhaled a long breath. "I'd consider it a personal favor."

"I'll think about it," she said.

"How about if I sweeten the deal with dinner?"

She looked around. Other than the champagne party, the dining room was empty. "It looks like the chef is done for the night, Mr. North."

"Who needs the chef?"

"You will cook?"

Moss nodded. "I'm capable."

"I was hoping someone in this hotel would be."

Now he laughed. "Come with me," he said, standing up and holding out a hand for her. "Will one chicken suffice, or should I make two?"

"Chicken?"

"Fresh roasted chicken with potatoes and herbs," he confirmed.

She drew conspiratorially close. "If you're trying to buy my silence, you are using the right currency."

He led her to the door. "Step into my kitchen, Miss Berget. Let's negotiate."

CHAPTER FIVE

The Thaw

Della watched Moss's hands as they fluttered over the chopping board. He cut up a carrot in less time than she could write the vegetable's name. He took a potato, stood it on one end, and whizzed down the side with a knife. In ten seconds, the whole potato was peeled.

"You should have been a chef," she said.

He waited for her attention before replying, a kindness that even her family did not always extend. "My menu is limited," he explained. "And I definitely cannot bake."

She almost blushed at the memory of the afternoon's scene, but then she remembered that she had not been the one humiliated in front of half of Manila. "You could learn."

"Luz will take the job," he said, shaking his head. "I will pay her twice what Clarke does, and she can run her own staff."

Della understood the draw of opportunity; she had followed her own across the Pacific. "Is baking that hard?"

"Harder than it looks. In this heat, it is hard to keep carabao milk fresh, so you have to make do with condensed," he said, wrinkling his nose.

He turned to throw the peeled, cut potatoes in a boiling pot with garlic cloves and a few local lemons that looked more like tiny limes. He had long since taken off his cotton duck jacket and rolled up his shirtsleeves. He threaded the tail of his black tie through his shirt buttons, keeping it from contaminating the raw chicken that he was rubbing with salt and pepper.

"Clarke figured out how to use the canned stuff," he added, looking at Della again. "The problem is he's not telling—not willingly."

Hence the culinary espionage, she thought. "Well, I'm glad you're trying to improve the food here. It's pretty bad."

Moss stopped his work long enough to laugh. "Do you even know how to be polite?"

Della looked down at the fork she was twirling in her fingers. "I suppose so," she said. "I spent most of my life being polite—"

She felt the table jolt and looked up to see Moss, wrists deep in chicken, knocking on the wood with his elbow. He had gotten her attention the only way he could. "Define polite."

"I was nice."

She thought he huffed out a chuckle. "You think 'polite' is not telling people to their faces that they're fools."

She shrugged. "Everyone thinks I am the fool."

"Like I did."

She raised her eyebrows. "You don't assume all your customers are new to indoor plumbing?"

"Had there not been water coming down your walls, how long before you would have put me in my place for some other reason?"

Della had no idea. The way that hearing people judged the deaf was predictable, and whenever possible Della used that predictability to her advantage. If people wanted to ignore her, she let them. Meanwhile, she observed their every move. Strange to think of it now, but she would not be sitting here if Mrs. Helen Cooper had been a little more discreet with her guest.

Moss tapped the table again. "Interesting answer."

She tilted her head. "I didn't say anything."

"Exactly." He set the chicken upside down and worked the other side.

"Where did you learn to do all this?" she asked. "Your mother?"

"I don't remember my parents. They died when I was a baby."

He turned away again before she could read his expression. She waited patiently while he finished the chicken and washed his hands. Then he picked up a sharpening stone, dabbed a bit of oil on it, and began dragging a knife diagonally across its face.

"The six of us, my brothers and sisters, were split up," he explained. "The eldest three were almost old enough to take care of themselves, so they went with our grandparents. The next two went with my father's sister. My mother's only surviving relative, her brother, took me, the baby."

"Why?" She asked, and then thought how that sounded. "I don't mean why would he want you, or anything. I just mean…"

Actually, she did not know what she meant.

He smiled, though it was strained. "It seems odd to me, too, especially since my uncle was a widower, but he had a daughter not much older than me, and he earned a good income from his business."

"What business?"

"The Queen Left Hand."

Usually Moss was easy to lip read—he spoke slowly and in complete sentences—but not this time. "The Queen Left Hand?" she repeated.

She knew that was wrong the instant she said it, but Moss did not laugh. Instead, he stopped sharpening his knife long enough to pull out a worn, misshapen card. It read: *Moses J. North, Assistant Clerk, White Elephant Hotel, St. Paul, Minnesota.*

"Ahh." A hearing person would never confuse "white" for "queen," but it was an easy mistake for a lip reader.

"The place took ten years to build—the design was a little too grandiose—and people took to calling it a 'white elephant.' By the time my uncle opened its doors, that was the only name people would use." He slipped the card back in his pocket.

"You carry that card with you," she observed. "You must have liked your uncle."

"He was fine."

She caught one side of his mouth tightening. "Fine?"

"Busy, demanding, difficult…but fine. People liked working for him. We had one porter who stayed for twenty-two years, another for twenty. The headwaiter lasted seventeen, and the bartender fifteen. Uncle Carl was a dependable boss."

"My grandfather is dependable. It's not always a recommendation."

"I can think of worse things. My uncle did not treat me any differently than his own daughter."

Now Della felt bad for the girl. None of Moss's evasions were very convincing, but neither was she going to get anywhere by asking questions head-on. "So you lived in the hotel?"

"Along with my aunt's sister, Mrs."—the name was garbled—"who was supposed to keep an eye on me and Abigail."

Della figured that the fact that Moss called his caretaker Mrs. Anything gave some idea of where this was going. "How well did she do?"

"Fine."

"More 'fine.'"

"Abigail was blood."

"But you weren't," Della concluded.

"No," he said, finishing with the knife. "She left me with the staff most days, and I'm thankful for that. They were my family: Howard, the assistant manager; Billy, the chief clerk—"

"And a cook?"

"Several," he said with a smile.

"How much time did you spend in the kitchen?"

"A lot," he said, fishing a potato out of the water to test it. "As soon as I could hold a knife, I was on spud duty. It was the best way to keep me out of trouble. It mostly worked."

Earlier she would have had trouble believing that the too-accommodating, too-patient man Moss had become was once a thorny little orphan. But Della knew a lot about little boys—and girls for that matter—who were separated from their families. She had known children who befriended everyone, from gardeners to mailmen, in search of affection and acceptance. Others became bullies, and still others, charming tricksters. She figured that Moss was the last type.

Moss said nothing. She watched him work in silence—it was all silence to her, of course, but she found that the hearing usually found long pauses uncomfortable.

Moss drained the potatoes and let them steam dry. Then he poked the boiled lemon with a fork before stuffing it in the chicken with the garlic cloves. He worked so efficiently that it was hard to believe he had been a young ne'er-do-well.

"I'm wondering what kind of trouble you caused," she finally said.

"Trouble is a strong word."

"I suppose a hotel can be quite a playground for a young man. There are maids, waitresses, laundresses…?"

Moss blushed. The color rose from his starched collar up to his spiky hairline. "What are you suggesting?" His eyes looked especially bright in their feigned innocence.

"I've lived in a boarding house most of my youth, and I know how these places are," Della said.

Moss stubbornly shook his head, but smiled. "I'm not going to talk about this." Not with you, his eyes said.

"I would have thought that a man who grew up in a fine establishment like the White Elephant"—she put dramatic emphasis on the name of the heretofore unknown hotel—"would have put the Oriente in shape by now."

"Is your stay not to your satisfaction?"

He was in the process of putting the chicken in the oven, so he did not see her smile until he turned back around.

"If it tells you anything about my stay," she said, "I am sure this will be the best meal ever to come out of this kitchen."

"You've not eaten it yet."

"Oh, believe me, I can tell. A half-starved woman knows her food."

"Half-starved, huh?" He grinned. "I should charge you for dinner, then."

She shrugged. "Fine."

"No, it would be too easy to put it on your grandfather's tab. I want a payment from you that is yours alone to give." He tapped his finger against his chin with a great flourish.

Della straightened her spine, unwilling to let him see that the suggestion rattled her a little.

"Secrets," he finally said.

"What?"

"I told you mine."

She sat up straight. "Being an orphan is hardly a secret!"

"No one else here knows about it."

"It is just a fact, like me being deaf—though that used to be a secret."

She turned from him, but he touched her hand to keep her attention. When he did not pull his hand away, she felt the contact all the way up to the back of her neck.

"What do you mean?" he asked.

"My grandfather paid my school bills, but even that he did anonymously. For a while, it was really important to him that no one find out."

"He was embarrassed?"

"He was careful." She struggled to find a way to explain the most confusing tribe in America: Congress. "You see, some of his colleagues thought that higher education for the deaf was a waste of the government's money."

"Your grandfather could not have agreed with them."

"What he actually thought was less important than what he could trade for his vote. If people had known he had deafness in the family, he would have been pigeonholed, written off. Instead, they competed for his support. I don't know which way he voted, though in the end the school kept its funding."

Moss shook his head.

She sighed. "This is the way things work in Washington. My grandfather is good at deals, which is how he maneuvered his way onto important committees. This trip might turn him into something more, something national, if he can draw enough attention from the players back home."

"And you don't mind being dragged around for show?"

"It is why I'm here."

He shook his head. "You are unbelievably passive when it suits you."

"Why fight it? Sure, there was a day when I wanted my grandfather's approval." It was embarrassing to talk about this, to admit how hopeful—and naive—she had been as a girl. But if Moss wanted secrets, this was all she had. "Once a month, he sent his driver to fetch me. His Brewster brougham was so fine, with the black exterior buffed into a mirror shine and the interior all cozy leather. None of the other girls at Kendall had ever seen anything like it. I used to let them come and sit in it briefly before I left. But when the congressman found out, he got angry—he demanded that I be more discreet about his patronage. He said lots more, too, but I was not as good at reading lips back then."

Moss gripped the edge of the table. "Where were your parents all this time?"

"I visited them sometimes."

"Sometimes?"

"My grandfather sent me back home when he remembered to make the arrangements." At Moss's raised eyebrow, she added: "The rail doesn't go all the way to Morgantown, and hiring a coach took some doing."

"You're making excuses for him."

She sighed. "No, I am being realistic. I know who he is, believe me, but without him I would not have gotten an education. I would not be able to understand you at all."

"So you pardon your grandfather for his sins."

She rolled her eyes. "He's a congressman, not a rebel."

She did not feel like talking about this anymore. Maybe she was just tired. Lip-reading for over an hour was exhausting, especially with someone she cared enough about to get it right.

Moss must have read the reluctance in her face—quite perceptive for a hearing person—and let it drop. He glanced down at his pocket watch to time the chicken.

After a few minutes, she realized that he was letting her choose when and what to say next. So she did. "How are the preparations for my grandfather's reception?"

The congressman was throwing a party in his own honor the next week, and he had decided to do it at the Oriente, despite its lackluster catering.

Moss threw a towel on the table in mock surrender. "Why he chose us, I don't know. He doesn't think any more of this hotel than you do."

"It's still the Oriente. The name means something in Manila."

"I only took over last week. You should have seen this place before."

She did not doubt its edges had been that much rougher before Moss took hold of it. "Just do what you would have done at the Queen Left Hand."

He laughed, as he was meant to. "We didn't host grand occasions at the White. The wives' auxiliary of train engineers, that kind of thing. Nothing very fashionable. And my time with the Minnesota

Volunteers trained me to police the streets of this city, not entertain its high society."

"Society," Della said with a smile. "The Americans here are hardly that. Carpetbaggers, more like, trying to make a buck off the Asian frontier."

"What does that make you and me?"

"Oh, we're the same," she admitted. "That's my point. Plan a party that would impress you—and, when in doubt, just make sure there is lots and lots of liquor."

He laughed. "What would you know about that?"

She slid her coffee mug over to him, the one she had brought from the dining room. It was mostly empty, but the fragrance would be enough. Moss sniffed the cup. "Crème de Cacao," he said.

"Mmm."

"You've been drinking all night?" he asked.

"You assume that I'm boring, just because I am—"

"A lady?"

She laughed. "I'm not a lady."

"So I'm learning," Moss said.

CHAPTER SIX

The Scandal

Della was sure that she had never tasted anything as magical as lemony potatoes smothered in roasted chicken fat. She had barely finished eating when her grandfather entered the dining room and sat down next to her.

"Here's where you have been hiding," he said, gesturing to his entourage to follow. He signaled the waiter. "Boy! Bring us a nightcap. Four." He held up four fingers.

Della was not one of those four.

The Filipino left a bottle on the table so he could end his shift and go to sleep behind the bar. It was late, even by local standards.

Her grandfather introduced Della to the lieutenant seated on the other side of her. Della knew that the soldier's mustache would make conversation impossible. Besides that, Della thought mustaches bad hygiene, a trap for half the food a man ate. Della was further unimpressed by the lieutenant's crooked, brown teeth and chapped lips.

The other men at the table—both of whom also had bad teeth—began competing for her attention, though they clearly did so to win over her grandfather, nothing else. Della knew that she was no prize. She had already been told by one brief suitor that she was not worth the trouble, and that was when she had been a more pliant girl of eighteen.

The older man, a civilian, spoke to her, but his exaggerated mouthing of words actually made him as unintelligible as Mustache Man. To her relief, no one actually expected her to respond. Once they felt they had paid her enough attention to be polite, they moved on to their own conversation.

A tall, bald man kept talking about a "water pastor," which had to be wrong. The water in this city did not need divine intervention, though it was a miracle that people survived drinking it. She ran through the possibilities until she figured it out: quartermaster. "Von" or "fawn" was really fraud. Quartermaster fraud. Once she had those key pieces, she had enough context to follow fairly easily.

Bald Man listed off staples—biscuits, flour, bacon—before asking: "How can someone make a hundred grand off flour?"

Mustache Man said something that Della could not decipher.

"A thousand sacks of flour," her grandfather said. "And wagon loads of bacon"—though it looked like "making loafs of baking." The ensuing debate about how much cured pork could fit into a wheeled cart cleared up her confusion, but many proficient lip-readers would have given up on this conversation already.

"All pears in cavern men pets," her grandfather concluded. Or didn't. Usually, he was easier to read, but the whisky was making it difficult.

"Who else is involved?" Bald Man asked. He and the other guests seemed to be less drunk than the congressman.

She caught the end of her grandfather's answer: "…and three of the largest bakeries in Manila."

"Clarke's?" Bald Man said. "Usually our friend is smart enough to smell a trap."

Mustache Man said something.

The congressman waved a hand to interrupt. "Not public"—his next words were slurred—"investigation is announced."

The men readily agreed. Della knew that a quartermaster scandal could damage the reputation of the military. Though the congressman would want to limit the damage, he was also eager to see a civilian government installed, so he would not want the Army to emerge completely unscathed.

"We need strong government," he said. "Permanent authority over these islands. Anything else will result in disaster." It was the clearest she had seen his speech all evening.

Bald Man agreed. "It would be folly to give the natives any consequence," he said, meaning self-government. "Not more than a half a dozen have the necessary capacity."

"They're like buffalo bulls—they struggle, whether right or wrong. You cannot possibly deal with them by gentle means. They must be fought, fought, fought ceaselessly and remorselessly." Her grandfather rammed his fist against the table. "No negotiations, no amnesties. Like raising children," he concluded, sending a fond smile Della's way.

The men's conversation continued, rambling from the topics of commerce in the islands to the incompetence of the previous Spanish administration. Della pulled out her little red notebook and started taking notes. She wrote without looking—the men probably thought she was doodling out of boredom. It created a mess of a page, but the alternative was losing some of the conversation.

Eventually, the bottle of whisky ran out, so the congressman's guests took their leave. He motioned Della to stay for a moment, which she did reluctantly. She had a daisy of a headache.

"You cannot tell anyone about this," he said. His articulation was remarkably clear now, which meant that his drunkenness had been, at least in part, an act.

"Tell anyone about what?"

"The investigation on the supplies."

"Oh."

"When I came in, you were chatting with that manager, Mr. West—"

"North."

He waved his hand at the irrelevancy of the man's name. "You don't know him. Not really. He could be in on it."

It took her a second to figure what out he meant. "You think he stole bacon?"

Her grandfather shrugged. "Where do you unload flour by the sack full? Places like this"—he motioned to the empty dining room—"where they cook for dozens, if not hundreds."

Della did not know Moss well enough to defend him, but she sensed his honesty in her gut. "I really don't think he would."

"He's been in Manila for three years. He's already half-Oriental by nature, I bet."

"But—"

"The evidence is all around you. Who could work with these people and not be corrupted?"

"Why don't you ask him yourself?"

The congressman looked shocked. "That's the last thing I want to do, not while I'm staying here, eating the spoils."

The chicken sat heavy in her stomach.

"You hear me, Della? No hints or warnings."

CHAPTER SEVEN

The Reception

Moss looked around at the tables of hors d'oeuvres and hoped there would be enough to feed the unexpectedly large crowd. The *Manila American* had reprinted Congressman Holt's invitation to all military officers stationed in the city and in the nearby provinces. Given the resulting crush, Moss wondered if there was anyone left to guard Fort Santiago or Bilibid Prison, let alone the rest of Luzon.

Fortunately, he had successfully poached Luz from Clarke's to be his baker, and she had learned the quirks of his ovens in no time. The tables overflowed with bread. Moss had taken her early experimental loaves, now stale, and diced them into his gazpacho. But he knew that he might have a hard time getting his guests to eat such an adventurous soup, especially since most Americans in Manila would only eat tomatoes from a can. For those folks, he had prepared boiled ox tongue and mashed potatoes. He made the mashed potatoes himself, fortified with butter, salt, and—his mentor Louis's secret ingredient—a little French mustard, which he personally procured from a commissary sergeant in Ermita.

Moss was not sure whether Della Berget had inspired him or embarrassed him over his past lack of leadership in the kitchen, but either way he had decided to make a change. In the last two weeks, he had heard praise ranging from "welcome change" to "about time." But he had never before been responsible for an occasion like tonight's reception. What would they say tomorrow?

He tried to relax, but the more he tried, the less he succeeded. He clasped his hands behind his back and feigned calm, as if he was not jumping out of his skin with anxiety. It helped to watch Della. She was wearing an off-white silk and lace dress with metallic threading along the gauzy neckline. It was more sensible than the other women's hot, high-necked frocks, and she looked dazzling in it. The cut of a talented dressmaker emphasized her long torso. Someone else might think her a maypole, but Moss had never been keen on the Camille Clifford hourglass-type.

Congressman Holt was talking with Mrs. Cooper. He was sympathizing with the plight of the brave Army wives who endured such worry while their husbands were out in the field. Della kept a plain face, but Moss thought he knew her well enough to detect the ripple of a swallowed laugh. Moss did nothing to acknowledge her—he kept his spine straight and his hands to himself—but he smiled. He counted the beats while Della stubbornly tried not to smile back. It took only five "one-thousands."

Someone tapped Moss on the shoulder: the staff was running out of mashed potatoes. It was an easy enough problem to solve, but the assistant chef did not like the mustard and had to be ordered to use it. Moss explained that Americans had different tastes than Filipinos— they diverged somewhere between Dijon mustard and fermented fish paste—but the lesson had not yet sunk in.

When Moss returned from the kitchen, Della was no longer at her grandfather's side. Moss looked around the packed hall. All of the chairs and tables had been pushed aside to make room for the crowd. He would have to watch how José, Fernando, and Anastasio put it all back together again in the morning, lest he ignite another furniture war.

A few proud Filipinos fidgeted in the crowd, impatient with standing. The old Spanish *bailes* had been formal seated dinners, but the Americans changed all that—they preferred to gulp down conversation on the move.

Once the band started playing, a space cleared for couples eager to dance. Greatly outnumbered by soldiers, every woman in the room was invited to join in—every woman but Della. Moss still did not see her anywhere.

It was not until he went back into the kitchen to deal with a shortage of cold beer that he found Della hiding behind the open door. She was gazing into the dining room, watching the young people with a mix of curiosity and skepticism as they acted out the latest cotillion fad: the "Dewey Figure." At the cry of a horn, men and women dashed to the middle of the floor and grabbed confetti balls for a manic bombardment. The battle waxed hot, confetti sparkled in the air, and Moss's dining room was turned into a mess worse than the real Spanish wrecks in Manila Bay. Della could not have looked more alarmed had she witnessed the actual battle.

When one side capitulated, the laughing couples paired off and began a lively two-step over the papered floor. Della watched dispassionately, but her attention betrayed her envy.

Even though Moss did not need to touch her to get her attention, he did so anyway. He gently brushed his hand down her arm, feeling goose pimples form under his fingers as he went. "Do you want to dance?" he asked.

She looked at him like he was crazy. "No! In front of them?"

"Which is your objection: dancing—or dancing in public?"

"I…"

Moss took a liberty and let his hand drop from her arm to her waist, where he tapped out a beat slower than the ragtime vibrations coming from the dining room.

"Your timing is off," she said.

"This is better."

He held out his other hand, which she took. He exaggerated the tilt of his hips and shoulders as he stepped to the side. Della moved with him. They rocked gently back and forth together to the pulse of his tapping finger.

Moss knew they were too close to read lips, so he let his body speak for him. He could hear her, though. "You smell like whisky and lime," she whispered. "The local lime, *calamansi.*"

The whisky was recent—a fortifying drink to calm his nerves—while the *calamansi* lingered from his earlier kitchen preparations. Few of his staff had the knife skills he did, so he had pitched in.

"Your hands," she whispered, rubbing his palm. "They're rough."

Running a hotel was a more physical job than most people understood. A good manager had to do everything, from cooking to moving furniture to spot-cleaning rooms. Fortunately, Della did not sound disappointed about his calluses. Moreover, he liked her rubbing his hand.

Moss could see the eyes of his kitchen crew upon them, so he danced Della through the swinging door into the back hall used by room service. She laughed as he twirled her into the darkness, only the light from the round porthole window illuminating their faces.

Moss gentled their sway, almost to the point where they were not moving at all. He drew her closer so that her forehead rested against his cheek, and he placed a soft kiss on her head, right above the hairline. Instead of protesting, she nuzzled in for another, which he gave easily.

And then her lips were on his. He hoped that this was not a dream, though if it were his dream, she would not have been so timid. After a few seconds of frustrating closed-mouthed kissing, Moss touched her chin and gently opened her lips. He pressed a little with his tongue to let her know what he wanted.

All his senses were focused on the moment: the taste of champagne on her tongue, the citrus lingering on his fingers, and the touch of her hands in his hair.

Moss traced along her spine with his free hand, all the way down to her rear end. Her shiver encouraged him so he kissed her neck, occasionally grazing her skin with his teeth. How easy would it be to pull her through the back hall to the storeroom? To go from there to his private quarters?

She rested her cheek against his collarbone and sighed as he worked his way back up to her ear. Then he found a ticklish spot, and she jerked away.

He reached for her, but she caught his hands and stopped him. She said nothing, but she was right. Moss could not do any of the things he wanted, certainly not now. And if he continued to think about them, his interest would be obvious to more than just his dancing partner.

He squeezed her hands in his. Della focused on his lips, waiting for some sort of declaration.

"I have to get the mutton out of the oven," he said, knowing it was a flimsy excuse—Moss could see that his chef was taking care of things just fine.

He tried again: "There's a mint sauce that I've prepared specially." That was true, but it was already made, and the sous-chef was now placing it in a crystal bowl.

Della nodded sadly.

He wanted to tell her the truth, that if he stayed in her arms any longer he would be tempted to leave with her. The party could hang, for all he cared.

She pulled her hands from his—not fast like he was on fire, but slowly, reluctantly, like she was forcing herself to give up Crème de Cacao forever. "Go and tend your party," she said, a small smile on her lips. The woman had gotten so used to people giving up on her that she had learned to make them feel less terrible as they did it.

"And then I'll—"

She shook her head. "I'll be fine."

And she would. The dreamy look in her eyes was gone. Della Berget, commodore of reality, was back. She pushed open the door and returned to the reception.

CHAPTER EIGHT

Refusal

Americans in the Philippines had taken to Spanish party hours, if nothing else. The final guests left the reception just before one in the morning. Moss had gotten up well before dawn every morning this week and was exhausted, but he could not go to bed right away, not until he spoke to Della. He felt like celebrating. He felt impulsive. He knew what he would tell her this time, and it would have nothing to do with mutton or mint sauce.

He saw the congressman alone in the dining room. The man was finishing his whisky and writing in his own little red notebook. Had Della's been his gift? Maybe the older man was not as unfeeling a cur as Moss thought.

Holt did not look up from his book when Moss approached. No doubt he kept careful notes of those he met because one never knew when a connection might be needed. Publicly, the congressman credited his career to an enviable Civil War record and a colorful stint as a steamboat captain, but Moss figured that neither of those experiences had really gotten him elected. Behind the man's populist facade was a meticulous and calculated ladder-climber. How else had a West Virginian earned a seat on the Insular Affairs Committee? Now, if all went well in Manila, he was poised for a bid at national office.

It seemed impolitic to interrupt a congressman at such a moment, especially if he hoped to woo this particular congressman's granddaughter, but Moss did it anyway. He seated himself.

Holt looked up. His eyes, his most distinctive feature, seemed a half-size too large for his narrow face. "Well, Mr. North, you should be congratulated for a successful evening."

It had been successful. Moss had even gotten some compliments on the food. Not every dish out of the kitchen had been popular, of course—he had ended up feeding the extra gazpacho to his staff. "Thank you, sir."

"Good little brownies you hired," the congressman said, using one of the less creative epithets that Americans had coined in their short colonial history.

"I'm glad you were pleased with the service."

"A damn sight better than the celestials I met our first day. The Chinaman works hard, but he's most resistant to English."

Not as resistant as Americans were to Chinese or Tagalog.

"Sir, there is something I would like to talk to you about, if you have a minute."

"Oh?"

"It is personal."

The congressman smoothed down a few imaginary strands of hair but said nothing.

"It's about your granddaughter," Moss began, hoping that a direct approach would be appreciated. "I would like your permission to court her."

Holt stared.

"If you're worried about us out in Manila," Moss kept on, hoping to win the man over by sheer zeal, "we can dine here—with a chaperone, if necessary. And only if she is interested, of course, but I believe she will—"

"No."

"If you ask her—"

"I have no intention of doing so."

"Why?"

"Della is my family."

"And?"

"She deserves better," the congressman said.

"I was only a private in the Minnesota Volunteers, it's true, but before that I was a long-time employee of the best hotel in the Midwest, the White Elephant."

"Strange name."

It was. It was also a good story, especially when well told, but this was not the time. "My uncle owned the hotel until very recently. He was a respected member of the St. Paul business community."

Holt's face stayed blank.

"I'm from a good family," Moss insisted. The death of his parents was an accident, not a condemnation of their lives. He knew little about them, actually, but he assumed they were good people—not thieves or drunkards.

Nevertheless, the congressman sighed and spoke slowly, as if to an idiot. "My granddaughter needs to be protected from the ugliness in this world. She cannot be exposed to ridicule and shame."

"I would not—"

"You want to get close to me, and you are using her to do it."

"No, I—"

The congressman waved the objection away. "I meet your kind all the time."

People who despise arrogant politicians?

"And don't go around me on this," the congressman continued. "You think you can charm her into disobedience, telling her she's special and—"

"She is special." But Moss instantly regretted speaking up. This man wouldn't understand—he did not think his granddaughter was unique in any way other than her deafness or her inheritance.

"Della is not yours to judge," Holt said.

"Believe me, I learned my lesson on that score. She is frank when she wants to be, but I would not change that, nor anything else about her." It was true. Della's deafness had made her fierce, but she was grudgingly charming at the same time.

"And I want Della to follow her ambitions," Moss continued. "She can be the writer she wants to be."

"Ha," the congressman scoffed. "What do you know about her writing?"

"I know that she sees what the rest of us miss. I'm halfway sure she can read a lie on a person's face. What better skill is there in a journalist?"

"Her tuition at that asylum was high enough that she might have been studying dental surgery, as far as I know." Holt paused for a chuckle. "Lord knows what they published in that silly newspaper of theirs."

"You haven't read her articles?"

"It was a charity project! They printed those 'articles' to wheedle out another donation from me." He pointed at Moss's chest. "That's what I mean—people use her to get to me. They always have. You are no different."

None of this was progressing as Moss had imagined. Was he as unworthy as the congressman believed? The thought settled around his heart like lead. What could he offer Della beyond a small apartment in the catacombs of a faux-luxury hotel? Even in America, he had no place to call home. He barely knew his brothers and sisters, nor had he been close to the family who raised him. The men he considered fathers were hotel staffers and Army officers, most of them dead by now. What could Moss offer a bride?

Respect. He could offer her that.

"I am sorry that you don't see what I see, sir, but your granddaughter is smarter than either of us. Any man she chooses will be lucky..."

Moss trailed off when he saw Della at the entrance of the dining room. Even at this distance, Moss could plainly see her surprise that he was sitting with the congressman.

"What are you doing?" her eyes asked.

Moss glanced back at the congressman, who had already returned his attention to his journal, before raising his own eyes to her. "I tried," he mouthed.

Her lips turned down, and she wrung her hands—not the reaction he was expecting. She spun and went into the lobby.

Assuming that he had been dismissed, Moss got up from the table. He walked with as much self-restraint as he could muster, but it was not long before he ran after Della.

She was halfway through the lobby and almost at the stables door. Where the devil did she think she was going?

Moss followed.

She led him through a maze of hallways that no guest should know, and into Moss's own office, which was dimly lit by a single electric bulb. It did not surprise him that Della had been lurking around the bowels of his hotel, investigating God-knows-what. She leaned against his desk.

"I don't know how to tell you this gently," she said. "But tomorrow you're going to be arrested."

CHAPTER NINE

Trust

"**A**rrested?"

Moss repeated himself twice more, and Della wondered if hearing the word again and again helped it sink in for him.

"He's that vindictive?" Moss shook his head. "Just because I show interest in his granddaughter, he's going to have me hauled away?"

Della remembered the way Moss had nibbled her neck during their "dance," and she blushed. "You told him about the kiss?"

"No, I'm still alive—for now. But I did declare my intentions."

Intentions. She let the word roll around in her mind for a quick second. She liked its implied determination.

"That's not why," she said. "It's because of the flour—"

"Flour?" Moss ran a hand through his hair. "Who cares about flour?"

"And more. You have hundreds of dollars of government supplies in your storeroom."

"We buy surplus goods, sure, like for the reception. I got some mustard and—"

"Mustard?"

"Just one jar. Okay, a big jar. Maybe they shouldn't sell to veterans, but I think it's a regular practice. Nothing illegal."

He rubbed his hand over bloodshot eyes, and Della realized how exhausted he was.

She reached up and touched his face. "Look at me," she said. "Listen."

He moved his head into her hand, and she caressed his cheek. He closed his eyes and relaxed into her care. "I am listening, sweetheart, even if my eyes are closed."

She did not understand how he could trust his ears that much, but she talked to his closed eyes, as he wished. "The quartermaster of Southern Luzon is a man named Captain Barrows," she began softly. She rubbed her fingers in his hair above his ears, and he breathed on her wrist. "Barrows has made a lot of money selling supplies—like bacon, flour, and the like—from the Army depot. Only he did not report the sales. He pocketed the cash. He made as much as $100,000 before one of his accomplices got scared and turned him in to the military police."

Moss opened his eyes. "That's a lot of money."

"Yes, it is."

"What does this have to do with me?"

"How often do you get deliveries from the quartermaster?"

"Why?"

"There's something I need to show you." She left his side and lit a kerosene lantern with an unsteady hand. She gave Moss the light and gestured for him to lead the way through another narrow passage—past the empty kitchen, and into the storeroom. He went to the shelves and placed the lamp at eye level. The glowing white mantle illuminated every corner of the small room.

Flour, Wheat. U.S. Army Issue. 50 lbs. Net. Contract No. NXS-16007.

There were six of them. Della had already counted.

"There's rum and brandy here," she said. "Vinegar there, salt there, and then there's all that." She pointed to a line of cans—Mother Fuller's corned beef hash, Heinz baked beans, and Armour fried bacon—all with U.S. Army purchase labels pasted across them.

Moss looked at the sacks. He touched a can. "You think I stole this?"

"No." But she knew that she was not convincing.

"Why were you poking around here to begin with?"

"Because that's what I do." She would not apologize for trespassing into forbidden areas of his hotel. She had done it for him. "They are going to search the whole place tomorrow with list in hand of the most pilfered items—these things here are on the list."

"All hotels need these things."

"Well, you can tell that to Colonel Wilder, the Chief of Police. He's the one who downed a quarter of a bottle of whisky in your dining room tonight."

"Damn it." Moss shook his head. "Why tomorrow?"

"Grandfather asked them to wait until the reception was over."

"Can't let my incarceration get in the way of his big affair. When did you first hear this?"

"Tonight."

"But you've been poking around longer than that."

"I knew about the scandal, but I didn't think you were involved, not until I saw this stuff coming and going." She spent her whole day watching and counting. "Do you have any idea how many deliveries you get a day?"

"Della, what do you expect? This flour"—he patted a bag—"could have come from my new baker, Luz. She probably bought it from Clarke's."

"Clarke is not implicated."

Moss did not look surprised. "As if the police would know where to look. That man has more warehouses than the Army itself. I'll talk with Luz."

Talk with her? "If she is involved, would she tell you anything? Better to leave you holding the bag—literally."

"She wouldn't do that."

"How do you know?"

"I just do."

Della knew that an angry American policeman could probably terrify Luz into giving up the Virgin Mary herself. "I hope you're right."

"Why did you wait to tell me this now?"

She held out her hand, but he did not take it. It was the first time he had rejected her since they became friends.

Della felt herself mentally dig in. "I had to piece together a lot of different conversations. I looked for you after but…"

"I was easy to find. I was with your grandfather."

It was hard for Della to watch both lips and eyes at the same time, but she did it well enough to recognize Moss's anger. "So you are telling me that you have more faith in your baker's intentions than in mine."

"No, I"—he paused—"I think we're just missing something here."

"Missing something?" She narrowed her gaze. "You think I couldn't figure out what the officers said right in front of my eyes?"

Moss paused. He tried to hide his suspicions, but she had seen the look on his face a thousand times before.

"That's it, isn't it?" she said. "You don't trust my lip reading."

"Everybody makes mistakes. You said yourself it was difficult to follow—"

"It's always difficult. You never doubted me before. But now suddenly there's a limit to what I can be expected to understand." She clenched her fists. "I won't be treated like a child, not by you."

"Della, the last thing you are to me is a child. All I'm saying is that there has to be another explanation."

Della pulled her gaze from Moss's mouth and looked straight into his eyes. "Then I'll leave you to find out what that is. Good luck." And she walked out.

CHAPTER TEN

Old Friends

Moss was angrier at himself than at Seb, but his assistant probably couldn't tell the difference at the moment. Moss had stopped Seb as he was about to go home for the night. "You can't leave yet," he had said. "Not until we sort this out."

"Sort what out?"

"You know what!"

Seb's bewilderment did nothing to soothe Moss's temper. He had to remind himself that two and a half years of friendship outweighed three hundred pounds of flour, no matter what the kitchen scales said. Moss wouldn't let anyone carry Seb away in chains. He hoped Seb felt the same way about him.

For most of their friendship, Seb had been the one doing Moss the favors. There was the night when Moss mixed local coconut wine with Cyrus Noble Rye Whisky. Not caring for God, man, or devil, Moss thought midnight the perfect time to sing an off-key serenade to the lovely Marita two streets down. When he failed to attract Marita to the window, he pounded on the door, so loaded for bear that he shrugged off all of Seb's tugs and warnings. The door finally opened to reveal an angry, silver-haired patriarch—a man Moss later learned was a spy for the Filipino army.

There were a dozen similar stories from their policing days—a history that made the present conversation much more difficult. Moss dragged Seb to the storeroom and asked only one word: "Why?" He pointed to the flour, the canned goods, and the booze.

Seb looked confused. "You needed flour for Luz. It is good quality, just like the soldiers use."

"Not just like the soldiers use, Seb. Exactly what the soldiers use!"

"So?"

"The flour is stolen."

Seb did not seem surprised. "I did not steal it. If the soldiers did, that is their problem."

"Who sold it to you?"

Silence.

"Shit, Seb," Moss whispered. "What have you gotten us into?"

Moss's friend took a step back, like the question itself was a blow. "I filled the empty shelves when you told me to. You did not ask questions then."

"Don't tell me this is the 'local' way of doing business—"

"No, it is the white man's way!" Seb shook his head sadly, as if all foreigners were beyond hope. "This is how the Oriente did business before you and I came. I had no choice."

"With whom did you make this arrangement?"

"Officers." In other words, men more powerful than either Seb or Moss.

"Which officers?"

"Captain Barrows and others—"

"Why is their stuff in our storeroom? What did you give them for it?"

Seb held up his hands. "I gave nothing. They gave it to us."

Moss looked over the plentiful cans and bottles. "Why?"

Seb shrugged a single shoulder, a gesture Moss read too well.

"*Amigo*," Moss said, "If we're going to work this out, you have to tell me everything."

"Your ignorance protects you."

"I don't need protection, especially from you." It was supposed to be the reverse. "Tell me."

"Suites 30 and 31—"

"Are empty."

"Not always."

Moss sighed in frustration. "The Army rents the rooms, so they can use them or not, as they see fit."

"They are used every Saturday night." Seb leaned in. "Only not by the same men who signed the contracts."

"They're not Army?"

"Oh, they are officers, like Barrows and his friends. And contractors—"

"—and girls," Moss finished.

There had been a regular flock of "low-flying doves" flitting up to the rooms, but Moss had looked the other way. A paying customer could choose his own guests. He should have known better. "Damn it."

"We didn't give them the girls."

"We didn't run a prostitution ring from within the hotel. I'm glad to hear it."

Seb frowned. Moss had never turned his sharp tongue against him before, and he regretted doing so now, no matter what was at stake. He took a breath before speaking again: "What did we give them?"

"Room service. Cleanup. Discretion. This is how they paid."

Moss had to admit it was a neat scheme—but he did not want to go to jail for it. "So you accepted contraband from thieves 'entertaining' in stolen rooms? Because that is how our friends at the station will see it." Actually, since Moss's regiment had gone home, they had no friends with the police anymore. The new chief was busy proving the chops of his civilian force. Embarrassing Moss and Seb would suit him fine. "Why didn't you tell me?"

Seb looked and sounded his age as he responded. "You did not need to know. The city has always been this way—Spanish or American, it is the same."

If there was anyone who would know the history of crime in Manila, it would be Seb—but Moss had never imagined the man would go along with any of it. Father, friend, employee—Seb was all three and more. Moss wanted to hug and throttle him at the same time.

"We could end up at Bilibid because of this." There were still inmates there who would remember Seb, and they both knew it.

"We did nothing wrong!"

"'Nothing wrong' would have been buying from Larry Gong, as I thought you were doing."

Gong owned the largest grocery in the city, right behind the open-air market in Quiapo. Moss liked Gong because he had been a U.S. Navy man and understood the American way of doing business, but Seb had never trusted him.

There was an awkward silence, one that made Moss feel more colonial than he had during his time policing the city.

"Yes, sir," Seb finally said. He had never "sirred" Moss before.

"Seb, it's just that…" The assistant looked at him expectantly, but Moss did not finish the sentence. What could he say? "Never mind."

If Seb had not trusted Moss enough to tell him about Barrows, then Moss had not been as good a manager or friend as he wanted to be. He pointed to the shelves. "We have to get rid of all of this by tomorrow morning."

"We can put it in the stables."

"No, that's the first place they'll look. And my apartment will be the second."

"The Army rooms?"

Moss laughed at the irony, but shook his head. "They will search anywhere Barrows has been."

"He never came to my house—"

"God, Seb, no. The last thing I need is for the Army to seize your house. Besides, we can't carry sacks of flour through the streets at night."

Moss had an idea, but it was a long shot. "Send the boys out to gather as much of the kitchen staff as possible."

"Gather them here?"

"Tell them they will work all night. Pay them a bonus. And then tell the boys to set up the dining room as it was for the reception, with one long banquet table."

"You want to hide the food under the tables?"

"On the tables." Moss smiled when he saw Seb catch on. "It's going to be the best breakfast ever offered at the Oriente—with enough fresh bread to feed an Army."

CHAPTER ELEVEN

Spelling

Moss stood in front of room 27 lacking both confidence and courage. The light under the door was a promising sign, but even so it was far too late for an evening call. At least he brought a peace offering Della would appreciate.

There was a string that extended from the door handle up and over the door. Next to the string was a note in big block penmanship: "Tug string to knock."

Moss juggled the heavy tray he carried with one hand and obediently tugged the string with the other. It gave several inches and then snagged. Now what?

He almost turned back. He could find her tomorrow. He shouldn't be here. She did not want to see him—

The door opened. Della was still fully dressed in her evening gown, which was a relief. Mostly.

He held out the tray in supplication. "May I bring this in? I want to talk."

"Just talk?"

Was that relief or disappointment on her face? She turned away, which could be a dismissal if he let it be. He didn't. He waited.

When Della noticed that he had not followed her into the room, she turned again. "Coming?"

Invited, Moss nearly dove into the room. He looked around, saw her notebook on a small table, and set the tray down next to it.

He watched as Della reset her string. An India rubber ball was pierced through and rested snugly on the thread. The other end was tied to the room's largest chandelier.

For his benefit, she pulled the string taut—as he had done from the other side of the door—and it set the ball and crystal bouncing.

"Genius," he said. Maybe it should have surprised him more, but it didn't. Of course she would have such a contraption.

"Is it breakfast already?" she asked, looking greedily at the tray.

Actually, it was so early for breakfast that no one would be blamed for thinking it was still time for supper. Nevertheless, he pulled a chair and gestured for her to sit.

Moss handed her the place card from the tray. It read: *Crêpes Suzette with dalandan butter sauce, poached eggs, baked beans, corned beef hash, fresh toast, and egg nog.* He removed the cover plate to reveal her banquet.

"That is the most absurd mix of food I have ever seen," she said. "Do I smell brandy? Isn't that a little extravagant for breakfast?"

"Let's hope it goes quickly. I don't like having the bottles everywhere."

Moss glowed when he saw a smile of realization turn up Della's lips. "I see—very clever. Flambéed *crêpes* to use up the brandy." Della looked at the drink. "And egg nog?"

"Best way to get rid of the Army's rum, along with a lot of condensed milk. We're calling it a Continental tour—a special promotion today only."

"How much?"

"A half Mex for as much as your belly can carry."

"That's nothing!"

"Which is what I hope to have left after the third seating at nine."

That was five hours away. It did not give him much time with Della, but the kitchen was under control for the time being, and he had something he wanted to say. "I'm sorry for not trusting you—"

"I should have told you about the arrests earlier."

He might not have reacted any better then. "I should have believed your eyes, Della, more than my ears. You knew something was going on. I didn't."

She picked up her fork and tugged at the *crêpe*. "Let me see if I will accept your apology."

He smiled as she savored the bite. He liked feeding this woman. "Forgiven?"

She set down the fork. "Only if I am, too."

"I don't know. What did you cook for me?"

She laughed that bubbly, slightly-too-loud laugh that made his chest swell. He wanted to hold her, but the food was in his way, so he stood and extended a hand. "Before I leave you to your meal, may I have this dance?"

"Is there music?" She looked toward the window, as if maybe he had hired a band. He should have thought of it just so that she could feel the vibrations—though waking the rest of the hotel would have been counterproductive.

"You are my music," he said, bringing her to her feet. When his thumb rubbed the thin fabric of her dress next to her wrist, she looked up at him.

The gold in her eyes sparkled in the lamplight. "Is that what you said to my grandfather?"

He drew her closer. "Maybe I said that I was falling in love with you."

"Did you?"

"I would have, had he let me."

He drew her hair away from her face and leaned down to kiss her forehead, but she offered her lips instead. She was less shy this time, opening her mouth and drawing him in. If it were up to him, he could fall into the kiss without ever hitting bottom. But there was a right and a wrong way to do this, so he pulled away.

"Della," he began, intending to finish his sentence with some form of the verb to marry.

But she reached up and pressed a finger across his lips. "No more talking. I'm tired," she explained. "It's been a long day of reading faces."

What could he say to that? He wouldn't force her to read her proposal. "You rest. I—"

"Quiet," she said. "That's not what I mean. I don't want to read you, but I still want you."

She turned off the electric light—really a glorified candle—and then blew out the kerosene lamp. They were left standing in a fading orange halo.

The streetlights from out front of the hotel only reached the high corner of the wall. She would not be able to read Moss's lips in this; she would have to trust him enough to be truly deaf. That was a lot of power, and he did not know where to begin.

She leaned into the comforting space of his neck, and he wrapped his arms around her. "Please," she whispered.

He swallowed.

"Don't think too much about it," she said against his skin. "I want to know what it's like. Tell me you know how."

He nodded, rubbing his cheek against her temple.

"I want to know, too."

Still, he hesitated. The first time was important for women, in a different way than it was for men. It could be awkward, even painful for her. Did she know that?

"I'm a grown woman," she said, anticipating his concern. "I want this to be with you. I won't expect anything afterward, I promise."

He expected something. He wanted to tell her that.

"Please?"

He couldn't refuse. He had hoped for this since she turned out the light; he just had not talked around the rest of his conscience yet. But he would make sure that Della would not regret asking. Fortunately, growing up in a hotel, even a respectable one, had broadened his education in just the right ways.

Moss circled around her to lift the lace drape that covered her back fastenings. He pulled the fabric tighter to create enough give so that he could loosen the buttons out of their holes. The dress slipped to the floor at her feet. He thought he could hear her breath quicken. Or maybe it was his.

He lifted the camisole over her head and tossed it to the side. The low, straight cut of Della's corset pushed her breasts together to create a mirage of cleavage. He tucked his fingers into that cleft and heard a tiny gasp in return. He pulled the two sides of the stays together to release the top snap, and then let his fingers drag down each corset bone to the next. Soon the criminal contraption joined its mates on the floor.

Moss raised one hand to her cheek, thinking to reassure her. When she turned into it and kissed his palm, he found that he was the one reassured.

He slowly unbuttoned her chemise, revealing two tiny, beautiful breasts. They barely tented from her chest in soft triangles, but they were more exciting to him than heavy, rounded flesh would be. He reached for one and brushed the nipple with his thumb. Della closed her eyes and gave a breathy exhale. Encouraged, he leaned down and took it into his mouth. As he sucked the nipple to a hard point, she cried out and leaned against his shoulder.

He righted her before continuing to peel off her chemise. Finally, Della stepped out of the circle of clothes at her feet.

He kissed her mouth again, holding her against him with an arm around her waist. With the other hand he drew a finger through her curls below. She sighed into his kiss and whispered him on. "Yes."

That was a good sign. She wanted to feel, and so she would. He led her over to the *sillon* in front of the window. The planter chair was a deep recliner made out of wood and rattan, and it had long, wide arms that stretched out in front of the seat. The *sillon* was built for napping, but Moss had not brought Della here to sleep.

She sat, and he gently lifted one of her legs to rest on the extended arm of the chair. She relaxed there, wanton, ready for him.

He started with a gentle kiss to her knee and then moved his lips up her inner thigh. Della gave a deep moan, vibrating her entire chest.

"I love you," he mouthed against her skin. He said it a second time. And a third.

His answer was a soft giggle. "I understood you the first time. I love you, too."

It was good that he would not need to repeat himself because he was running out of room on her leg. He did not ease her into anything, but licked his way up her opening. New to this, she pulled back, but he held her hips and gave no quarter. And when he flicked his tongue against her sensitive center, she shifted and pressed back into him.

At every touch, she grew louder. His fingers joined the effort, and occasionally he drew his teeth lightly across her flesh. Her moans became grunts and whines, none of which she had any idea she was making. It was the most glorious noise Moss had ever heard, but he knew it would carry easily through the night air.

He leaned over and pressed one dry finger against her lips. It was the same command she had given him earlier.

"Sorry," she whispered.

He kissed her thigh to let her know she was forgiven. When he returned to his pleasant task, though, it did not take her long to start moaning again, so Moss paused to close the window. The loss of light was a fair trade for her full voice.

He settled at her feet and resumed his worship. When he reached two knuckles inside, she let him know he had found the right spot. He sucked harder at her clitoris until he felt, heard, and smelled her pleasure. He did not stop until her body no longer squeezed and pulled at him. By that time, they were both out of breath.

His eyes had adjusted to the blackness, but even so he could not make out her expression. She remained in the chair, leg raised, worn out. He picked up her hand and drew letters on her palm: *more?*

"Yes," she said quickly. "More."

He began removing his own clothes, and she watched as best she could in the dark. By the time he pulled down his drawers, Della's eyes were riveted to one spot. She held out a hand, but she was still too low in the chair to reach. Moss helped by walking into her grasp.

She reached down and cupped him. The coolness of her hands gave him a little jolt, but by the time she reached his shaft, she was all warmth. And so soft. He stood as still as he could while she fumbled and explored, even though every touch drove him a little more crazy.

And then she did something unexpected. She leaned in to his pelvis and took a deep, long sniff.

He chuckled, which she felt. "This smells like you," she explained. "Not your cooking, not your laundry, just you."

Just his need.

She sat up to kiss him. He shouldn't have let her serve him as he had her, but he ran his hand through her hair as she did. When she sucked hard, he gripped a handful before he could stop himself. He tried to pull away, but she reached up and held his rear end in place.

"Della," he whispered vainly, but he lacked the self-control to stop her.

When he felt the warm tickle start in his heavy sac, he knew he was too close. He pulled out of her reach—firmly this time—because he had a better idea than she did what would happen if he didn't.

He tugged at her hand, and she rose from the chair without hesitation. She tilted her head to kiss him but stopped an inch from his lips, a little startled.

She sniffed again. "That must be me," she said.

He nodded and let her give him a quick, investigative peck. Bolder, she flicked her tongue against his soiled lips. He welcomed the deeper kiss and pulled her hard against him, his erection pressing impatiently against her stomach.

As they kissed and groped, Moss walked Della to the bed. Or, more likely, she walked him. Moss lifted the mosquito net for her, and she crawled in first.

He nudged her legs wide so he could settle in between—skin to skin, cock to cunny, mouth to mouth. She would be a little sensitive yet, so he kissed her from her ears to her nipples as his hips gently thrust against her, wetting the tip of his penis. Soon he had her moaning again.

"Will this feel as good as your mouth?" she asked.

He was sure that it would not—not right away. She could help him, though. He placed her hand over her clitoris, but she pulled away, self-conscious. Because he had no soothing words for her, he put her fingers back and pressed. He traced circles, showing how she could make this better for them both. When she kept on of her own accord, he rewarded her with more kisses.

Slowly he pushed inside. It was easy for the first inch or two. The warmth of her body was almost too tempting, and the rutting animal in him wanted to spear her through. He needed to distract them both. He worked at her nipple with his tongue and teeth, reading her noises as she relaxed underneath him.

He bit just a little—not hard, but not soft—and at the same time thrust all the way in. Both moves caused her a little pain—her scream of surprise was not delicate—but the discomfort did not seem to last long. He stayed fully inside her and began gently tonguing her abraded breast by way of apology.

Her hand froze at the initial pain, but now he felt her fingers rotating beneath him again. He felt her push up against him, drawing him in even deeper.

So, of course, he pulled back.

"Don't go," she began.

Happy to oblige, he pushed back into her.

"Yes," she whispered.

His buttocks bounced slowly as he repeated the motion again and again. He began kissing her neck, her ear, her temple, whatever he could concentrate on while he felt the pleasure coil in his balls again. She rocked her hips in counterpoint, making the thrusts faster and harder than he could do alone.

He would not last much longer. Moss reached down and helped her apply pressure with her fingers. He would have loved to let her dance on the edge a little longer, but he couldn't risk it.

She screamed off key as her walls pulsed around him. He bent his head back, eyes shut, concentrating, still thrusting. Her body tried to coax him into giving up his seed, but he gritted his teeth and held on. Finally, when she quieted, he pulled out and rocked against her hip a few times before spilling on her stomach. It had been a near thing.

He ducked out of the bed to grab a napkin for the mess. After, he settled at her side and ran his fingertips over her smile. He brought her hand up to his mouth so she could feel the same on his.

Now would have been a good time for a proposal, but he would have plenty of time tomorrow once he was rid of the inspectors. It was only a matter of a few hours. He could wait.

CHAPTER TWELVE

The Grand Tour

Della awoke when the first crack of light snuck around the edges of the closed windows.

She was alone, naked, and hungry. Poor Moss, though, had not slept at all. After their second time, he had said a sweet goodnight and then headed back to his mad kitchen.

Della imagined what it would be like to sleep—really sleep—with him. Did he snore? She hoped so. It seemed a waste for her to fall for a quiet sleeper.

She walked over to the covered tray. Moss had cleared most of the food before he left, leaving only toast and jam. She was sorry that her plate had gone to waste, but then again, that was sort of the point. Moreover, she could get a whole new breakfast downstairs. She was a paying customer—and a very satisfied one.

She ate the toast and then headed into the bathroom to erase the traces of Moss from her body. She hung up her clothes, ruffled through her toiletries, threw a nightgown over her head, and climbed into bed. She was down barely long enough to settle her breathing when the door opened.

A maid crept into the room just in time for Della's requested wake-up. Usually Della would be truly asleep at this hour, but today she pretended to naturally waken just as the Filipina opened the netting. With a quick nod, the maid backed out of the room, her frightful job done.

Della rose, performed her real morning toilette, and dressed. She was quick, but not quick enough. By the time she knocked on her grandfather's door, he was already agitated.

"We've got to go," he said. "The dining room is flooded with commoners."

Della smiled. Moss's evidence would be consumed in no time.

"I tell you, this hotel gets worse and worse by the day," he continued. "A nasty business."

By that he probably meant the police inspection more than the madding crowd.

If getting the congressman out of the hotel would help Moss carry off his caper, though, she would gladly leave. "I'll grab my bag. Clarke's?" She could use some coffee.

"Town," her grandfather said. "The Palace."

The Marble Palace, or Ayuntamiento, was not really a palace. It was not even the residence of the governor-general, an honor reserved for Malacañang. No, it was just a municipal hall, albeit a grand one, fashioned after two Renaissance *palazzos*.

Whatever the building was called, Della had never actually seen it. So far, she had not been allowed to venture farther than the Escolta. "You'll take me with you?"

For the first time the whole trip, her grandfather did not look annoyed by one of her questions. "Unless you don't want to go."

"No, I—"

"I have made plans for us. For you."

Della did not believe her eyes. "You have?"

Her grandfather nodded unambiguously. "I have a friend at a paper. A contact. He's willing to meet you, maybe give you some advice."

"Me?"

"Yes, Della." The congressman seemed more annoyed by her surprise than her parrot-like repartee. "I told you that I would help you meet the right people while we were here, and I keep my promises. It has just taken me a while to set it up."

"Why?"

"Well, I first tried the *Manila Times* but—"

"No," she cut in. "I mean, why would you do this for me?"

He drew back as if offended. "You are my daughter's daughter."

Della knew that Holt had not seen her mother in years. In fairness, neither had she. No one in her family had ever come to Washington. In fact, no other Holts had been farther east than Morgantown, West Virginia, let alone the Philippines. Della realized that she and her grandfather were both strangers to everyone who mattered.

Suddenly, everything from her eyeballs to her nostrils tingled, but she straightened her back and swallowed the sentiment whole. She would not look back. Her grandfather was offering her a way forward, and she had to take it. "Thank you," she said.

"You're welcome." Her grandfather actually smiled, and the hallway felt a little brighter for it. "Now get your things and meet me downstairs. We're late."

If they were late, so was the rest of the city. The streets were packed with carriages. Vendors blocked the sidewalks. From teenage boys to bow-legged old men, these footpad salesmen balanced everything from baskets of bananas to water buckets on their bamboo sticks. It took longer to ride past Clarke's than it would have to walk.

When their *calesa* reached the Bridge of Spain, the horse slowed down a bit—whether because of the slight incline or equine nervousness, Della did not know. She was happy to lend the beast some courage, though, since she felt invincible today. She watched the dance of lighters on the river, and even the wafting tang of fish, coal smoke, and sewage did not put her off.

They entered Intramuros through a Romanesque gate, a portal to some kind of Catholic wonderland. If she glanced up, the city was all domes, crosses, and oyster shell windows. If she kept her eyes on the sidewalks, though, she could have been back home with so many Yankees on the street.

The Palace lived up to its name: it was a beautiful two-story stone building with awning-covered windows and a large American flag hanging by the arched entrance. Della happily followed her grandfather on his rounds through the building, from the health inspector's desk to the office of the treasurer. He let her sit in on his meetings, most of which she stopped lip-reading once she realized how boring they were. If she was impatient for her own appointment, she could hardly be blamed for that.

Lunch was brought into the hall, and Congressman Holt sat Della next to him as if she were the guest of honor. She understood snippets of the conversations, which were on subjects as diverse as troop movements and school curricula. One of the men even said that some Filipinos advocated for American statehood.

After lunch her grandfather made good. She had not doubted him, but like a child promised a sweetmeat, she had almost resorted to begging. Finally, he introduced her to Mr. Burt Dorr, manager of the *Manila Freedom* newspaper.

"I have two daughters," Dorr said. "Just about your age. I doubt they even read a newspaper."

Not a promising start. "I would very much like to meet them," Della offered. "Maybe we can take a tour of the editorial offices together."

Her grandfather brushed his hand through the air. "We don't have time for that. Just show Dorr your notebook."

With that impatient cue, Della handed over her clippings. She held her breath as he paged through—it didn't take long, so she was hardly in danger of expiring. The only article he lingered over was an interview of a deaf artist, who, like Della, was saddled with a political family.

"A typical collegiate operation," Dorr said of her paper. "No worse."

That last statement may have been meant as a compliment. "Thank you?"

Dorr sat back and thrust out his chin. Whatever he was considering, when he reached a decision his fist hit the table like a gavel. She felt the tremor beneath the soft skin of her wrist.

"Tell you what," he said. "If you think you have something, send it on to me. I'll probably need to rewrite it, of course. But your style is less tortured than I expected."

It took a moment for Della to process that as a compliment, too. "Okay, thank you."

"Send them to me until I tell you to stop."

Had she just gotten a job? Sort of. She would write for him for free until he fired her. But maybe, just maybe, he wouldn't.

Almost before she could thank Mr. Dorr, her grandfather hustled her outside. "Why are we in such a hurry?" she asked.

"They're waiting on us."

"Who?"

But Della's question died in the confusion of finding their driver among the multitude seeking a plump fare, so she let it go. Besides, she was tired. Dozens of conversations from a jumble of mouths, and all at one speed: fast. The hearing made such a day look effortless. If only they knew.

She was ready for a wordless ride—a twenty-minute nap for her mind until they arrived "home" at the Oriente, where she could check on Moss.

But instead of turning right off the bridge into Binondo, their calesa went left and stopped at the dock, where only two weeks ago she had first stepped foot on Philippine soil. Della followed her grandfather to the riverside, hoping they were just picking up a mailbag. But no—Holt motioned her to jump into one of the thatched houseboats.

"No," she said. "Where are we going?"

The stony look in her grandfather's eyes told Della he had anticipated resistance. "We're leaving."

"Why?"

No answer.

"To go where?"

She hated it when the hearing pretended to be deaf. They did it so badly.

"Grandfather..."

"The grand tour," he said finally. "You knew that was our plan."

"Your plan." The congressman may have told the public that he would guide Della around the islands, but privately she knew that he had always planned to leave her behind.

"I thought you would love this," he said. "It's what you want, isn't it? To see as much of the islands as possible? Send your impressions back to a bona fide newspaper?"

Just days before, she would have jumped at the opportunity. Her grandfather knew it, too. "Why now?"

"I told you. I'm doing what is best for my granddaughter."

"What is best for me is to know where I am going, and why."

The congressman motioned for their American entourage to wait, and then steered Della back into the relative privacy of the Filipino crowd. "You were in more danger at that hotel than you realize."

Danger? Was Moss being marched off to jail? A seed of panic swelled in her gut as she struggled to think of an excuse, any excuse, to get back to the Oriente. "What about our belongings...?"

He pointed to the rear of the lighter. "They're already packed."

They were—her grandfather's many trunks and Della's one were piled next to huge clay jars. "How do I know that's everything? I need to check—"

"Don't worry, Della. I have taken care of it all. Trust me."

"But—"

"You have your portfolio, right?"

That was true. Everything else she owned was replaceable. "But I—"

"Forget him."

That brought her up short. "Who?"

"That hotel manager. He didn't touch you, did he?"

That was not a question she could answer honestly, not without landing Moss in more trouble. "No."

"Look, I know it is not easy being you," he said. "And I don't mean being deaf."

No, he wouldn't. He meant being a Holt, a name that was Della's almost as much as Berget was. "Not everyone is using me to get close to you."

"Are you sure?"

"I know Mr. North isn't like that. He's a hardworking man in his own right."

"It is the hardworking ones you have to watch out for. They're that much more ruthless."

"You came from nothing, too."

"Why else do you think I am protecting you? Do you remember when your mother asked me to take you?"

Della did not like to remember anything about the time she awoke from meningitis to face the jarring silence of her mother's tears. Only five years old, she could not read words on the page, let alone lips, so no one could explain to her what had happened. Finally, people stopped talking to her—what was the point? With her frightened cries, they had assumed she had lost her wits as well as the use of her ears.

An older man was eventually summoned, and he took a confused and screaming Della from her home. Only at school later that year did Della learn that this older man was her grandfather.

Holt took a step closer and placed a hand on her arm. "You should have a man with nothing to prove. They are easier. They don't hurt the ones they love, not as much."

"I want him," she said over her sigh.

"He's a criminal. In prison. And if, by some miracle, he is released, he will be arrested again tomorrow, or next year. His kind is always caught."

"Or elected to office."

The congressman smiled sadly. "If so, that's a hard road, too. Della, you are my first and last responsibility, and I will see you safe."

A tear escaped, and she wiped it away quickly.

"I wanted to make it easier for you with the offer of a newspaper job," he added. "That is the best I can do."

He had given her the chance for one type of happiness, but it came at the cost of another. "I still won't go."

"You will."

"No, I—"

But as she moved to step away, she realized that the caring hand on her arm had become a shackle. For an older man, her grandfather had an iron grip.

"Don't make a scene." He grasped her other arm. "I don't want to hire men to carry you to the boat, but I will if I have to."

"He's a good man—"

"Don't test me," her grandfather warned. "Think of it—he's a felon and a traitor. If you stay with him the papers will run with the scandal for weeks. You would be in the news, Della, not reporting it."

She considered her options. Even if she could run away, her grandfather would give chase. And it was hard to hide with no money, especially with all her belongings on the lighter. Besides, where would she go with Moss in jail?

With his newfound strength, her grandfather put her on the boat.

By the time her tears dried up, all she could see was the walled city of Manila shrink from view as the rowers made good time into the bay. Della knew disappointment and she knew shame, but this feeling was different. She felt sick to her stomach, an illness that had nothing to do with food, nor the motion of the boat. Love: she had never imagined it could be so wretched.

CHAPTER THIRTEEN

Crossed Wires

22 JANUARY 1901 08:14
TO: MOSS NORTH, HOTEL ORIENTE MANILA
HOLT REPORTED YOUR ARREST STOP WILL RETURN DIRECTLY
IF ADVISED
DELLA BERGET

* * *

22 JANUARY 1901 15:38
TO: DELLA BERGET, SORSOGON
HOLT MISTAKEN INSPECTION CLEAR HOPE FOR YOUR
IMMEDIATE RETURN
MOSS

* * *

31 JANUARY 1901 14:02
TO: MOSS NORTH, HOTEL ORIENTE MANILA
WHY NO ANSWER STOP MISS YOU
DELLA

* * *

31 JANUARY 1901 20:49
TO: DELLA BERGET, DUMAGUETE
ALL CLEAR PLEASE RETURN MARRY ME
MOSS

* * *

2 FEBRUARY 1901 11:27
TO: MOSS NORTH, HOTEL ORIENTE, MANILA
STILL NOTHING FROM YOU WORRIED
DELLA

* * *

3 FEBRUARY 1901 09:43
TO: DELLA BERGET, DUMAGUETE
RESENT ALL MESSAGES STOP WILL MEET ANYWHERE FOR
VOWS PLEASE
MOSS

* * *

18 FEBRUARY 1901 15:12
TO: DELLA BERGET, CEBU
STILL AWAITING ACCEPTANCE PLEASE SAY YES
MOSS

* * *

20 FEBRUARY 1901 09:02
TO: WARDEN, BILIBID PRISON MANILA
REQUEST INFORMATION PRISONER MOSES NORTH REPORT
HEALTH LEGAL STATUS DIRECTLY
DELLA BERGET

* * *

20 FEBRUARY 1901 17:59
TO: DELLA BERGET, CEBU
STAY THERE DEPARTING MANILA TONIGHT
MOSS

CHAPTER FOURTEEN

Bread Crumbs

Moss stood by the rail of the S. S. *Aeolus* and scanned the Camotes Sea for steamers heading the other way. It had taken great effort to get this close to Cebu, but it might all be for naught if Della had already left.

Nothing had been simple since the night of the reception. Moss should have expected Holt to pull something shady, but he had been too busy feeding all of Manila to pay the man close attention. Moss and Seb had stashed the empty cans and bottles—the only remaining evidence—in the stables' manure cart. Only Americans could make such a fuss over a day's worth of groceries, Seb pointed out.

After the unsuccessful but time-consuming police inspection, Moss waited impatiently for Della to return from her day's errands so that they could celebrate. When she still had not returned that evening, he discovered from his clerk that the Holt party had checked out.

For the next few days, Moss waited for Della to contact him. Meanwhile, the Oriente was frequented by an unusual number of policemen. Moss was not surprised by the additional attention; after all, the police were embarrassed by the unsuccessful raid. But the police never left. Someone was paying these coppers a full day's salary to watch Moss watch them. And then a second day's salary. And a third.

When Della's first cable came, Moss was at the hotel to receive it. But his relief was short-lived. The cable told him two things: first, that she was far away; and, second, that she believed he had been arrested.

It did not matter, Moss told himself. He could fix this. He would recall Della to Manila with a simple "all clear." She would come. He convinced himself in the subsequent week of silence that she needed time to make return arrangements.

And then her second cable arrived. Maybe she was moving from city to city too fast, or maybe Holt was interfering, but it was clear that she had not received Moss's response. Worst of all, she probably thought that he had given up on her.

So when Moss overheard customers talking about the deaf woman who wrote for the *Manila Freedom*, he immediately subscribed. With each edition, he assembled a byline bread crumb trail, marking each city onto an oversized map on his office wall. But each of these bylines went stale too quickly: by the time he could have reached any of these places, Della would be gone.

What else could he do but propose over the wire? Repeatedly. He did not mind the telegrapher's snicker the first time, but the third time he did wonder if he was making an ass of himself. Had Della given up on him? She had said that she expected nothing from him; maybe she wanted nothing, as well.

The congressman was making a big circle throughout the islands, which should have meant returning to Manila. But when Moss checked with every other hotel in the city worth the title, he found that no reservations had been made for Holt's party. The congressman would not leave something like that to chance. There were two other cities from which he could leave the islands: Iloilo and Cebu, both ports of call for Hong Kong-based steamers. Moss could wait for Della at one of them, but which one?

He didn't know, which meant he had no choice but to stay where he was. Each passing day made the Oriente as much of a prison as Bilibid. He sulked. He could not walk into the kitchen without wanting to throw a pot at some innocent dishwasher, so instead he sat at his desk and stared at Della's clippings. The employees avoided him. Seb avoided him.

Her stories were good, but too many of them featured the congressman. Moss had trouble even looking at the man's name in print. His eyes glazed over at the details of receptions and parades and speeches…

And then something caught his attention. Moss had skimmed the description of the Cebu banquet a few times, but now he scrutinized every word: "The people of Cebu laid the richest table outside of Manila. Congressman Holt told his hosts that grilled fish and roasted pig would make a Filipino of him yet, as long as he never had to give up his favorite treat from home: roast chicken with lemony potatoes."

Moss did not believe that any of those words came out of the congressman's mouth. The man was not that likeable, nor did he give a whit about local cuisine. It was Della who missed chicken and potatoes. Della missed him.

But what was Moss supposed to do about it? This article was three days old. She could be anywhere by now. He dropped his head in his hands and tugged at the roots of his hair, the dull pain surprisingly cathartic.

He was interrupted by a knock at the door.

Moss didn't look up. "Whatever it is, ask Señor Lopa."

"Who else would be here but me? No one else likes you so much." Seb dropped a folded piece of paper on Moss's desk. "For you."

TELEGRAM shouted from the brown paper in big red block letters.

"You opened one of my cables?"

"Not me. Look who it's addressed to."

The new warden of Bilibid Prison. Why would Della expect to find Moss there?

Unless she still had not received any of his messages. A wave of fury surged through Moss. How could Holt be so selfish and controlling?

But then he realized that the cable actually brought good news—it meant Della had not rejected him. Moss looked at the sending station. "She's still in Cebu! How long ago did you get this?"

"It came to my friends at the prison today. They brought it by after work to tease me. They wanted to know why my boss is supposed to be behind their bars." Seb looked at him sharply. "So much for being bottom key."

"Low key," Moss corrected absently, but his mind was elsewhere. If he left now, he could catch her. "I'm going to be gone for a few days."

Seb handed him another piece of paper. On it was written: *Aeolus*, 18:30.

"What's this?"

"The next steamer for Cebu. You must hurry. I sent one of the boys ahead to the dock to hire you a *casco*, and another is upstairs packing your bag."

"I don't know what to say."

"Say you'll bring back a smile and the *Americana* wearing that ring you bought. Or else I may throw you in Bilibid myself."

Moss laughed for the first time in weeks, though he didn't draw it out for more than a few breaths. After all, he had to hurry.

But now, three days later, all he could do was wait, albeit not patiently. The steamer under his feet was ignorant of its important mission, and its staff definitely did not have the requisite sense of urgency. Moss paced the ship relentlessly for two days, unable to sleep, while the deck hand ran from his questions.

This morning, another sailor assured Moss that they would arrive soon. Only eight hours, he said hopefully. Only? Moss wondered if he could wait that long, or if instead he might dive off the boat and swim. Della could be in Hong Kong by the time he landed.

The eight hours felt like eighty, but eventually the *Aeolus* made it to Cebu. Moss scanned the port, which—as the oldest Spanish settlement in the Philippines—was better laid out and more efficient than Manila's. The wide-open squares were lined with shops, big churches, whitewashed buildings, and airy warehouses. But today Moss focused his gaze on the large shuttered government building flying Old Glory. It looked like the kind of place that attracted pompous politicians. Holt would be there, if anywhere.

Moss pushed his way to the front of the line of disembarking passengers. Filipinos yielded because they didn't know whether or not he was someone important; the Americans didn't yield because they knew he wasn't. Nevertheless, Moss was first off the ship.

Once his feet touched solid ground, he was off. It was really too hot to run, but Moss was in too cold a sweat to care. He burst into the hotel's grand banquet hall to find an actual banquet in progress. The special guest's eyes rose to meet his.

Congressman Holt stiffened.

Funny, Moss was actually happy to see the windbag—until he realized that Della was not next to him. She was nowhere in the room.

He strode up to Holt and demanded: "Where is Della?"

"I don't know how you found me, but—"

"Let me talk to her. One question is all I need."

"Do you think to impress me with your persistence?"

Moss did not give two shakes what impressed Holt. But he needed to find Della, so he tamed his voice to sound reasonable. "You know that I wasn't involved in any of that quartermaster nonsense, and—"

"I know no such thing."

"Well, I'm here," Moss said. "Not in prison, despite your best efforts."

"I don't know how you escaped justice," Holt said. "But a glorified bellhop will get no quarter from me."

"If I had to escape 'justice,' I would not come here." Moss nodded in the direction of the full complement of Army and Navy command staff at the table. In a time of martial law, these men were judge, jury, and executioner.

"I fought in four battles around Manila," he continued. "Yet in all that time, I never attracted the attention of any brass whatsoever. But if I have to make a scene now, I will."

"What unit were you with?" a half-drunk colonel yelled out.

"Thirteenth Minnesota, Company E." That was enough information to guess which battles, and the man nodded soberly.

"I won't humble myself for you," Moss said to Holt. "Only for her."

He pulled an envelope out of his pocket. He laid down the clippings, one after another, neatly in a row. Della was now one of a handful of female reporters in the English-speaking world, and the only one Moss knew outside of New York. "For this woman, I would do anything."

"So? She didn't write those for you."

Moss pointed at the quip about the chicken. "I think she did."

Holt looked at the marked paragraph, but then just as quickly dismissed it. "An inconsequential fabrication, so what of it? Dorr prints her because her subject is worthy. He doesn't expect her writing to be perfect."

Not perfect? It was brilliant. Della had revealed Holt's tour of condescension for what it was. Most of Manila was chuckling at the congressman's gaffes, but he was too pompous to know it.

That made it harder for Moss to do what he had to do. "Give me a chance," he said, lowering himself after all. "Let me ask her, at least. If she says no, I will leave you both alone. Forever."

Hughes Holt was determined. Moss could see it in his eyes. He would not soften, let alone bend.

Another throat cleared. It was the colonel.

"I believe I saw her," the man said slowly, drawing out the words as if he enjoyed a career on the stage, not the battlefield. "She went to cable one of her latest tales."

Moss started toward the door without another word.

Chairs skidded against the floor as men behind him rose to follow. Moss turned briefly to see the military command at his back—everyone but Holt.

This time when Moss ran across the big, empty square outside, he did sweat. He made it to the customs building before realizing that Della would not use the government's cable. She would have to use a commercial firm.

The crowd came to a collective halt behind Moss. The colonel nodded toward a long street of shops.

Moss was off again, with the officers close behind, displaying all the raucous enthusiasm of boys at a parade. They turned the corner next to the American Shoe Store, and there it was: The Eastern Extension Australasia & China Telegraph Company. As Moss approached, Della stepped out the door and onto the sidewalk.

She was thinner. Her eyes looked darker against her pale skin. Had she been sick?

"Della!"

When she saw him, her whole face lifted into as beautiful a smile as ever. He took her into his arms and held her tight. Only when she snorted with laughter at his possessiveness did he loosen his grip.

"You're here," she whispered.

He looked down into her warm eyes with genuine relief. "I would have left earlier," he said, "but I didn't know where to go."

She shook her head as if excuses were unnecessary, yet she offered her own. "I didn't want to leave Manila at all. I was going to come back—I even bought a ticket—but then I didn't hear from you."

"I sent a half dozen cables."

"I didn't get any." Her eyes glassed over. "I thought—"

"You know I love you," he mouthed so that only she could read it.

"Yes, but…"

She was such a smart woman and yet so unaware of her own value. "I'm glad I found you here," he assured her. "But if I had to follow you to Hong Kong, San Francisco, or even Washington, D.C., I would

have. I don't care how many newspaper subscriptions I \
buy to do it—I would have found you."

"Sounds like love to me," drawled the colonel behind
much for privacy.

But then a less welcome voice cut in. "Della," Congressman Holt
said, stepping into his granddaughter's line of sight. "Don't do this."

She left Moss's embrace. Though he could have stopped her, he
had to trust her—and he did trust her. But he didn't trust himself, so he
held his fists at his side, lest they stray too close to the congressman's
face. Della did not deserve to have her name attached to scandal. At
least in that, Holt was right.

"I have to make my own choices," Della said to her grandfather.

"And avoidable mistakes?" Holt asked. "I want better for you."

"There is no better."

"But I must keep you safe—"

"And bored?" Della asked. "Is that why you became a politician?
Because it was easy, predictable?"

"We're talking about you," Holt said.

"Don't you know me at all? Why do you think I came out here
with you?"

"If I had known you were going to stay—"

"You'd rather tuck me away in the attic like you did your own
children?"

"You were my second chance," Holt said, his voice halting, cracked.
He sounded sincere, but Moss assumed that like everything else the
man did, such emotions were for public consumption. "I made promises to your mother—"

"She doesn't have the right to choose my life for me, either." Della
looked over to Moss. "I really do have my ticket for Manila. I was going to leave tonight."

She was probably scheduled to leave on the same ship that brought
him in.

Holt pulled on Della's arm, drawing her attention back to him. "You didn't even know whether North was in jail or not. How could you take such a risk?"

"I knew he was innocent," she said. "He wouldn't be there long."

"It's just a matter of time with a man like him. He'll drag you down like an anchor."

"You're the one holding me back."

The congressman winced. Maybe he was thinking of Della's articles laid out on the banquet table. Holt had only been able to see himself in them; Moss saw a future for Della.

Several emotions rippled across the congressman's face, and this time Moss believed them. First, there was the implicit threat: if you hurt her, you will pay. Then came worry. And, finally, there was grudging respect—for Della, not Moss. After all, Holt was a man who understood ambition. Recognizing it in his granddaughter merited his respect—at some level, her ambition ensured that she would always do what was best for herself. And if she believed that Moss was best for her, then maybe he was.

All of this went unsaid, though. Holt only nodded, ever so slightly.

It was as close to a blessing as Moss was going to get. Moss lowered himself to one knee in front of Della and pulled out a small sapphire ring. It was not an expensive piece of jewelry; it didn't even have a fancy velvet box. It was not worthy of this woman. Holt had to notice the same, but he stayed silent.

"Della Berget, will you…"

He trailed off because he realized that Della was not looking at him. She was watching the growing crowd around them.

Moss tried to wave off the officers. "Do you mind?" he called out.

No one minded, but no one left.

"Say it, man," the colonel called out. Others shouted in a similar vein, though they used more colorful language. Clearly, Della could read some of this because she blushed. The congressman crossed his arms and stood unmoving, offering no help.

"I will get to it," Moss explained to their audience. "But I can't do it while you're distracting her. She has to watch my lips, not yours."

"Come on, men," the colonel said. But instead of leaving, he simply turned his back. The others followed suit, including Holt. They were close enough to hear the drama but would not distract the actors.

Good enough. Moss stared down some of the civilians in the crowd, but the women and children were a lost cause. A few even pointed.

Moss turned back to Della. She was laughing a little, but at least she was looking at his mouth. The crowd probably expected a lot of flowery language, but this proposal was for her, not them. "Marry me."

Smiling, she took the ring and put it on. Then she took his hand and flattened it against her own. As she looked into his eyes, her finger traced three letters into his palm. Those three letters were no one else's but his, and together they were the best thing he never heard in his life.

Clippings

FIRST AMERICAN NAVAL WEDDING IN PORT OF CEBU: WEST VIRGINIA CONGRESSMAN'S GRANDDAUGHTER WEDS ORIENTE MANAGER

Manila Freedom, February 28, 1901

Della Berget and Moss North were joined under an arch of silver swords on the U.S.S. *Marietta*. A boatful of white-uniformed sailors witnessed the event as they sailed over the blue-green waters of the Mactan Channel.

The ceremony was the best-attended event of the year in Cebu, with the entire Visayas command in attendance. At the wedding breakfast afterward, Congressman Hughes Holt praised the match as his own doing: "The fact that I entrust my deaf granddaughter to married life in these islands proves how successfully the Philippines have been brought under a stable and secure American government." Colonel Isaac De Russy then toasted the congressman, saying that if Mr. Holt meddled in the affairs of state as successfully as he did in love, the insurrection would soon be all wound up.

Colonel De Russy, a friend of the groom, made a final toast to the marriage as a marker of the new American century in the Pacific. As a tribute to their international lives, the bride wore a gown of French silk and local piña. The couple will honeymoon in the captain's cabin on the way back to Manila. Once there, the bride will continue to report for the *Freedom*, taking up residence with her husband in the halls of the Hotel de Oriente.

Their friends in the newspaper profession extend their heartiest congratulations.

* * *

TALK AROUND TOWN

Manila Freedom, September 30, 1902

They say…that a correspondent of this very newspaper gave birth to her first child, a boy, at home in the Hotel de Oriente, this past weekend.

They say…that the correspondent had just returned home from reporting on a cholera fire in Binondo when her husband called for the doctor.

They say…that the correspondent's husband, the manager of the Oriente, named the child Aidan, which means fire, in appreciation of his son not being born in one.

The following is a preview from *Under the Sugar Sun*, the first novel in the *Sugar Sun* series. To receive announcements of new Jennifer Hallock stories, send an e-mail to news@jenniferhallock.com

First Encounter

Georgie was not lucky—never had been—but even she could not believe her poor timing. The growing fire was only a few streets away. In this city made almost entirely of wood, the buildings separating her from the fire were a mere appetizer when compared to the towering three-story Hotel de Oriente, where she was now standing. If the Oriente burned down, it would kill scores of Americans who chose this very hotel to protect them from the dangers of the city. None of this was part of Georgie's plan: she had come to the Philippines to start a new life, not end the one she had.

She blew out the candles, pinched the wicks between her fingers to be safe, and fled the room. She ran down two flights of polished wood stairs, almost flattening a bell-hopper in the empty lobby as she charged the door. Where were the other guests, and why was no one evacuating the hotel?

Once in the street, Georgie took a moment to get her bearings. She'd had a clear view from above, but now the eastern horizon of the plaza was blocked by the La Insular cigar factory. The dull light of petroleum lamps did not help much either. She ran toward the open square in front of Binondo Church to get a better look and then followed the glow of flames down a dirt road. She had just arrived in this city, but she could still guess that tall, redheaded white women should not race through the streets of Manila at night.

She wound her way down to the canal where the fire was digesting rows of native houseboats. Families stood on shore and watched helplessly as their homes burned. Women comforted children and men cradled prize roosters as houseboat after houseboat disappeared into the flame. A dozen Filipino firemen in khaki uniforms and British-style pith helmets stood idly, their shiny engine from Sta. Cruz Fire Brigade Station No. 2 sitting unused, too far from the water line to do any good. Judging by the men resting casually against the cool iron, no one had lit the pump's boiler yet.

Georgie had read that the natives here were natural fatalists— a long-suffering, impassive people—but this was just ridiculous. She approached the firemen.

"Put water there," she demanded, pointing to boats that had so far escaped the flames. If doused heavily enough they might only smoke a bit. She struggled to remember the word for water she had learned earlier that day. "Tabog, tabog," she said.

The men looked at her blankly. She tried again, working out the mnemonic device in her head: the Philippines were islands too big in the sea...too big...*tubig*.

"*Tubig*," she said, pointing. "*Tubig, tubig.*"

They shrugged but kept staring at her, more interested in the novelty of a hysterical *Americana* than in the fire. Looking for help elsewhere, Georgie slipped around the front of the engine to find two men arguing loudly in English.

"I've warned you before not to interfere with the quarantine, señor. I'll not explain myself again, especially to the likes of you."

The speaker, a squat American policeman, had comically bushy eyebrows that did not match his humorless tone. No doubt he had been interrupted from his evening revelry to carry out this duty, and he planned to finish the job quickly and get back to the saloon. Georgie had grown up around men of his stripe, their ruddy noses betraying a greater exposure to alcohol than sun.

She did not have a good view of the man the policeman was speaking to, but she heard the fellow give a short cluck before responding. "There's nothing in your law to prevent me from standing here, and I'll do it all night if I have to." His British accent amplified his condescension.

"You're interfering with a direct order of the Bureau of Health," said the policeman, "and that could cost you five thousand dollars—gold, mind you—and ten years in Bilibid."

"You can't be serious."

"That's the law—need I translate it into goo-goo for you?"

Sensing she was missing something, Georgie edged forward to get a better look at the Brit and discovered that he was not a Brit at all. His angular face bragged of Spanish blood, but the blackness of his hair and eyes revealed a more complicated ancestry. She had heard about these mixed-blood Filipinos, many of them wealthy and powerful, but she had not expected to meet one shirtless on the shore of the canal.

"I read law in London," the Mestizo said. "I need no lectures on the King's English from a blooming Yank."

Proud words from a naked man. Well, not naked exactly, but the black silk pajama bottoms—Chinese-style, embroidered with white stitching—did not hide much. He was the tallest man in the crowd by half a head, and his powerful torso betrayed some familiarity with labor, yet he spoke to the policeman with the studied patience of a man used to commanding those around him.

"Put out this inferno," he continued. "If you don't, there'll be nothing left to disinfect. The entire city will burn."

"That's hardly likely. We're protected by water." The American waved his fat hand toward the walled-in core of Manila and the bay settlements beyond, the places where the colonial regime was headquartered and most foreigners lived. The wide Pasig River in between would buffer the elite from the "sanitation" of this canal.

A tall flame bit noisily into the woven roof of a houseboat, devouring the dry grass in seconds. Georgie followed the Mestizo's gaze from the grass to the bamboo-pile pier, nipa huts, and market stalls. Wood, wood, and more wood—it was all bona fide fire fuel straight up the street to the Oriente, the hotel that contained all her possessions in this hemisphere.

The Mestizo turned back to the policeman and tilted his head toward this path of destruction. "I'm sure you've considered every possibility," he said acidly.

"I don't have to listen to this." The American stalked away, still eyeing his adversary, and nearly collided with Georgie. In something close to relief, he directed his frustration at her, a new and easier target. "Miss, this is no place for a woman. What are you doing here?"

Georgie wondered the same thing—though her concern had little to do with her gender and more to do with the fact that, in the thirty hours she had spent in Manila so far, she had been temporarily abandoned by her fiancé, maybe permanently abandoned by her missing brother, and now threatened by a fire that her own countrymen would not even bother to put out. That last part bothered her the most right now.

"Why aren't the wagons being used?" she asked. "You have enough equipment to douse the flames."

"The fire's a necessary precaution, I assure you," the policeman said.

Georgie frowned. "A precaution?"

"I have orders from the Commissioner to sweep this district—"

A loud crack interrupted him as another boat frame split under the strain of falling debris.

"You set this blaze?" she asked, still not sure she was getting it right.

The policeman looked quickly at the fire and then back at her. "We did what we had to do. After we burn out the spirilla in this nest, the entire area can be disinfected with carbolic acid and lime."

Georgie knew from experience that fire was a risky ally. She had grown up near the tenements of South Boston, twelve acres of which burnt down in the Roxbury Conflagration. "Isn't that a rough way to go about it?"

Her skepticism exasperated the policeman. Clearly, he had not anticipated this challenge from a fellow American.

"Rough?" he cried. "People should be thanking us for our help. For months we've been distributing distilled water all over the city for free. We've built new encampments and staffed them with doctors and nurses to treat the stricken. We've even reimbursed people for the loss of their filthy, worthless shacks. Are these efforts appreciated? Instead, savages like him"—he crooked his thumb at the Mestizo—"stir up trouble, talking of tyranny."

The dark-eyed man in question did not respond, but crossed his arms across his bare chest. When he caught her looking at him, she turned away, embarrassed by the impropriety: his in dress and hers in curiosity.

"And what's the natives' answer to the cholera?" the policeman continued. "Candles? A few prayers? Carting some wooden saints around?"

Georgie thought he had a point, albeit one badly made. It took no more than an hour in the city to realize that Manila had no sewage system, making it ripe for plague. Nowhere that she had wandered today had been out of olfactory range of the Pasig River, its estuaries, or the Spanish moat. Using the same water for drink and toilet did not make for a pleasant bouquet, never mind good health. That thought gave her some sympathy for the beleaguered Insular official. This morning's *Manila Times* had reported that cholera deaths were down to a quarter of their July high, so something must be working.

"Maybe he's right," she said hopefully to the angry man. "They're killing the germs, after all."

The Mestizo ran a large hand through his short hair and sighed. "His plan would've been better if he hadn't chased off the infected people who used to live here, spreading the disease farther. That's not just stupid, it's bad policy. Do you know what the people will say tomorrow? 'The Americans are burning the poor out of their homes to make room for new mansions.'"

"That's absurd!" she said.

The policeman did not deny it, though. "These brownies are like children, always looking to blame someone else. I can't control what they think, nor would I deign to try."

The Mestizo clenched his fists at his side, unconsciously tugging at the silk pajamas. Georgie wished he would not do that, especially since it was clear he was not wearing anything underneath. She turned away to watch the flames.

A piece of fiery thatch floated through the air near her head. A fresh gust of wind blew it up and over the street toward a cluster of neighboring homes whose occupants were still in the process of pulling out their belongings. The fireball rose and fell, dancing through the dark sky in slow motion, until it landed on the grass roof of one of the huts, igniting in seconds.

Everyone, including the firemen, rushed to warn those inside, but somehow Georgie got there first. She climbed the ladder into the hut and found a small boy holding a baby. He looked at Georgie with wide eyes as if she, not the fire, was the monster devouring his home. She inched forward, hoping her exaggerated smile would bridge the language gulf. She motioned him forward, her hand outstretched, palm up, fingers beckoning—but to no avail. The boy backed farther into the bamboo wall, acting like he had never seen such a gesture before.

Georgie looked up and saw that the whole roof was in flames. How had the fire grown so quickly? "Please!" she shouted, even though she knew her English was worthless. "You have to climb down with me." She waved her arms furiously, only adding to the boy's terror. She couldn't will herself to crawl more deeply into the hut, though. That would be suicide.

"*Ven acá*," a deep voice said. She turned to see the Mestizo behind her on the ladder. "*Dito.*" He motioned with this hand, too, but his palm faced down, brushing his fingers under like a broom. It seemed a dismissive gesture to Georgie, but the boy responded right away and crawled toward them.

The man handed the baby to Georgie before scooping up the boy. "Now go!"

The Mestizo swung back on the ladder to let Georgie down first. Just then the fire surged out of the hut, raking the big man's back. Grunting in pain, he shoved everyone the rest of the way down and pushed them all to the ground. He fell last on top of the human pile, providing cover as the platform of the house gave way in a single explosion. The flames reached out to claw at them one last time before retreating. The Mestizo pulled Georgie and the boy onto their feet and dragged them farther from the burning hut, just to be safe.

After a few moments Georgie started to breathe again, devouring air in large gulps. She could feel the heavy sobs of the boy wedged into her side, but she did not have a free hand to comfort him. The baby, on the other hand, made not a sound. Georgie looked down at the little one, wondering what kind of life the infant had led so far if tonight's episode was not even worthy of a good bawl.

A single beat of peace passed before a throng of excited Filipinos descended on them. A young woman swooped down to grab the two children, leaving Georgie alone in the Mestizo's arms. He continued to hold her close, brushing the ash and dirt off her ruined white shirt-waist. It was a useless attempt, but she didn't stop him.

"Are you all right?" he asked. He was still sweating—a musky, sweet scent that distracted her from the smoke. When she looked up at his face, she noticed details she had missed before: the dimple in his chin, prominent among his dark stubble; his full bottom lip, swollen a little from an accidental elbow in the face by the boy; and his low, dark eyebrows that framed his strong, straight nose. He was handsome but unrefined—too urbane to be a blackguard but too unruly to be a gentleman.

"Are you okay?" he asked again, shaking her lightly. "Can you hear me?"

She was embarrassed to be caught staring. "Yes," she answered. "I'm sorry. I'm fine."

"Not hurt?"

"No, I'm okay now. I've just...I've never felt so useless. The boy couldn't understand me."

The Mestizo shrugged. "Believe me, had you spoken his language, he would have been more scared."

Georgie laughed, surprised at her ease. "I don't know how your heart isn't racing."

The man paused, his smile not softening the look in his eyes. "Who says it isn't?"

So he might be a bit of a blackguard after all, she thought.

Georgie noticed that the natives had stopped watching the fire and instead were watching her. She glanced over to the American policeman. The man did not need to speak to communicate the extent of his disgust. No self-respecting American woman would allow herself to be held this way by a half-naked Filipino. Upper-crust accent, Spanish features, and English law degree notwithstanding, he was still a "brownie."

Georgie tried to loosen the Mestizo's grip by twisting away. When that didn't work she gently nudged him with her elbow, but he didn't take that hint either. A seed of panic bloomed in her stomach. If they did not separate, there was liable to be more trouble for them both. She planted both palms on his chest and pressed lightly, but no one on the outside could see her resistance. All they saw was a suggestive caress.

The policeman's eyes darkened. A small man like him—diminutive in both stature and intelligence—would no doubt resort to the power of his office to reestablish authority. Dash it, he had said as much even before the Mestizo had gotten his hands on a white woman.

Georgie summoned her strength and shoved the Mestizo away, hard. His heel caught on a rock and he fell, grimacing as he landed flat on his injured back.

A few bystanders laughed. Some would have laughed at anyone's misfortune, but others relished the embarrassment of a proud man. Not surprisingly, the policeman's guffaw was the loudest.

The Mestizo's cheeks flushed red, but fury trumped pride. He got up immediately, rising in a single fluid motion while glaring at Georgie. She wanted to say something to defuse the situation—to explain, apologize, something—but the moment passed before she got up the courage. The man pivoted on his heel and walked away, not bothering to brush the gravel from his burned, torn flesh.

Georgie sighed in regret. Her first full day in Manila had not been a success by any measure. Unfortunately, it was too late to turn around now.

Made in the USA
Charleston, SC
27 February 2016

Cover illustration: Actor Edwin Forrest in the role of Metamora; photograph by Mathew B. Brady, 1861; collodion glass plate negative; courtesy of National Portrait Gallery, Smithsonian Institution; gift of the Edwin Forrest Home for Retired Actors

THEATRE SYMPOSIUM (ISSN 1065-4917) is published annually by The University of Alabama Press, Box 870380, Tuscaloosa, AL 35487-0380. Subscription rates for 2020 are $25.00 for individuals and $35.00 for institutions; please include an additional $10.00 for subscriptions outside the United States. Back issues are $34.95.

Paperback ISBN: 978-0-8173-7013-8
eBook ISBN: 978-0-8173-9207-9

THEATRE SYMPOSIUM
A PUBLICATION OF THE SOUTHEASTERN THEATRE CONFERENCE

Theatre and Citizenship

Volume 28

Published by the

Southeastern Theatre Conference and

The University of Alabama Press

THEATRE SYMPOSIUM is published annually by the Southeastern Theatre Conference, Inc. (SETC), and by the University of Alabama Press. SETC nonstudent members receive the journal as a part of their membership under rules determined by SETC. For information on membership, visit the SETC website at www.setc.org, send an email to info@setc.org, or write to SETC, 1175 Revolution Mill Drive, Suite 14, Greensboro, NC 27405. All other inquiries regarding subscriptions, circulation, purchase of individual copies, and requests to reprint materials should be addressed to the University of Alabama Press, Box 870380, Tuscaloosa, AL 35487-0380.

THEATRE SYMPOSIUM publishes works of scholarship resulting from a single-topic meeting held on a southeastern university campus each spring. A call for papers to be presented at that meeting is widely publicized each autumn for the following spring. Information about the next symposium is available from Andrew Gibb, Texas Tech University, School of Theatre and Dance, Box 42061, 2812 18th Street, Lubbock, TX 79409-2061, andrew.gibb@ttu.edu.

THEATRE SYMPOSIUM
A PUBLICATION OF THE SOUTHEASTERN THEATRE CONFERENCE

Volume 28   *Contents*   **2020**

Introduction

Andrew Gibb

I N THE PLACES WHERE THE craft of theatre is taught as part of a college or university curriculum, requirements often include some exposure to the history of the field, whether offered through a designated course or sequence of courses, or in a more integrated fashion within classes intended to teach acting, design, directing, or any number of production-related skills. The intentions behind this requirement are frequently multiple, dependent on the unique mission of the institution and the population(s) it serves. One frequently expressed goal of history coursework is the fostering of a sense of artistic and professional community through the inculcation of what is conceived as a common genealogical narrative. Such an argument may be borrowed, consciously or not, from the rhetoric advanced to support the teaching of national history as a key component of primary and secondary education.

In the case of theatre history instruction, a traditional practice (though by no means a universal one, and a habit that has been increasingly challenged in the last few decades) is to begin the assumed common narrative with the study of the drama and theatrical practice of fifth-century BCE Athens. A statement frequently made by textbooks and instructors alike regarding performance in that place and time is that the ancient Athenians considered attendance at, or sponsorship of, theatrical festivals to be something akin to a civic duty—an activity that declared one's citizenship.[1]

Perhaps this embrace of an origin story that places theatre at the center of civic discourse is the result of a sense of injustice, as theatre makers often believe that they are being treated as second-class citizens within the halls of academia. What better claim of relevance could be made than to point out (however accurately or Eurocentrically) that theatre began in the cradle of democracy and philosophy? Despite the strategic usefulness of this particular historical claim, however, when the long arc of history is considered, are theatre folk truly justified in claiming a fundamental connection between theatre and citizenship?

No doubt the editors of and contributors to this volume would answer that question affirmatively, though it is worth noting that our stance is likely dependent upon a broader definition of "citizenship" than might be endorsed by other academic or legal traditions. The call for the scholarly conference from which this publication emerged was circulated in the waning months of 2018, following a summer of urgent and emotional debate surrounding new US immigration policies regarding immigrant family separations, arguments fueled on one side by fears about the loss of social cohesion, and on the other by photographs of incarcerated children.[2] Given the then-prevailing political atmosphere, the present editor anticipated that a good number of submissions might draw connections between the patterns, policies, and histories of immigration on the one hand, and theatrical or otherwise performance-centered expressions of citizenship, whether inclusive or exclusionary, on the other. In retrospect, what could have been foreseen is that theatre scholars, educators, and professionals would interpret recent events against a wider and more complex backdrop. The ultimate result of that initial call is the work you now hold in your hand, a collection of essays whose authors reach beyond simple definitions of citizenship as determined by documents and legal rights, and who engage in larger conversations about what citizenship can mean, and how such meanings are expressed through theatre and performance.

Interestingly, while none of the authors published herein take up immigration as a central issue, they all make use of some combination of three particular analytical frameworks, all of which happen to be pertinent to the current immigrant experience and attempts to regulate it: bodies, institutions, and technologies. A focus on bodies in performance (whether the physical bodies of humans, animatronic figures, or puppets, or the less tangible examples of bodies of literary work or digitally embodied presences) represents in part a continuation of the rich conversation surrounding "Theatre and Embodiment" distilled by editor Sarah McCarroll into the publication of last year's volume of *Theatre Symposium*. Institutions (here taking the form of theatres, schools, prize boards, and theme parks) have always been of interest to theatre scholars, as they concretize collective cultural values, not the least of which is a particular group's sense of citizenship. Technologies (including in these pages photography, the printing press, the personal computer, animatronics, and the techniques of clothing construction) are another perennial focus of performance analysis, though it is perhaps only recently, thanks to new digital methods of monitoring and control, that such considerations have entered so prominently into the discourse on citizenship. Through their consideration of technologies, institutions, and bodies, the contributors to this volume participate fully in the project of redefining citizenship for a new era.

As befits a keynote address, Charlotte M. Canning's opening essay provides a broad historical overview of the shifting meanings of citizenship within US social and political discourse as they have been shaped by theatrical and performative means, an analysis appropriately framed by the opening words of the US Constitution, "We, the People." Anchored by readings of Edwin Forrest's performance in *Metamora* and Lin-Manuel Miranda's *Hamilton*, Canning's piece reminds us of the importance of bringing a historical perspective to the urgent issues of our day. Her essay provides the inspiration for our cover image, Matthew Brady's (in) famous photograph of Edwin Forrest, arguably the nineteenth century's most famous American actor, made up in redface. The incongruity of that spectacle, painted over by period oil portraits of Forrest in the role, serves to further make strange the morally incoherent phenomena Canning treats so ably.

Sarah McCarroll furthers our understanding of what Canning calls *Hamilton*'s "myth of citizenship" by elucidating how that myth is generated not only by the musical's book and score, but through the show's production choices. While many have commented on Miranda's intentional foregrounding of the actors' raced bodies, McCarroll takes that analysis a step further by highlighting the work of the show's costumer and choreographer. Through a close reading of elements including faux-hawks and corsets, rap battles and snaps, McCarroll helps us to see how *Hamilton*'s reinterpretation of the US origin story relies upon a doubling of the audience's historical vision of the bodies before them. This doubling is at the core of the musical's genius, but it is also the source of the show's troubling erasures, a fact established by McCarroll's analysis of the costuming and choreography of the female actors/characters.

McCarroll's and Canning's focuses on US examples are mirrored in most of the contributions to this volume, an understandable development given the intensity of current debates surrounding citizenship in the United States. That said, a handful of presentations at the 2019 Theatre Symposium did venture beyond US borders, challenging those in attendance to think in more global terms. A fine example of such exhortation is Shadow Zimmerman's treatment of divergent representations of citizenship in Benito Mussolini's Italy. Zimmerman pushes additional boundaries by nearly exclusively focusing on the visual iconography of performance, through examples that range from the prominent display of hagiographic postcard images of Il Duce before and during World War II, to the public mutilation of his executed body in Milan in 1945, and the subsequent photographic record thereof. Zimmerman grounds his performance studies analysis in the theoretical writings of Filippo Marinetti, arguing for a direct and mutual exchange of influence between Futurist and fascist performances of citizenship.

Zimmerman's treatment of the performativity of photography turns our attention fully upon the place of technology in our discussion of theatre and citizenship. Following that strand, Becky K. Becker takes us on a leap forward from the twentieth to the twenty-first century, updating our technology from photography to that of the internet. Becker works the theoretical line between live performance and the digital presence enabled by social media, positing a "cyber-citizen performativity," the implications of which she explores via the example of a performative social media response to a live theatrical performance. As befits a contemplation of new technologies, Becker's essay raises as many questions as it answers, and will no doubt serve as a springboard to many future conversations, not only about the liveness of performance, but about how the questioning of basic notions of presence undermines our traditional theorizations of theatre's relationship to social constructs like citizenship.

David S. Thompson continues our meandering path through the history of technology by referencing the cutting-edge mass media of the nineteenth and early twentieth centuries—the newspaper. Thompson's focus is not on printing per se, however, but on the institutions that arose to justify and protect the concentration of wealth that printing technology enabled. The particular institution that draws Thompson's attention is the Pulitzer Prize for Drama, unquestionably a key driver of high-art critical discourse about theatre in the United States. As might be expected of such a prominent prize, the Pulitzer rewards artistic expressions that align with hegemonic values. Thompson is particularly interested in how founder and immigrant Joseph Pulitzer sought to use his legacy to promote a particular construction of US citizenship. As Thompson points out, the prize board has historically used the selection process as a tool for monitoring which playwrights can claim model citizenship and which cannot.

Alex Ates shares the story of another immigrant, Alexander "Xanti" Schawinsky, who seized the opportunity offered by a different kind of institution—the experiment in higher education known as Black Mountain College—to advance his own ideas about artistry and citizenship. Ates argues that Schawinsky's contribution to the theatrical culture of his adopted nation, a process and perspective that Ates labels "Schawinskian

Space," was not only shaped by the artist's immigrant experience but was enabled by Black Mountain's iconoclastic pedagogy. Furthermore, Ates believes that the development of Schawinsky's artistic and educational philosophies was uniquely shaped by Black Mountain College's location in the southern United States, thus introducing the lens of regionalism into this volume's exploration of theatre and citizenship.

Jennifer Toutant's position as director of education at the Milwaukee Repertory Theater affords her a unique perspective from which to view the interconnection of region, institution, education, and the collective body of the audience. For her, the most pertinent questions of theatre and citizenship revolve around the duties she believes that artistic institutions owe to their audiences and their communities. A critical responsibility of her position is to consider who constitutes the regular audiences of her institution and who resides in the neighborhood surrounding its facilities. In the case of the Milwaukee Rep, the collection and analysis of such data reveals a historical gap, one that Toutant sees as all too common among major regional theatres. Over the course of more than a decade of service, Toutant has worked closely with the surrounding community, making significant strides to address this historical discrepancy in audience makeup. With her essay, she shares many of the successful strategies that she and her team have developed over the years.

With the final piece of the volume, Chase Bringardner brings into alignment all three of the major analytical lenses employed by his fellow authors: bodies, institutions, and technology. Bringardner examines two competing performances staged at Walt Disney World's Magic Kingdom, an entertainment destination that has attained the status of institution. Moreover, the performances Bringardner treats—the Hall of Presidents and "Great Moments in History"—themselves rely upon a familiarity with particular US institutions: the presidency and the Muppets, respectively. Interestingly, neither of these performances is embodied by human beings, but rather by simulacra, in the first case animatronic figures and in the second puppets, each brought to life by their own particular performance technology. Bringardner argues that these two performances, located adjacent to each other within the theme park geography, present visitors with starkly divergent interpretations of US citizenship. The author reminds us that such a public debate is taking place in the heart of "the happiest place on Earth," revealing the extent to which the questions of citizenship have migrated to the forefront of popular discourse in the United States. Bringardner's study also shows how performance can be a preferred method for dealing with such thorny social questions, a technique first mastered by the citizens of Athens some 2,500 years ago.

To the extent that citizenship entails an active investment in the success and well-being of the collective, no one is more deserving of the title of "good citizen" than those who labored tirelessly to bring about the 2019 Theatre Symposium and the collection of essays drawn from it. Charlotte M. Canning generously put on hold her teaching and administrative duties at the University of Texas at Austin in order to serve as the *princeps civitatis* of our gathering, delivering our charge with her keynote and weaving together the weekend's various insights with her response. While a full recounting of the symposium's work could not be captured within the pages of this volume, the contributions of all the gathered presenters and attendees of our on-site event shaped the pieces that were ultimately published.

For some time now, Theatre Symposium has enjoyed a congenial and civil home once a year among the welcoming administration, faculty, and staff of Agnes Scott College, represented most ably by David S. Thompson, the college's Annie Louise Harrison Waterman Professor of Theatre and a former editor of *Theatre Symposium*. Agnes Scott catering manager Katy McKinney and her dining services team provided the delicious fuel that enabled our debates, inviting us to their table and into their community.

The yearly gathering and publication of *Theatre Symposium* would not be possible without the continued investment of the Southeastern Theatre Conference, and we are most grateful to its executive director, Susie Prueter, and the entire staff of the SETC administrative offices for their ongoing support of our endeavors.

In my first year as editor, I relied heavily upon the wisdom and sage counsel so freely offered by the *Theatre Symposium* steering committee and editorial board, and I cannot thank them enough for their service to the symposium and for their personal support. I could not have been luckier than to serve my editorial apprenticeship under Sarah McCarroll, whose inspiring example I strive to emulate, and whose friendship I cherish.

It was a very great comfort for me during this past year to know that I could rely on the partnership of associate editor Chase Bringardner, who throughout the process has given unsparingly of his valuable time, his extensive experience, and his considerable expertise. I eagerly anticipate working with him again as my editorship continues.

The pressures associated with my transition to editor this year have been tremendously eased by the team of consummate professionals at the University of Alabama Press, especially editor-in-chief Dan Waterman, assistant managing editor Joanna Jacobs, and copyeditor Eric Schramm. The volume you hold in your hands is a testament to their skill and dedication. In an age when university presses are being threatened on all sides, there is no greater argument for their necessity than the work of these dedicated academic citizens.

Finally, I would be remiss if I failed to recognize the leadership of my own personal Texas Tech polis, especially Mark Charney, director of the School of Theatre and Dance, and Dean Noel Zahler of the J. T. & Margaret Talkington College of Visual and Performing Arts. Their support has enabled me to travel in pursuit of my duties, making my editorship possible.

Notes

1. See Tobin Nellhaus, Bruce McConachie, Carol Fischer Sorgenfrei, and Tamara Underiner, eds., *Theatre Histories: An Introduction*, 3rd ed. (New York: Routledge, 2016), 53. Also see Oscar G. Brockett and Franklin J. Hildy, *History of the Theatre*, Foundation Edition (Boston: Allyn and Bacon, 2007), 26–27.

2. A timeline of the crisis, stretching back into 2017 and forward through July 2019, has been compiled by the Southern Poverty Law Center (https://www .splcenter.org/news/2019/09/24/family-separation-under-trump-administration -timeline).

Theatre and Citizenship

Performing the Myths of We, the People

Charlotte M. Canning

Prologue

Beautiful evening at a #MAGARally with great American Patriots. Loyal citizens like you helped build this Country and together, we are taking back this Country—returning power to YOU, the AMERICAN PEOPLE. Get out and Vote. GOP!
    —Donald Trump, Twitter, November 1, 2018

I WANT TO ACKNOWLEDGE WHAT a harrowing time this is in US history, as well as an especially challenging one in which to be thinking about citizenship. The current multiple calamities—election fraud, numerous violations of both the Hatch Act and the emoluments clause,[1] the courts packed with unqualified, ideologically driven judges, the appointment of incompetent cabinet officials, and the open embrace of white supremacy are just a few of the horrors the country has endured since 2016—have forced everyone in the United States to confront what the rights and responsibilities of citizens are and should be. Perhaps nothing has prompted that confrontation more than the treatment of immigrants, particularly those seeking to cross the United States' southern border to request legal asylum. The federal government has separated families at the border, caged children, and opened concentration camps.[2] Fear is palpable—especially within Latinx communities—and that fear has been met with utter callousness from those who believe the camps are necessary. During a 2018 episode of the conservative television show *Fox and Friends*, host Brian Kilmeade argued: "Like it or not, these are not our kids. . . . These are people from another country."[3] The idea that those who are citizens of a country deserve better treatment or at least different treatment in that country is not new to the twenty-first century nor unique to the United States. The tension between citizen and non-citizen has been part of the United States since its founding.

Introduction

> We, the People of the United States, in Order to form a more perfect Union, establish Justice, insure domestic Tranquility, provide for the common defense, promote the general Welfare, and secure the Blessings of Liberty to ourselves and our Posterity, do ordain and establish this Constitution for the United States of America.
> —Preamble, US Constitution, 1789

From the "beginning," a word I put in quotations since there are no singular beginnings (only deeply ramified origin stories), citizens were interpolated through live performance. Written in 1776, the Declaration of Independence first reached the public as a broadside created by John Dunlap, a twenty-nine-year-old Irish printer in Philadelphia. The initial run of about two hundred copies was distributed as widely as possible at the time and read aloud to the public. Most of those who within a few years would cease to be subjects of the king and be cast as citizens of a democratic republic never read the Declaration. For them it was not a written document but an oral performance. The ideas it promulgated were embodied by the reader, and the nation it called into being populated by the same multitudes gathered together in towns and cities across the thirteen colonies, each person straining to catch every fateful word. Thirteen years later a more attenuated performance called forth "We the People of the United States" as the Constitution was defended by the Federalist Papers and debated on its way to ratification by the states. In 1789 "the people" could be taken for granted as an already existing discrete body hailed into being by the Declaration. "The people" were vaguely assumed to be citizens as the Constitution did not define them in any practical way. In her general history of the United States, written as an "old-fashioned civics book," historian Jill Lepore asks, "What is a citizen? Before the Civil War, and for rather a long time afterward, the government of the United States had no certain answer to that question. 'I have often been pained by the fruitless search in our law books and the records of our courts for a clear and satisfactory definition of the phrase "citizen of the United States,"' Lincoln's exasperated attorney general wrote in 1862."[4] Needless to say, Attorney General Edward Bates did not find anything that helped him resolve the citizenship question that faced the nation as the Civil War reinvented who was included in "We, the People.".

Citizen, in the US context, has always had multiple meanings from normative actions as decided on by the individual citizen (voting or participation in local governance) to the possession of specific rights determined by the state (such as those enumerated in the Bill of Rights). The definition of citizenship has always been vexed and can be productively labeled what political scientist W. B. Gallie termed "essentially contested concepts," which, as political scientists Elizabeth F. Cohen and Cyril Ghosh elaborate, are ideas with "no settled consensus on their specific meaning."[5] That citizenship is constituted through and as contestation means that there must always be public ways to reflect and represent how citizenship is constituted at any given historical moment. The inherent contestation is fertile ground for theatre. Theatre is an affective and live art, which means that it can represent ideas that, like citizenship, have what Cohen and Ghosh describe as "a powerful emotional appeal for many people."[6] Part of that appeal is that citizenship is often represented as evidence of the legitimate and deserved membership in the affective community. Over its two hundred–plus years of nationhood, nothing has been more controversial within the United States than who "We, the People" are, and we are no closer to unanimity about who a citizen is than we were in the eighteenth century.

Throughout the republic's history, theatre has provided a space for accountability and assessment denied and/or suppressed in the official spaces of the dominant discourse. The US Congress and courts of law may possess the legal power to define citizenship, but cultural spaces, not the least of which is theatre, have always been where the aspirations for, arguments over, and articulations of citizenship have been publicly aired and evaluated. One of the earliest plays to articulate a vision of how US citizenship is unique among nations was *Metamora* (1829). Written as a vehicle to showcase the talents of Edwin Forrest, the play justifies, from the perspective of white supremacy, the genocide of Native Americans as necessary for the birth of a nation far greater than indigenous people can imagine. This mythology places indigenous people in the distant past and reinvents their lives as tragedy, thus granting the US a classical past. Just about two hundred years later, a very different theatre artist took up what is, in the twenty-first century, the classical mythology of the US origin story—the founding fathers. *Hamilton* (2015) explores the eighteenth-century origins of the US by reinventing the key characters that populate the story. The history and representations of the early nineteenth century and twenty-first centuries are productive places to look for understanding how theatre was and is essential to the debate over citizenship through its ability to advance and embody ideas less well suited for legislative chambers or a court of law.

The Nineteenth Century

The eternal spirit of the red man wakes from its long sleep. It shakes off the fetters that have weighed it down and rushes forth on wings of fire! . . . Thus, white man, do I smite your nation and defy your power!
—Metamora, *Metamora*, 1829

This section's epigraph comprises the final lines of a character of color written to be played by a white man. The text's content—resistance and abjection—is revealing about how the dominant culture's white supremacy needed to define and represent indigenous inhabitants. Native Americans were heroic but doomed, the play demonstrates, and they served as a precedent for principled opposition to hegemonic powers. The source for these lines—*Metamora*—was the most influential US play until it was superseded by *Uncle Tom's Cabin* in 1852. The play's impact stemmed not from its literary merit, as it has almost none, but from the ways in which it articulated the concerns of the historical moment, provided audiences with a means to think about the nation-state, and became a trope for the issues the play explored. *Metamora* depended, as would *Uncle Tom's Cabin* twenty-three years later, on the assumption that white authors and performers had the authority to offer authentic representations of the people of color who were the focus of national debate.

That national debate can be summed up in two words: Manifest Destiny. Journalist John O'Sullivan coined the term in 1845, but he had been popularly writing in this vein since at least 1839 when he predicted that "our country is destined to be *the great nation*" of the future.[7] Manifest Destiny was as much a grievance as an arrogant prophecy. The United States was as sure about its right to expand as it was offended that any nation might stand in its way. Manifest Destiny was an argument for territorial expansion by any means. Historian Steven Woodworth observed that "Americans seized eagerly on O'Sullivan's term . . . as the perfect expression of how they had for some time seen their drive for westward expansion."[8] As Woodworth indicates, the term stood in for people and their feelings. Manifest Destiny was not simply about territorial expansion but also about who got to live in and possess those lands—enslaved and free, indigenous and settler colonist—and on what terms. In short, Manifest Destiny was a struggle to articulate citizenship. Theatre took up the banner of Manifest Destiny by representing its affect with stories that audiences were assured were true, as true as the fact that God had intended the United States of America to cover the continent.

In 1828 Edwin Forrest ran a contest for "a tragedy, in five acts, of which the hero, or principal character, shall be an aboriginal of this country."[9] The winning submission was Charles Stone's *Metamora*. In the forty years following the play's 1829 premiere, Forrest would perform the eponymous character over two hundred times, and it became his best-known role. Audiences for *Metamora* were assured that what they were seeing was an authentic representation of Native American lives and experiences. The play was based on King Philip's War of 1675–1678 between the Puritans and the Wampanoag. The eponymous character is a tragic, noble figure turned violent only because of the Puritans' duplicity.

The play may have dramatized an almost two-hundred-year-old war, but it rode the wave of one of the most popular trends in the early nineteenth century. Literary scholar Theresa Strouth Gale notes: "Beginning in the 1820s and continuing through the next decades, 'Indian dramas' . . . plays written by whites about American Indians, were one of the hottest phenomena on the American stage."[10] Forrest alleged a great advantage—he based his performance of Metamora on his friend Pushmataha, the great Choctaw leader and diplomat respected in both the United States and Europe—and this assertion was repeated endlessly to set *Metamora* apart from other "Indian" plays. Scholars in the twentieth and twenty-first centuries would dutifully repeat the contention as evidence of Forrest's skill and the accuracy of the play. Theatre historian Bethany Hughes has debunked the claim, however, pointing out that "Pushmataha died in Washington DC on December 24, 1824, more than six months before Edwin Forrest . . . allegedly [spent] the summer with him."[11] Most likely Forrest elided the famous Native American with a Choctaw he had met in 1825 who in turn became what Hughes identifies as the "foundation for the theatrical mythmaking about the Indian."[12] No one was particularly concerned that Stone and Forrest conflated Choctaw and Wampanoag because what was being represented onstage was not so much actual Native Americans as mythic Native Americans on whom the United States could invent a much-needed traditional heritage.

"Indian" plays are crucial to understanding how theatre articulated citizenship. What US citizens needed was a glorious national past, and theatre helped invent one. Lepore points out that "without its aboriginal heritage, America was only a more vulgar England, but with it America was its own nation with a unique culture and its own ancestral past."[13] *Metamora*, like other plays in the genre, gave the United States of America the tragic heroes it needed—ones who were indigenous but gone. Native Americans onstage allowed white America offstage to re-solve the contradiction of the genocide going on all around them by re-inventing slaughter as sacrifice. The imagined past they celebrated, Sayre reminds us, "required that there be no Indians in the present, or at least not anywhere near by."[14] Audiences could weep for that tragic necessity as they sat in the theatre and then commit to carrying it out after the show ended.

Representation made Manifest Destiny real for most US citizens. The radical reinvention of the United States was happening, Woodworth in-dicates, "with a speed and strength that dazzled even those who were carrying out the expansion."[15] Theatre provided a space to reflect apart from the hectic pace. It also was where the meanings and implications of such growth could be worked out. Literary scholar Gordon M. Sayre argues: "These plays thus worked to reconcile political and ethnic dif-ferences in the interests of a hegemonic US national purpose."[16] That purpose was just and right, the theatre was arguing. The death of Na-tive Americans was the necessary sacrifice that allowed the United States to fulfill its sacred destiny, white US citizens could reassure themselves. Metamora's curse was not a reference to contemporary white people— it was a curse on Europeans who would forestall destiny. The removal/ death of the actual Metamoras, as historian Greg Grandin summarizes using key phrase from a legal scholar from 1906: "opened the floodgates, allowing, 'an irresistible tide of Caucasian democracy' to wash over the land. King Cotton extended its dominion through the South, creating unparalleled wealth, along with unparalleled forms of racial domination over both enslaved and free blacks. At the same time, Native Americans were driven west, and the white settlers and planters who got their land experienced something equally unprecedented: an extraordinary de-gree of power and popular sovereignty. Never before in history could so many white men consider themselves so free."[17] White freedom was pur-chased through the dispossession and death of people of color. Citizens were defined—not in a court of law, but in a court of popular sentiment which had bearing on legal thinking—as white and male. Those were the most obvious arguments *Metamora* made to its approving audiences. They were not the only ones, however.

More complexly, the figure of Metamora, as with all Native American protagonists, embodied the kinds of people citizens should strive to be-come. These leaders—Metamora was the most popular but plays were also written about others, including Montezuma, Pontiac, and Tecumseh— were, as Sayre argues, "the tragic heroes of America."[18] They were prin-cipled leaders, reluctant but skillful warriors, and devoted family men. Most of all, they loved their land and dedicated their lives to it. They could be models because, like Achilles or Hector, they were long gone beyond living memory. If they were not, they were soon to be. Collectively these plays presented the myth of a glorious US past.

Like all myths, the ones created by plays like *Metamora* explained and justified choices made in the historical moment. As Forrest selected, rehearsed, and opened *Metamora*, Congress was crafting what would become the Indian Removal Act of 1830. The law authorized President Andrew Jackson to uproot Native Americans in the South and force them onto federal territory west of the Mississippi River. The ancestral lands of the indigenous people were then made available to white settlers. Historian Jeffrey Ostler summarizes the removals of the 1830s as typical of the history of the United States and the indigenous people whose land the settlers seized. "Americans have seldom confronted the fact that their version of democracy required the dispossession of the continent's indigenous people. Nor have Americans ever really acknowledged the costs to Native people of building the United States on Indigenous lands."[19] Nor have they acknowledged that Native Americans did not achieve full US citizenship until 1948.[20] In her award-winning history of King Philip's War, Lisa Brooks cautions, "It is . . . dangerous to regard the history of Indigenous resistance as an exercise in futility, with successful colonial 'replacement' the only inevitable outcome."[21] Such approaches align themselves with *Metamora* and its like, with the concomitant emphasis that white supremacy is inevitable. Brooks insists we look to stories of kinship, diplomacy, and survival as rebuttals and resistance to the tragic myths that enthralled the nineteenth century. After all, the Wampanoag may have lost the 1675–1678 war, but they survive to this day, in their words, as a "strong culture" with "over 12,000 years of history culture and tradition."[22] Metamora's final words may have been more prophetic than Charles Stone intended.

The Twenty-First Century

> We studied and we fought and we killed for the notion of a nation we now get to build.
> —"Non-Stop," *Hamilton*, 2015

In the last half-century, no single piece of theatre has penetrated as far beyond the borders of the theatre world as *Hamilton*. It premiered at New York's Public Theater in 2015 and moved to Broadway that same year. The show's lines have become catchphrases, and its author, Lin-Manuel Miranda, is ubiquitous on social media and throughout the public sphere. Academics have not lagged behind the general public in their engagement with the show. The show has been scrutinized for accuracy, lauded for its genius, and derided for its politics. It collected a record-setting sixteen Tony nominations, won an impressive eleven, and was the 2016 Pulitzer Prize winner in the drama category. *Hamilton* has become a ubiquitous lens through which the United States of America has discussed the nation's history, politics, and future. One of the show's taglines—"America then, told by America now"—anticipated and shaped public engagement with *Hamilton* as being about "us" and "now."

Hamilton was a myth-making enterprise from its first public presentation. Almost immediately after its transfer to Broadway, the production became one of the chief vehicles for a "new American civic myth," as historian Renee C. Romano described it.[23] Encomiums came from all parts of the political spectrum, as well as from critics, journalists, and audiences—even those who had never seen it, but its own origins are those of myth as well. Its origin story is not that of a typical show— endless workshops, numerous out-of-town tryouts, multiple backers' auditions—but seemed to have sprung fully fledged from Lin-Manuel Miranda's reading of Ron Chernow's biography of Alexander Hamilton to his performance of what would become its opening number on the stage at the White House. This heralded start made the show seem inevitable, and the sense of inevitability made it all the more authentic and authoritative.

No small part of *Hamilton*'s mandate was derived from where it first reached the public, the White House, one of the most symbolic and mythic sites in the country. In May 2009 the Obama administration, at the behest of First Lady Michelle Obama, hosted an evening of poetry, music, and spoken word. Ten years later, Miranda looked back at that evening as a moment out of time, one of mythic proportions. "The whole day was a day that will exist outside any other day in my life. . . . I was the closing act of the show and I had never done this project in public before so I was already nervous. . . . Afterwards, George Stephanopoulos came up to me and said, 'The President is back there talking about your song, he's saying "Where is (Secretary of the Treasury) Timothy Geitner? We need him to hear the Hamilton rap!"'" To hear that the President enjoyed the song was a real dream come true."[24] Miranda's self-description as humble and star-struck (he wonders at sharing a van with James Earl Jones) starts to build the myth of *Hamilton*. That he was invited in the first place as an established and successful artist—largely due to his 2008 musical, *In the Heights* (nominated for thirteen Tony Awards and winning four, including Best Musical)—is and was positioned as an irrelevant distraction to the truths that underlie the show's start.

The performance at the White House set *Hamilton* apart from theatre history. No other show has been as inextricably linked with a president during his administration—the identification of *Camelot* (1960) with President John F. Kennedy came after his 1963 assassination—in the history of the American musical. The Obamas would take an active role in promoting the show. Miranda would subsequently be a frequent guest at the White House, the Obamas introduced the show's performance at the 2016 Tony Awards, and (by then former) President Obama read George Washington's farewell address in "One Last Time (44 Remix)" on the 2018 *Hamilton Mixtape*. Like *Hamilton*, *1776*, which opened on Broadway in 1969, enjoyed fulsome praise from across the political spectrum because it "found hope, pride, and patriotism in [a] lively depiction of the signing of the Declaration of Independence."[25] President Richard Nixon invited the cast to perform at the White House in 1970, but nowhere did anyone suggest that the musical offered a transformative sense of history or challenged any theatrical, cultural, or political norms. Similarly, *1776* made no claims to pointing our attention toward an overlooked figure or a musical form absent from musical theatre.

Miranda introduced his contribution that evening at the White House as the start to "a concept album," but the essential ingredients of the show to come were already in place by that evening's performance. The album was to be, he continued, "about the life of someone who I think embodies hip hop, Treasury Secretary Alexander Hamilton." At this the audience laughed loudly and PBS, recording the event for television, cut to the Obamas, who were rapt. The laughter that greeted Miranda's introduction marked the perceived distance between the remote white founding father and the contemporary African American cultural form. At that point the casting for which the production would become known—actors of color playing the white founding fathers—was being foreshadowed. Miranda's Latinx body represented the white one of Alexander Hamilton. What he also embodied was a virtuosity that would seem to close the racial gap. Miranda "blew them all away" (to paraphrase the musical) with his argument for Hamilton as an eighteenth-century hip-hop artist, as well as with his literary mastery and charismatic stage presence. His performance said to the audience that this is an authentic depiction of what the event felt like and meant at the time. What was actually authentic, however, was less the argument about historiography and more the way in which Miranda's prodigious talent was dazzling the audience. He was conflating his genius (in the MacArthur sense) with his charismatic racialized body to give new life to the meritocracy's fallacy: I did it, you can too.

Just as *Metamora* did in the nineteenth century for a fledgling democratic republic, *Hamilton* staged in the twenty-first a founding myth of citizenship and of destiny for a nation poised uneasily on the cusp of a new century. The then-concept album and future show provided the United States with the heroic past that culminated in the first African American president. In this formulation the presidency of Barack Obama is not an outlier but the inevitable fulfillment of the founder's dreams. No matter that those who enslaved people and those who were willing to overlook that fact to create a nation would never have dreamed of an African American president, *Hamilton* suggests that the idea has been with us all along.

The neoliberal, multicultural compromise—you can hold full citizenship if you embrace US history as a positive story of individual achievement and beneficial progress and agree to understate or omit slavery, prejudice, and discrimination from the narrative—has a very high cost. The nineteenth-century version of this promissory myth that *Metamora* dramatized elided the genocide necessary to deliver on Manifest Destiny. *Hamilton* has been the focus of thoughtful critiques that point out that Alexander Hamilton was far more comfortable with slavery than the musical admits, that the cast of color elides the fact that there are no characters of color, and that the historiography it promotes is yet another version of hagiography or "founders chic."[26] Among the most rigorous of these critics has been Ishmael Reed, who has for decades fought assiduously for the inclusion of diverse voices in the cultural sphere. Reed has not been willing to agree to the citizenship compromise and perpetuate the foundational myths that have defined "We, the People."

Reed has been in a very public conversation with *Hamilton* since 2015 when, in his oft-quoted piece in *CounterPunch*, he asserted: "Establishment historians write best sellers in which some of the cruel actions of the Founding Fathers are smudged over if not ignored altogether. They're guilty of a cover-up. This is the case with Alexander Hamilton whose life has been scrubbed with a kind of historical Ajax until it sparkles."[27] Even the much-lauded casting received a caustic appraisal. "Can you imagine Jewish actors in Berlin's theaters taking roles of Goering? Goebbels? Eichmann? Hitler?"[28] Reed has long scoured US history to reveal its violent white supremacy, a commitment he described as "artistic guerrilla warfare against the Historical Establishment."[29] This has now extended to a full-length play, *The Haunting of Lin-Manuel Miranda*, which had its first staged reading at New York City's Nuyorican Poets Café in June 2019.

The play confronts Miranda with a reckoning for the myths he perpetuates in his global smash hit. As the show begins Miranda, the protagonist, is struggling with writer's block. While possibly under the influence of Ambien supplied by his agent, he is visited, reminiscent of *A Christmas Carol*, by ghosts or hallucinations of those omitted from the musical. Enslaved people (including Harriet Tubman), Native Americans, and white indentured servants all lecture Miranda on the consequences of omitting them. Ron Chernow, rather than Miranda, is the focus of Reed's fury, however. The play's antagonist is responsible for the rehabilitation of Alexander Hamilton and is thoroughly unapologetic about his role in sanitizing US history. In the *New Yorker*, cultural critic Hua Hsu observed about Reed's play in progress: "If 'Hamilton' is subversive, Reed asks, what is it subverting? Though the musical overthrew Broadway orthodoxy with its casting and music, the version of history that it presents is arguably quite old-fashioned, despite its success in making that history seem hipper. Rags-to-riches stories celebrate exceptions, distracting us from the crookedness of a system that dooms the rest to misery."[30] Myths about the past provide necessary legitimation for actions in the present.

Hamilton's ability to offer a veneer of inclusivity—especially though its casting choices—and contemporaneity diverts audiences from seeing the myths it perpetuates as myths. Reed remarked, "These were human beings—they weren't gods."[31] Seventeenth-century Metamora was rendered for nineteenth-century audiences as belonging to the pantheon of ancient heroes whose legacies could inspire citizens to see themselves as uniquely of the United States. Similarly, eighteenth-century Hamilton, Jefferson, and Washington (and others) were reinvented for a twenty-first century audience as forward-thinking men whose unrivaled foresight anticipated the challenges that would face their nation two hundred plus years hence. In both cases, theatre makes the claims and the myths that justify those claims more urgent and accurate because of the immediacy of live performance.

Conclusion

> For better or for worse, America is a country in which entertainment defines whose story is heard.
> —Elizabeth Vincentelli, *New York Times*, June 2, 2019

Myth and history are long-entangled discourses, as indeed are myth and performance. Following the thinking of theorist Claude Lévi-Strauss on narrative, historian Hayden White observed that myth as history "consisted of the mistaking of a method of representation, narrative, for a content, that is, the notion of a humanity uniquely identified with those societies capable of believing that they had lived the kinds of stories that Western historians had told about them."[32] Myth does not just urge its audiences to identify with its narratives and see the stories as applicable to their own lives. Instead, myths are told, White specifies, as accurate and truthful representations of the lives of those in the audience. The citizens *Metamora* and *Hamilton* urged and urge us to be are already us, the myth reassures. Origin stories demand myth to endow them with affective appeal. The acceptance of the disappearance of indigenous people as a tragic necessity or the founding fathers as hip as hip-hop helps audiences believe their citizenship has an empowering and positive history to guide them into the future.

Origins are themselves myths, and pernicious ones at that. It is important to be wary of origins. Theorist Michel Foucault cautions us that "what is found at the historical beginning of things is not the inviolable identity of their origin; it is the dissension of other things." These plays, when taken together, offer a (partial) history of the "dissension" of citizenship. As the US faces its current challenges, citizens and residents can draw strength from historical discord and dissent to advocate for another revision of "We, the People." Theatre may no longer be the primary engine of the entertainment industry, as it was in Edwin Forrest's day, but performed representation still plays an enormously influential role in influencing which myths are perpetuated and which ones are disavowed. Performance is not a court of law or a legislative body, but it is a public forum that has historically played a role in attending to the voices of those silenced in government and the judicature. It can and will continue to be an essential space in which citizenship is contested and reinvented.

Epilogue

I'm calling these ICE raids what they are—an act of terrorism. Just days after the El Paso massacre where a gun-wielding maniac parroted Trump's anti-immigrant hate, a battalion of ICE agents abducted 680 Latinx and immigrant men and women on Trump's orders.
—Greisa Martínez Rosas, Twitter, August 7, 2019

As I revise this keynote I delivered four months ago as an article, the national news has not appreciably changed. On Saturday, August 3, 2019, a gunman, inflamed by the kind of racist rhetoric promoted by Trump and his administration and specifically targeting Latinx people, slaughtered twenty-two people in an area Walmart and wounded more than twenty others.[33] Four days later, on Wednesday morning, August 7, 2019, ICE targeted seven workplaces in Mississippi and arrested more than 680 people for working without authorization.[34] Newspapers and social media were flooded with pictures of devastated children sobbing as they came home from the first day of school to find one or both of their parents missing. Writer Myriam Gurba stresses that these kinds of violent acts have a long history in the United States, and she connects them to the same ideas and historical myths that produced *Metamora* and *Hamilton*. "The manifesto posted by the El Paso killer roots his motives in the 1845 American doctrine propounded by John O'Sullivan."[35] The idea that the continent belongs to white settler colonists is no less pernicious and deadly now than it was 174 years ago. "Manifest Destiny," Gurba concludes, "has yielded to Manifesto Destiny."[36] Citizens who wish to resist the totalitarian and oppressive direction the United States has taken since 2016, as well as address the nation's long and ongoing history of racial oppression, should look to the 2020 election. Citizenship continues to be an incendiary category—essentially contested—but its past does not have to be its future.

Notes

1. The Hatch Act of 1939 prohibits federal employees from engaging in partisan activities while working in an official capacity. See Office of Special Counsel, Hatch Act, https://osc.gov/Pages/HatchAct.aspx, accessed August 21, 2019. The two emoluments clauses—foreign in Article I of the Constitution and domestic in Article II—prohibit office holders from profiting from that office. Scott Bomboy, "An Update on the Emoluments Cases," *National Constitution Center*, August 1, 2018. Online. Accessed August 21, 2019.

2. Aaron Montes and Rick Jervis, "'We've Never Seen Anything like This': As Trump Threatens to Close Border, Migrants Overwhelm Texas Cities," *El Paso Times*, March 30, 2019. Online. Accessed August 10, 2019.

3. *Fox and Friends*, June 22, 2018. Online. Accessed August 10, 2019.

4. Jill Lepore, *These Truths: A History of the United States* (New York: Norton, 2018), xviii and 311.

5. Elizabeth F. Cohen and Cyril Ghosh, *Citizenship* (Cambridge, UK: Polity Books, 2019) 11.

6. Cohen and Ghosh, *Citizenship*, 4.

7. John O'Sullivan, "The Great Nation of Futurity," *The United States Democratic Review* 6, no. 23 (1839): 426. Emphasis in the original.

8. Steven E. Woodworth, *Manifest Destinies: Westward Expansion and the Civil War* (New York: Alfred A. Knopf, 2010), 103.

9. Scott C. Martin, "Interpreting 'Metamora': Nationalism, Theater, and Jacksonian Indian Policy," *Journal of the Early Republic* 19, no. 1 (Spring 1999): 77.

10. Theresa Strouth Gale, "'The Genuine Indian Who Was Brought Upon the Stage': Edwin Forrest's *Metamora* and White Audiences," *Arizona Quarterly* 56, no. 1 (Spring 2000): 1.

11. Bethany Hughes, "The Indispensable Indian: Edwin Forrest, Pushmataha, and *Metamora*," *Theatre Survey* 59, no. 1 (January 2018): 27.

12. Hughes, "The Indispensable Indian," 29.

13. Jill Lepore, *In the Name of War: King Philip's War and the Origins of American Identity* (New York: Random House, 1998), 200.

14. Lepore, *In the Name of War,* 193.

15. Woodworth, *Manifest Destinies,* 104.

16. Gordon Sayre, *The Indian Chief as Tragic Hero: Native Resistance and the Literatures of America from Moctezuma to Tecumseh* (Chapel Hill: University of North Carolina Press, 2005), 26.

17. Greg Grandin, *The End of the Myth: From the Frontier to the Border Wall in the Mind of America* (New York: Metropolitan Books, 2019), 67.

18. Sayre, *The Indian Chief,* 16.

19. Jeffrey Ostler, *Surviving Genocide: Native Nations and the United States from the American Revolution to Bleeding Kansas* (New Haven, CT: Yale University Press, 2019), 8.

20. Laughlin McDonald, *American Indians and the Fight for Equal Voting Rights* (Norman: University of Oklahoma Press, 2011), 18–19.

21. Lisa Brooks, *Our Beloved Kin: A New History of King Philip's War* (New Haven, CT: Yale University Press, 2018) 346.

22. Mashpee Wampanoag, https://mashpeewampanoagtribe-nsn.gov/. See also The Wampanoag Tribe of Gay Head (Aquinnah), https://www.wampanoagtribe .org/, accessed August 11, 2019.

23. Renee C. Romano, *"Hamilton:* A New American Civic Myth," *Historians on Hamilton: How a Blockbuster Musical Is Restaging America's Past,* ed. Renee C. Romano and Claire Bond Potter (New Brunswick, NJ: Rutgers University Press, 2018), 297.

24. Blake Ross, "Lin-Manuel Miranda Goes Crazy for HOUSE and Hamilton," *Playbill,* September 21, 2009. Online. Accessed August 12, 2019.

25. Elissa Harbert, "Ever to the Right? The Political Life of *1776* in the Nixon Era," *American Music* 35, no. 2 (Summer 2017): 237.

26. Ken Owen, "Historians and *Hamilton:* Founders Chic and the Cult of Personality," *The Junto: A Group Blog on Early American History,* April 21, 2016. Online. Accessed August 13, 2019.

27. Ishmael Reed, "'Hamilton: the Musical': Black Actors Dress Up like Slave Traders . . . and It's Not Halloween," *Counterpunch,* August 21, 2015. Online. Accessed August 10, 2019.

28. Reed, "Hamilton: The Musical."

29. Bruce Dick and Amritjit Singh, eds., *Conversations with Ishmael Reed* (Jackson: University Press of Mississippi, 1995), xv.

30. Hua Hsu, "In 'The Haunting of Lin-Manuel Miranda,' Ishmael Reed Revives an Old Debate," *New Yorker,* January 9, 2019. Online. Accessed August 11, 2019.

31. Helen Holmes, "Playwright Ishmael Reed on Why He Thinks 'Hamilton' Is a Total Fraud," *Observer,* January 15, 2019. Online. Accessed August 10, 2019.

32. Hayden White, *The Content of the Form: Narrative Discourse and Historical Representation* (Baltimore: Johns Hopkins University Press, 1987), 34.

33. Astrid Galvan, et al., "El Paso Deaths Climb to 22, as Mayor Prepares for Trump Visit," *Washington Post,* August 5, 2019. Online. Accessed August 10, 2019.

34. Miriam Jordan, "ICE Arrests Hundreds in Mississippi Raids Targeting Immigrant Workers," *New York Times*, August 7, 2019. Online. Accessed August 10, 2019.

35. Myriam Gurba, "The Mexplainer: A History of Anti-Brown Violence in the American Southwest," *Autostraddle*, August 14, 2019. Online. Accessed August 21, 2019.

36. Gurba, "Mexplainer."

"Back in the Narrative"

Creating the Citizen Body in *Hamilton*

Sarah McCarroll

How FAMOUS DO YOU have to be for your body to be recognizable in silhouette only?[1] The Statue of Liberty with her lamp raised high above her togated body. Sherlock Holmes's profile with a deerstalker hat and meerschaum pipe. Charlie Chaplin's Little Tramp, trousers bagging around his oversized shoes. Marilyn Monroe, her pleated white dress blowing up in the wind from a passing subway train. In order to be reduced to a form recognizable in outline alone, it helps to be an iconic creation or character rather than just a person, but that iconicity requires signifiers beyond the body, most usually in articles of dress. In recent years, a new group of bodies could be added to this list: the silhouettes that are the primary marketing graphic of the musical *Hamilton*.[2] These silhouettes, perched on a black star against a burnished gold background, raise some complex questions, however: Who, exactly, are we seeing—actor or character? What body is represented— period or modern? I argue that the answer to these questions is always both/and, and that this duality provides the basis for an alchemy through which *Hamilton* inscribes some of the modern bodies of its actors with the transformative narrative of its period characters. In the course of the musical, upon the founding of the American nation, we see the noncitizen bodies of the characters become citizens; in seeing the characters undergo this process, however, we also inescapably see the actors experience it, although in their non-character lives, presumably the majority are already citizens. Or at least we see *some* of the actor's bodies have this experience. Numerous statements by cast, artistic team, and audience members have made the point that what gives the production its power seems to be seeing this multicultural cast in positions that would have been denied to them in the historical moment the musical chronicles.

I argue that the creation of these transitive, transformative bodies is in large measure accomplished via the conflation of period and modern in the costume and hair designs of Paul Tazewell and the choreography of Andy Blankenbuehler, and in the interaction of those production elements with the bodies of the cast in performance. I first briefly review the development of what became the musical *Hamilton* and some of the critiques that the musical has faced from scholars, then turn to less scholarly statements from the artistic team, the cast, and audiences to explore the impact that *Hamilton* seems to have had on many of those who experience it. Through close readings of Tazewell's designs and Blankenbuehler's choreography, I suggest that this impact is built upon the performative impact of bodies that fluidly move between then and now. Thus, the audience witnesses black and brown bodies becoming citizens of the young American nation, an apparent granting to these bodies of a fuller citizenship because it includes them in the founding myths of the nation. Ultimately, however, I wish to trouble this narrative of *Hamilton*'s effect, through an examination of the widely differing treatment, in both dramaturgy and embodiment, of the male and female characters in the musical.

Lin-Manuel Miranda's idea for what would become *Hamilton* began when, while on vacation in the Caribbean, he read historian Ron Chernow's 2004 biography of Alexander Hamilton; he immediately recognized a synergy between Hamilton's life story—a man who wrote himself out of his circumstances and into a founding role in the American experiment—and those of contemporary rappers whose ability as MCs to play with language allows them to change their own circumstances. As Miranda said in an interview with MSNBC's Chris Hayes, "At the end of the second chapter, I was like, 'Oh, this is a hip-hop story. . . . This is an immigrant who wrote his way into the top of American society, that helped create the country. And then wrote himself out of it.'" As an example of Hamilton's brashness, Miranda notes that the young military officer designed uniforms for his command: "It's very Kanye."[3]

Initially, Miranda's idea was to produce an album about Hamilton's life. At the White House in 2009 for "An Evening of Poetry, Music, and Spoken Word," Miranda introduced his performance by saying, "I'm actually working on a hip-hop album—it's a concept album—about the life of someone who I think embodies hip-hop, Treasury Secretary Alexander Hamilton."[4] The line got a laugh from the audience, but as it turned out, Miranda wasn't kidding. His next performance of the material that became *Hamilton* was "My Shot," the second song on what was then called

The Hamilton Mixtape, performed at a June 2011 benefit for Ars Nova, a Manhattan theatre group.[5] From these two events, *Hamilton* moved to a Lincoln Center American Songbook concert performance of a suite of songs, and then into a workshop that became a sold-out full production at New York City's Public Theater in the 2014–15 season, and finally a smash-hit Broadway run that continues as of 2019. In 2018 alone, the New York run of Hamilton sold 526,773 tickets, and there are sister productions running in Chicago and San Francisco as a US National Tour and in London, all of which are likewise sold out.[6]

Hamilton's beginning as a hip-hop concept album is, of course, evident in the styles of music that remain central to the production; lyrical, musical, and even structural quotations or inspirations from rap and hip-hop blend with those from the history of musical theatre.[7] Using contemporary musical genres to tell this eighteenth-century story has seemed appropriate to others besides Miranda. Ben Brantley's *New York Times* review of the Broadway production proclaims, "It's the immoderate language of youth, ravenous and ambitious, wanting to claim and initial everything in reach as their own. Which turns out to be the perfect voice for expressing the thoughts and drives of the diverse immigrants in the American colonies who came together to forge their own contentious, contradictory nation."[8] The diversity Brantley perceives in the production's treatment of its historical subject has certainly contributed to *Hamilton*'s success. However, popularity with reviewers and audiences has not shielded *Hamilton* from stinging critique from some critics and scholars.

As early as 2015, while the show was still in its initial Broadway run, the *Village Voice*'s Tom Sellar noted that it "lacked heft": "For all the talent on display, it's surprising that a show hailed so widely as a watershed event wields no edge. *Hamilton* stays fairly anodyne. The production makes a joyful display of identity politics by virtue of its stunning cast—many of them African-American and Latino performers—and its fusion of hip-hop with Broadway ballads to tell the tale of the Founding Fathers. Although the show's built on this terrific discrepancy, it doesn't do much with irony. *Hamilton* narrates the war of independence from Britain, the drafting of the Constitution, and the formation of a new economic system, but it never elucidates a political critique."[9]

Many of the scholars whose work appears in *Historians on "Hamilton": How a Blockbuster Musical Is Restaging America's Past* articulate what they see as the dangers inherent in *Hamilton*'s refusal to engage critically with contemporary issues or with truly revolutionary choices in dramaturgy. Lyra D. Montero situates the musical as part of the genre of "Founder's Chic," in which hagiographic attitudes toward the founders create the impression that "the only people who lived during this period—or the only ones who mattered—were wealthy (often slave-owning) white men."[10] For Montero, the elision of people of color (and, to a lesser extent in the context of her essay, women) from the narratives of American creation that *Hamilton* presents means that the musical does more harm than good. For instance, she notes that while Hercules Mulligan, who became one of George Washington's chief spies, is played by a black actor, Mulligan's slave Cato, who was a part of his intelligence-gathering activities, appears nowhere on the stage. And Sally Hemings, the enslaved woman who bore Thomas Jefferson multiple children, is physically represented only briefly by a silent member of the chorus who delivers him a letter, an embodied replication of the service required of enslaved African Americans.[11]

As Montero sees it, because the musical is so overtly concerned with how the narration of history evolves—one of its central musical numbers is titled "Who Lives, Who Dies, Who Tells Your Story," and those are the lyrics that end the show—*Hamilton* abdicates a significant responsibility given the thematic claims its lyrics make. The erasure of the bodies, voices, and stories of black and brown people from the story is not compensated for through multicultural casting: "The idea that this musical 'looks like America now' in contrast to 'then,' however, is misleading. . . . America 'then' *did* look like the people in this play, if you looked outside the halls of government."[12]

It is important to accept the validity of these critiques and acknowledge the ways in which *Hamilton* elides portions of history from its narrative; and I am conscious of my own positions as a white, female scholar as I think about the work. However, I am also leery of historians, myself included, using their collective standing as scholars to dismiss audience members' authentic responses to onstage material, especially when I remember my own sense that I was seeing authentic and transformative theatre when I saw *Hamilton*. It's a tricky thing to tell theatregoers that what they're feeling is wrong.

Historians, of course, have perspectives that are created by professionally informed judgments, in addition to their own histories and emotions, and their assessments are important to making sense of artworks within large cultural and critical contexts. But we should not ignore the experiences articulated by cast and audience members who speak of the musical's powerful effect on them. *Les Misérables*, for example, enjoyed a successful Broadway revival between 2014 and 2016, although "the [original] London production had been panned by critics," and New York critics were also less than enthusiastic when the musical transferred to the United States; in the *New York Daily News*, Clive Barnes called the show "instantly disposable trash."[13] *Les Mis* may suffer from some of the same problematics as *Hamilton* in the way it frames the resistance at the heart of its story. Recent castings have seen multicultural actors in a variety of roles (Ramin Karimloo, an Iranian-Canadian actor, as Jean Valjean in the 2014 revival cast, along with African American Nikki M. James as Eponine and part-Maori Keala Settle as Madame Thénardier), although both Victor Hugo's source novel and the book of the musical present the uprisings of 1830s Paris as composed of exclusively white narratives. The production also homogenizes the revolutionary spirit of the novel. "*Les Misérables* has highly specific politics that aren't simply the politics of popular revolt and 'sentimental' liberty," Adam Gopnik reminds us, but are connected to Hugo's vision for a united Europe.[14]

Joseph M. Adelman and Renee C. Romano separately point out that there are perhaps more positive ways to think about the work the musical is doing on stage. Adelman notes that *Hamilton*'s creators "seek to understand the past not on its own terms but on those of the contemporary moment in the 2010s. . . . [It] emphasizes that we cannot fully know the past or even create a single narrative about it. It therefore presents a fascinating case study for understanding the complexity and contingency of the past, for seeing the essence of the historical narrative in new ways, and for learning about how to connect past and present through both form and content."[15] It is this contingency, this liminality of the past—its capacity for speaking of, to, and with the present via the always-contemporary bodies of the actors on stage—that gives *Hamilton* its power, but it may also ultimately point toward the gaps it does not seek to fill.

The musical has inarguably allowed people who have not seen themselves in the story of America's founding to become part of the national mythology in ways that are new and important to them. Actor Daveed Diggs, who played Jefferson/Lafayette in the original production, says that the show has given him "a sense of ownership over American history. Part of it is seeing brown bodies play these people."[16] And Leslie Odom Jr., the original Aaron Burr, claims that prior to *Hamilton*, "I was a student of African-American history. I cared way more about the achievements of and hard-won battles of black people in this country than I did about the founding fathers. But this show has been such a gift to me in that way because I feel that it's my history, too, for the first time ever. We all fought in the Revolutionary War. I think this show is going to hopefully make hundreds of thousands of people of color feel a part of something that we don't often feel a part of."[17] New York City high school students, who saw *Hamilton* at free student matinees as part of the Theatre Development Fund's Stage Doors program in partnership with the Public Theater, also connected to American history in new ways. Bill Coulter's sophomore English students at Fort Hamilton High School in Brooklyn, when asked how the musical's casting affected them, said, "It just made me really proud, and feel good about being American. Like I belong here."[18]

This is where Renee Romano finds the power of the musical. While it is true, she notes, that "*Hamilton*, regardless of its imaginative casting, does not in any way address the reality and experiences of people of color in the United States at the time of the founding," it does find "a way to rewrite America's foundational civic myths to allow people of all different backgrounds to claim full belonging in the nation no matter their race, ethnicity, or immigration status. . . . *Hamilton* allows people of color to see themselves in the country's history . . . by making the stories of the founders more universal and inclusive. Every night, it gives ownership of America's narrative over to blacks and Latinxs, peoples who have long been marginalized, persecuted, and denied full inclusion in the United States."[19] What Romano is saying, what Diggs, Odom, and those high school students are saying, is that *Hamilton* allows them to feel more fully as citizens of the United States because they can see themselves, through the bodies of performers whom they recognize as looking like them, becoming citizens in the new American nation. When we meet the characters of *Hamilton* in the first act, they are British citizens, subjects of a king none of them has ever seen, who lives in what is, for all the Anglophone influences on colonial America, a foreign land. Hamilton is the least established of these residents of the colonies, "just another immigrant coming up from the bottom,"[20] but every one of the principal characters is "young, scrappy, and hungry"[21] for something envisioned but not yet realized: a new nation. As the first act plays out, we see these British subjects rise up in a move explicitly positioned as analogous to Moses leading his people out of slavery to Israel. Hamilton raps, "Foes oppose us, we take an honest stand, / We roll like Moses, claimin' our promised land."[22] This comparison is all the more powerful for being articulated by a person of color. The word "roll" in this context comes from the lexicon of rap and hip-hop, but it also contains echoes of the Book of Amos as quoted by Martin Luther King Jr. in his "I Have a Dream" speech: "Let justice roll down like waters, and righteousness like an ever-flowing stream."[23] In claiming the justice and righteousness of the colonial cause, these young bodies lay claim to ownership in the American promised land; and like Moses and the Israelites, the claiming here is one not just of land, but of nation.

The inhabitants of a nation are its citizens,[24] and the course of *Hamilton*'s first act enacts this becoming—of nation and citizens. We see the

Revolutionary War fought through to the Battle of Yorktown, which ends the war but does not yet create the United States. As the British soldiers surrender, Hamilton cries that now he and his compatriots "Gotta start a new nation."[25] In "Non-Stop," the closing number of the act, we see the nation come fully into existence as the Constitution is written, Hamilton defends it in *The Federalist Papers*, and he is then tapped to be treasury secretary. And what happens in the six and a half minutes of "Non-Stop" encapsulates the transitive magic of *Hamilton*, because in the course of this song the characters cease to be subjects and become citizens. There is no naturalization process, none of them has an immigration status or a green card, and certainly none of them is held to be three-fifths of a person; by virtue of their presence in the moment that America becomes a nation, they are American citizens. The musical, via its casting, literally acts the bodies of black and brown people into the rooms where the founding acts of America happened.

I'm interested in how this embodiment is accomplished, and my contention is that it's not just the casting choices the musical makes or the musical styles it embraces that do this work; it is also the ways the bodies of the rapping, singing cast are presented through costume and choreography as simultaneously eighteenth and twenty-first century. Paul Tazewell's costume and hair designs, in concert with Andy Blankenbuehler's choreography, allow a mapping of the foundational moments of American democracy onto the specific bodies of the cast—a transformative act of becoming citizens at the end of *Hamilton*'s first act and living as citizens in its second.

Tazewell, who was part of the musical's artistic team from the first staging at the Public, says that drawing together the world of the script's events with the world of its music was the design problem of the show: "The challenge was figuring out where those two eras meet, and what percentage of this world is hip-hop and what percentage is 18th century."[26] He eventually settled on "two guiding principles: First, period from the neck down and modern from the neck up; and, second, strip away all the embroidered detail of the 18th century."[27]

As to the first principle Tazewell lists: Saving only King George III, whose character and attitudes are trapped irrevocably in the past, none of the cast wears period wigs (some actors wore wigs styled in contemporary fashions to save their hair from the wear and tear of daily styling). Thus, we see a chorus with mohawks, faux-hawks, buzzed sides, natural curls, or five o'clock shadow. Phillipa Soo, who is Chinese American, played Eliza Hamilton with her straight black hair pulled back from her face, but with no curl or powder. The knit watch cap that Oakieriete Onaodowan wore in rehearsals became an element of James Madison's curmudgeonly badass persona. Renee Elise Goldsberry's Angelica appeared with natural African American curls above her boned taffeta bodice. Tazewell has explicitly connected the effect of integrating period and modern on the actors' individual bodies; having modern hair and makeup allowed the cast to relate to the costumes as though they were part of contemporary dress: "We discovered that the clothes lay very comfortably on the actors. . . . They could relate to the costumes in a very contemporary way with a street exuberance and the beauty of contemporary face and hair."[28] Thus, performers' character personas, because of the presentation of their bodies, could exist in a both/and relationship with time period.

The modernity begun with hairstyle choices continued in Tazewell's design for the costumes of both chorus and principals. The clothing of the chorus is based on the cream breeches and vests that are an iconic part of the Revolutionary colonial military uniform; the cream is not only a historical reference but the color of the parchment on which Hamilton spent so much of his life writing, an act central to the musical. However, these chorus uniforms are clearly and explicitly not eighteenth-century ensembles; shirts have been dispensed with so that the sleeveless vests reveal the toned arms of male and female dancers, the male chorus's breeches are constructed to allow for contemporary choreography, while the female chorus member's breeches are actually constructed from a stretch fabric that mimics the leggings that are ubiquitous in "athleisure" wear today. The principals' costumes play with color more than those of the chorus. Miranda's Hamilton spends much of the middle portion of the show (bridging the intermission between acts 1 and 2) in a green taffeta vest and coat because, as Miranda said to Tazewell, "green is the color of money."[29] When we meet Thomas Jefferson at the top of the second act, he appears in a purple velvet and taffeta suit, the coat of which is nearly floor-length, much longer than would be historically accurate but which wonderfully reflects the exuberant swagger of the character. Tazewell has said that as Daveed Diggs's performance evolved, "It became apparent that Jefferson was better served to be represented as a Rock Star like Jimi Hendrix or Prince."[30]

While these costumes superficially appear truer to period than those of the chorus, their construction allows them to function rather like contemporary dress. The pose of the Schuyler sisters, arms aloft, snapping out a feminist "Work!"[31] at the thought of including women in the declaration that "all men are created equal" would not be possible without garment construction choices that allow those arms to be raised in ways that an actual period gown would render impossible. Close examination of the female chorus reveals that accommodations for contemporary movement have been made here, too. Gores have been added to the hipline of the corsets that the female chorus wears when they appear as women (the cream vests are worn when they appear as men). In addition, the corsets have been lengthened so as not to create a hard line that cuts into the waist as the women dance, and their shape reflects a more hourglass silhouette, rather than the hard, triangular torso forced by eighteenth-century stays.[32]

Theatrical modifications to period clothing to accommodate the movement needs of actors are certainly neither new nor exclusive to *Hamilton*. But the movement needs of *Hamilton* perhaps require even more consideration of how these modifications must be made than other period shows. Because the actors in this show, whom the action of the text largely positions in the eighteenth century, aren't just asked to dance the minuet. These actors have to dance hip-hop, have to execute lifts drawn from classical ballet, have to launch themselves into the air. As with the show's music and lyrics, Andy Blankenbuehler's choreography reveals a multiplicity of influences from a broad timeline of dance history: "Beyond several varieties of hip-hop dance, you can see little traces of Gene Kelly and Justin Timberlake . . . Jerome Robbins. But the movement of *Hamilton* reaches far beyond conventional dance steps, of any tradition. Andy devised a language of what he calls 'stylized heightened gesture.' It includes everything from the way a chair is moved to how a shoulder pops to the bows at the curtain call."[33] And Ben Brantley felt that "the gymnastic corps de ballet . . . gives further, infectious life to that feeling of perpetual motion, of a speeding, unceasing course of human events. (The use of a revolving stage . . . has seldom seemed more apt; this world never stops spinning)."[34]

And because the choreographic style is so wide-ranging and encompasses not just the "dance breaks" of the musical, but every element of how the actors move through the world, the effect that is created by these perpetually moving actors is that modern bodies are eighteenth-century bodies and that eighteenth-century bodies believably and naturally move in modern ways. The two worlds overlap, bleed together; there is a liminality in the world of *Hamilton*. It's not just that Hamilton's life is "a hip-hop story," as it struck Miranda, but that the modern movement of the bodies in this world, dressed in period garments, allows for the possibility that those bodies are both/and—they naturally inhabit both the moment of American creation and the moment of contemporary America. The interplay of costume design and choreography suggests that that process of creation is an ongoing one—a transitive process in which perhaps time is not fully linear but circles like the turntables on stage so that the bodies of the actors, citizens in the now, are also American citizens in the then. That, after all, is what happens to the bodies over the course of the story. Or is it?

It's possible to think of the American musical as creating a space for bodies that represent dreams and idealism. That's what Miranda gives us in *Hamilton*, but it's a dream for *his* body. The journey to American citizenship is marked on bodies in *Hamilton*, but not on all bodies; this empowerment is only fully granted to male bodies—to Hamilton, Jefferson, Madison, and even Burr. And perhaps this shouldn't be surprising. Lin-Manuel Miranda's Puerto Rican roots are close to the surface of his public persona (witness his calls for support for the island in the wake of Hurricane Maria)[35]—his lived experience is intimately connected with questions of immigration and belonging as they apply to brown and black bodies. But he is also a cisgender, straight man who worked with a wholly male production team, so no matter how aware of gender issues he may be, those questions are not part of his direct embodied experience. It has been clear since the musical's inception that Miranda connected in visceral ways with Alexander Hamilton's story, and the musical is a clear reflection of its creator and his perspectives. Perhaps it is not fair to ask the musical to be all things to all people. But just as historians have criticized *Hamilton* for not showing the presence of enslaved Africans in the origins of America, so too do I want to call attention to *Hamilton*'s lack of full female citizenship.

The major female characters in *Hamilton* are acted onto the bodies of multiethnic and multiracial performers just as those of the male characters are, but the possibilities of movement (literal and metaphorical) granted to women's bodies by the costume design and choreography of the first act are not upheld by the dramaturgy of the musical in act 2, and the design choices follow the lead of the text's story construction. The exclusions from the musical that Montero points to in terms of race (Cato, Sally Hemings) are reperformed in gendered terms via the disappearance from the story of the Schuyler sisters. In act 1, they are proto-feminists who take active agency to interact with the revolutionary spirit of New York City and demand that women be included in an imagined sequel to the Declaration of Independence; they are their own women, going downtown without their father's consent—he "doesn't need to know."[36] By act 2, they have ceased to be Schuylers—all have married—and have become adjuncts to men. Peggy has disappeared altogether; the historical woman died young and the actress is needed to play Maria Reynolds in the second act, thus transforming from ingénue to femme fatale, defined by the danger and downfall she represents for Hamilton. Angelica, who spits words with a facility that positions her as the intellectual equal of

Hamilton, Burr, and the other founding fathers, has sailed "off to London . . . accompanied by someone who always pays." Although she acknowledges that her choice of a marriage for the sake of financial stability means that she "will never be satisfied,"[37] the character does not reappear as a rapping intellectual, but only as a sister and support for Eliza. Eliza herself spends much of act 2 as "the best of wives, the best of women,"[38] and although she takes back agency to "put [her]self back into the narrative"[39] at the end of the musical, she does it to serve as keeper of Hamilton's legacy, not to write her own narrative.

This dramaturgical elision is repeated by the design choices of *Hamilton*'s second act. Here we find that the male characters are empowered by increased spectacle. Instead of the nearly identical blue-and-buff Revolutionary War uniforms that the men spend much of the first act wearing, by the beginning of act 2 their costumes have become increasingly elaborate. As noted, Hamilton first adds a green vest and coat and later matching breeches; Thomas Jefferson appears resplendent in purple velvet and satin; even George Washington trades his uniform for a black velvet coat. This flamboyance is reflected lyrically in the hyper-articulate cabinet rap battles of act 2; increased spectacle empowers the male bodies of the musical while it serves to further contain the women.

As the women's costumes and hair become more elaborate, that spectacle becomes dangerous to the freedom of their bodies. When the actress playing Peggy Schuyler becomes Maria Reynolds, with whom Hamilton has an adulterous affair, she exchanges her pale yellow satin gown for one of blood-red satin, literally becoming a scarlet woman. Angelica adds a vest and peplumed jacket to her gown, thus containing the arms that snapped above her head in "The Schuyler Sisters." Both her hair and Eliza's are put up; for women, "putting one's hair up" was historically a symbol of having become an adult,[40] and in *Hamilton*, becoming an adult woman means existing as wife and mother—adjunct to a man (and perhaps putting away foolish childhood ideas of women's equality?). Eliza is liberated from her eighteenth-century corset in the second act as the action moves into the early nineteenth century, but she trades it for an empire-style gown that arguably contains her legs much more effectively than the full skirts she wore in the first act. Further, following the death of her son Philip, she appears in a black redingote (a long overcoat), high at the neck and tight in the sleeves; at times its stiffness seems to actually hold her arms away from her body.[41] Where aesthetic spectacle in dress liberates the male characters of *Hamilton*, it represents the containment of some women's bodies and the dangers inherent in others.

In *Theatre and Citizenship*, David Wiles writes, "The citizen is at once the constitutive element of an abstract State, and the actor of a permanent revolution, endlessly calling for equality."[42] *Hamilton* provides an apt demonstration of this thesis, as it enacts revolutionary positions onto the bodies of black and brown men while the gaps in its revolutionary treatment of bodies point so clearly to the necessity for continued theatrical revolution. The multicultural male bodies in *Hamilton*'s cast, dressed in eighteenth-century costumes, are citizens of the new nation of the eighteenth century, here granted the power and agency of the founding American citizens; but because the hip-hop songs they sing are performed by recognizably modern bodies, they also constitute the contemporary state of our nation. Because these bodies are both/and, then/now, they carry ownership in the process of creating a citizenry with them. They are both the citizens of an abstract eighteenth-century American state, and citizen-actors in the twenty-first century calls for equality. And thus they also cannot escape demonstrating some of the continued gaps of agency/full-citizenship in the bodies of the American narrative. *Hamilton*'s ideals are largely based in racial redress of power, but how might the bodies of the musical behave had there been a woman's voice during its evolution? Hidden at the back of *Hamilton*'s success is the continued need for more women in positions of generative and creative power. We see the frustration this lack of agency causes Angelica—who repeats "I will never be satisfied"[43]—and Eliza—whose refrain is "let me be a part of the narrative."[44] More than once in *Hamilton*, George Washington tells Alexander, "Let me tell you what I wish I'd known / When I was young and dreamed of glory. / You have no control: / Who lives, who dies, who tells your story."[45] *Hamilton*'s women do not get to tell their own story. Perhaps it's not fair to ask that the show allow them to do so. But I'd like to see their bodies freed for that potential.

Notes

1. I would like to acknowledge the contributions to the development of this essay made by Dr. Charlotte Canning and other attendees of Theatre Symposium 28. Her keynote address and their questions and conversation during the conference greatly helped to clarify and expand my initial thoughts on this topic.

2. The *Hamilton* marketing graphics may be found on the musical's official website, https://hamiltonmusical.com/new-york/, along with many other sites that can be located with a Google image search of "Hamilton musical silhouettes."

3. "Off-Broadway 'Hamilton' Is A Smash Hit," *All In with Chris Hayes*, March 10, 2015, 2018, https://www.youtube.com/watch?v=EWo7VZ17iGA, accessed December 11.

4. Lin-Manuel Miranda and Jeremy McCarter, *Hamilton: The Revolution* (New York: Grand Central Publishing, 2016), 14. This performance can be seen on YouTube: "Lin-Manuel Miranda performs 'Alexander Hamilton' at White

House," https://www.youtube.com/watch?v=E8_ARd4oKiI, accessed April 17, 2019.

5. "My Shot," as Jeremy McCarter points out, is an "I want" song, in which a protagonist "tells the audience about the fierce desire that will propel the plot. . . . Without a song like this, you wouldn't get very far in a musical: A character needs to want something pretty badly to sing about it for two and a half hours. And you wouldn't get anywhere at all in hip-hop. For all of its variety of style and subject, rap is, at bottom, the music of ambition, the soundtrack of defiance, whether the force that must be defied is poverty, cops, racism, rival rappers," or, say, the British Empire (Miranda and McCarter, *Hamilton*, 20–21).

6. "Broadway Grosses—Hamilton," BroadwayWorld.com, https://www .broadwayworld.com/grossesshow.cfm?show=HAMILTON&year=2018, accessed December 11, 2018, and "Hamilton," https://hamiltonmusical.com/new-york /home, accessed December 11, 2018.

7. To provide a structural example: Miranda says that "Alexander Hamilton," the show's opening number, "owes a debt to the prologue of *Sweeney Todd*. All our characters set the stage for the main man's entrance" (Miranda and McCarter, *Hamilton*, 16). Other musical or lyrical references include: Mobb Deep, The Notorious B.I.G., Jay-Z, Rodgers and Hammerstein, Stephen Sondheim, and Gilbert and Sullivan, among others. These references are noted by Miranda in the printed marginal notes throughout Miranda and McCarter, *Hamilton*.

8. Ben Brantley, "Review: 'Hamilton,' Young Rebels Changing History and Theatre," *New York Times*, August 6, 2015, https://www.nytimes.com/2015/08/07 /theater/review-hamilton-young-rebels-changing-history-and-theater.html, accessed December 12, 2018.

9. Tom Sellar, "Lacking Only Heft, 'Hamilton' Bowls Over Broadway," *Village Voice*, August 18, 2015, https://www.villagevoice.com/2015/08/18/lacking-only -heft-hamilton-bowls-over-broadway/, accessed December 11, 2018.

10. Lyra D. Montero, "Race-Conscious Casting and the Erasure of the Black Past in *Hamilton*," in *Historians on "Hamilton": How a Blockbuster Musical Is Restaging America's Past*, ed. Renee C. Romano and Claire Bond Potter (New Brunswick, NJ: Rutgers University Press, 2018), 58.

11. Montero, "Race-Conscious Casting," 64, 62.

12. Montero, "Race-Conscious Casting," 62. "America Then Told By America Now" is one of the show's taglines and was repeated by Miranda in multiple interviews, including in the *New York Times* (https://www.nytimes .com/2015/02/08/theater/lin-manuel-miranda-and-others-from-hamilton-talk -history.html), *The Atlantic* (https://www.theatlantic.com/entertainment /archive/2015/09/lin-manuel-miranda-hamilton/408019/), and on the BBC (https://www.bbc.com/news/video_and_audio/headlines/42464676 /hamilton-creator-it-s-a-story-of-america-then-told-by-america-now).

13. Mark Robinson, "*Company, Les Mis*, and More: Which Musicals Got No Love From the Critics but Took Home the Tony?," *Playbill.com*, June 11, 2015, 2019, http://www.playbill.com/article/company-les-mis-and-more-which-musicals -got-no-love-from-the-critics-but-took-home-the-tony-com-351054, accessed February 26, 2020.

14. Adam Gopnik, "The Persistent Greatness of 'Les Misérables,'" *New Yorker*,

December 28, 2012, https://www.newyorker.com/books/page-turner/the-persistent-greatness-of-les-misrables, accessed September 7, 2019.

15. Joseph M. Adelman, "Who Tells Your Story: *Hamilton* as a People's History," in Romano and Potter, *Historians on "Hamilton,"* 279.

16. Branden Janese, "'Hamilton' Roles Are This Rapper's Delight," *Wall Street Journal,* July 7, 2015, https://www.wsj.com/articles/hamilton-roles-are-this-rappers-delight-1436303922, accessed December 11, 2018.

17. Qtd. in Montero, "Race-Conscious Casting," 66–67.

18. Qtd. in Miranda and McCarter, *Hamilton,* 159. For other responses from students in the same vein, see Renee C. Romano, "*Hamilton*: A New American Civic Myth," in Romano and Potter, *Historians on "Hamilton,"* 315.

19. Romano, "*Hamilton*: A New American Civic Myth," 317, 314.

20. Lin-Manuel Miranda, *Hamilton,* "Alexander Hamilton."

21. Miranda, *Hamilton,* "My Shot."

22. Miranda, *Hamilton,* "My Shot."

23. Amos 5:24 and "I Have a Dream," Dr. Martin Luther King Jr., speech delivered August 28, 1963, during the March on Washington.

24. I am aware that this is a remarkably simplistic statement, particularly given the political climate surrounding issues of immigration and citizenship in 2019. Those issues were no less fraught in the late eighteenth century, as the framers of the Constitution considered how to "count" the enslaved African Americans present in the colonies (they were partial "people" for census purposes but not citizens). I use this phrasing to reflect what I see as the musical's idealism, at least in racial terms. Because the musical's dramaturgy avoids presenting enslaved characters and showcases black and brown actors experiencing the birth of the nation, it neatly dodges the reality of racially based exclusion from citizenship. Perhaps a more realistic wording would be "inhabitants of a nation *ought to be* its citizens."

25. Miranda, *Hamilton,* "The World Turned Upside Down."

26. Miranda and McCarter, *Hamilton,* 113.

27. Patrick Pacheco, "'Hamilton' Costume Designer on How He Streamlined 18th Century Looks for a 21st Century Show," *Los Angeles Times,* June 11, 2016, https://www.latimes.com/entertainment/arts/la-et-cm-paul-tazewell-hamilton-costumes-20160610-snap-htmlstory.html, accessed December 12, 2018. Images of all the costume looks and choreographic moments referenced in the remainder of this essay can be found in the photographs included in Miranda and McCarter, *Hamilton.* In addition, portions of the choreography may be seen in "Hamilton's America," a documentary about the musical presented on PBS's *Great Performances* (2016).

28. Pacheco, "'Hamilton' Costume Designer."

29. Pacheco, "'Hamilton' Costume Designer."

30. Joe Kucharski, "The Costume Design of HAMILTON!," *Tyranny of Style: A Closer Look at Costume Design and the Language of Clothing* (blog), February 15, 2016, http://tyrannyofstyle.com/home/14202271/costume-design-hamilton-broadway.

31. See Constance Grady, "How the Women of *Hamilton* Are Changing Broadway," Vox.com, https://www.vox.com/2016/2/23/11058702/hamilton-angelica

-eliza-schuyler-love-triangle, accessed April 19, 2019, among numerous published versions of this image.

32. See especially pictures on pp. 18–19 and 66–67 in Miranda and McCarter, *Hamilton*. For discussion of how the shape of the female torso was constructed during the Revolutionary period, see Anne Cécile Moheng, "Whalebone Stays and Panniers: The Mechanics of Good Carriage in the Eighteenth Century," in *Fashioning the Body: An Intimate History of the Silhouette*, ed. Denis Bruna (New Haven, CT: Yale University Press, 2015), 108–28, published in conjunction with the exhibition "Fashioning the Body: An Intimate History of the Silhouette," held at Bard Graduate Center, New York, April 3–July 26, 2015.

33. Miranda and McCarter, *Hamilton*, 134.

34. Brantley, "Review."

35. See "Lin-Manuel Miranda's Passion for Puerto Rico," *New York Times*, December 26, 2018, https://www.nytimes.com/2018/12/26/theater/hamilton-puerto-rico-lin-manuel-miranda.html, accessed February 26, 2020, for information about Miranda's calls in support and philanthropic efforts on behalf of Puerto Rico.

36. Miranda, *Hamilton*, "The Schuyler Sisters."

37. Miranda, *Hamilton*, "Non-Stop."

38. Miranda, *Hamilton*, "The Best of Wives, the Best of Women."

39. Miranda, *Hamilton*, "Who Lives, Who Dies, Who Tells Your Story?"

40. See Hugh Aldersey-Williams, *Anatomies: A Cultural History of the Human Body* (New York: W. W. Norton, 2013), 94.

41. See picture on pp. 254–55 in Miranda and McCarter, *Hamilton*.

42. David Wiles, *Theatre and Citizenship: The History of a Practice* (Cambridge: Cambridge University Press, 2011), 18.

43. Miranda, *Hamilton*, "Satisfied."

44. Miranda, *Hamilton*, "That Would Be Enough."

45. Miranda, *Hamilton*, "History Has Its Eyes on You" and "Who Lives, Who Dies, Who Tells Your Story."

Mussolini and Marinetti

Performing Citizenship in Fascist Italy

Shadow Zimmerman

lose YOUR EYES AND imagine, if you will, Benito Mussolini, the infamous "first dictator." Picture him emphatically placed above an audience, speaking from a pedestal, striking an iconic pose—his arm struck forcefully out, his hand closed in a fist or perhaps thrusting a fascist salute, his barrel chest reverberating the echoes of his impassioned speech, his strong jaw lifted toweringly above all onlookers. This, Mussolini's public persona, was the "new Italian" citizen incarnate. Now, figuratively open your eyes, step back, and realize that you are not staring at Mussolini the orator himself, but rather at one of millions of postcards of his likeness—postcards purposefully hung around the homes of countless Italians. This act was one of many layers of Italy's communal performance of "new Italian" citizenship during the Fascist regime. However, Italy's final act of performed citizenship before the onset of its Republican era—the public display and mutilation of Mussolini's corpse—was its most iconic and, perhaps, its most definitive. Comparing the iconography of these two actions, specifically the positioning of Mussolini's body in each (strong and tall in postcards and photographs versus dangling from a service station in the end), serves to demonstrate the complete reversal of Italy's performed citizenship from the beginning to the end of Mussolini's Fascist regime.

The fledgling authoritarian government of Italy embraced Futurism because the artistic form meticulously defined, policed, and performed citizenship in both an artistic and sociopolitical sense—and Futurism's leader, Filippo Marinetti, did so according to a strict hierarchy. In defining and exploring the etymology of the term "avant-garde," Hans Magnus Enzensberger explains, "Every guard is a collective. . . . First the group, and only then the individual, whose decisions are of no consequence in the undertakings of the guard, unless he be its leader. For every guard is most rigorously divided into the one who issues the commands and passwords of the day and the many who receive them, pass them on, and obey them."[1]

As Enzensberger clarifies, the forms of the historical avant-garde mimic the structure of authoritarian forms of government—membership is strictly curated and guided by an individual with power. Benito Mussolini in particular harnessed the potency of the avant-garde by aligning himself with Filippo Marinetti and the Futurists, and he embraced the Futurist ideology, rhetoric, and definitions of citizenship accordingly. Mussolini carefully crafted his image through specific iconographic management—much in the way Marinetti curated the public perception of Futurism through membership control and advertising—and the Italian populace embraced that image during the first half of his reign, as evidenced by contemporaneous postcard collections. I'm particularly fascinated by the revelations these postcards offer regarding Italy's performance of citizenship during Mussolini's Fascist regime. In this essay, I explore the iconographic evolution of Italy's communal performance of citizenship. After explaining Futurism's foundations in themes of citizenship, I detail the iconography of Mussolini's performed citizenship, the "new Italian," replete with Marinetti's apparent influence. With this guide, I chronicle the iconographic evolution of Italy's performance of citizenship, defined by the populace's approbation or disapprobation of Mussolini's model, drawing from the aforementioned postcards and the public desecration of Mussolini's corpse as case studies.

As Mussolini's performed iconography as leader and paragon of "the New Italian" was directly inspired by the forms of Futurism and the art of Marinetti, it's crucial that we detail the relationship between the two and define the importance of citizenship to the forms of the historical avant-garde, especially Futurism. The earliest political usage of the term "avant-garde" is accredited to Henri de Saint-Simon, a French political theorist and early Socialist thinker, writing at the cusp of the nineteenth century. In his essay *On Social Organization*, Saint-Simon presents a utopia in which humanity "marches" toward "the well-being and happiness of all mankind"; he writes that "in this great undertaking the artists, the men of imagination will open the march: they will take the Golden Age from the past and offer it as a gift to future generations; they will make society pursue passionately the rise of its well-being, and they will do this by presenting the picture of new prosperity."[2]

Saint-Simon dreamt of a society in which artists had direct sociopolitical agency in their depictions (or performances) of "pictures of new prosperity" (i.e., ideal citizenship). Scholars like Matei Călinescu have noted that Saint-Simon's literature is highly romanticized, but the manner in which Saint-Simon positioned artists as a vanguard for political change directly inspired actual agendas within Mussolini's Fascist regime. Mussolini, who was a rising star in the Milanese socialist scene before he defected, is known to have referenced the writings of Saint-Simon in his speeches.[3] As such, Saint-Simon was clearly in the philosophical lexicon of the socialist communities of early twentieth-century Italy.

As Marinetti was also a devoted socialist at the turn of the twentieth century, we can reasonably assume that he was also familiar with Saint-Simon's philosophy. This influence can be seen mirrored in Marinetti's Futurist theory: Marinetti deliberately constructed a political voice ("We futurists name as our sole political programme the pride, the energy, and the expansion of our nation");[4] he described a utopia ("we . . . want to free this land from its smelly gangrene of professors, archaeologists, ciceroni, and antiquarians");[5] he prescribed ideal citizenship, both as a Futurist and an ideal Italian ("Let all freedom be granted to the individual and the people except the freedom to be cowardly");[6] and he enforced traditional gender roles ("[masculinity is that which is] free of every emotional morbidity, every womanly delicacy . . . [that which is] lively, pugnacious, muscular, and violently dynamic").[7] Marinetti defined citizenship through his writings, performed it during the Futurist *serate*, and policed it through the publication of seemingly endless manifestos and a discerning curation of Futurism's public image, leaning on the writings and theories of Saint-Simon.

Thankfully, the artistic and political relationship between Marinetti and Mussolini has inspired bountiful scholarship, and the palimpsestic layers of influence between the two men have been the focus of a great deal of critical engagement. To summarize a selection: in her book *Painters and Politics*, Theda Shapiro concludes that "the methods used by Mussolini in the initial stage of fascism—the bombast and threats, the street brawling, the disregard for truth and legality—were indeed Futurist and had been learned directly from Marinetti in the course of the interventionist manifestations of 1915 and thereafter."[8] Similarly, Anne Bowler writes in her essay "Politics as Art" that the Futurists "developed important forms in their performances, notably agitprop and the spectacle, that formed the basis of later [Fascist Party] methods for crowd provocation and control."[9] Even in an essay that largely refutes the connection between the two, arguing instead that Mussolini was more deeply influenced by his fellow Milanese socialists, Walter Adamson surrenders in "The Language of Opposition in Early Twentieth-Century Italy" that Mussolini's "manner of 'seducing a crowd'" and his "knack for sloganizing" were directly inspired by Marinetti.[10] Additionally, Mussolini proclaimed himself "at heart, a Futurist" in a 1914 letter to Paolo Buzzi, a member of the artistic party.[11] During their interventionist demonstrations (and prison time)[12] together before Italy entered World War II, Marinetti's bold and brash style left its mark on Mussolini, and Mussolini later turned to these inspirations as dictator.

Ultimately, Mussolini and Marinetti became public partners. They made their first communal appearance at a Fascio d'Azione Rivoluzionaria meeting on March 31, 1915.[13] In 1919, Marinetti led a gang of Mussolini's men as they burned the offices of the journal *Avanti!* and Mussolini reciprocated by propping Marinetti up as a political candidate in the General Elections of 1919—an attempt that failed.[14] Nevertheless, the pair's relationship continued well into Mussolini's fascist reign, and the result was a web of direct influence between the men, their theories, their politics, and their practices. Much as the ideals of Saint-Simon inspired the artists of the avant-garde, Marinetti's avant-garde art inspired Mussolini to rise above the crowd, to force it to eat out of his hand and to learn to like it. In her essay "Folla/Follia," Christine Poggi clarifies that the Futurists "understood the crowd to be 'feminine' in its malleability, its incapacity to reason, its susceptibility to flattery and hysteria, and its secret desire to be seduced and dominated."[15] Inspired by Marinetti, Mussolini targeted the "malleability" of the Italian populace, its desire to be "dominated" by a powerful, definitive force.

Mussolini, a professed Futurist, maintained a strict public image as the de facto head of the Italian Fascists and eventual exemplar for the "new Italian." Mussolini, like Marinetti and also inspired by Saint-Simon, sought to define ideal citizenship. In the manner of the Futurist *serate*, during which Futurists would read directly from their prescriptive manifestos and demand compliance,[16] Mussolini performed that ideal citizenship, the "new Italian," immediately in the form of his public persona. He supplemented this image with bombastic propaganda, and he laced schoolbooks with pro-Fascist rhetoric in order to create a highly specified iconography.[17] Ultimately, Mussolini sought to represent in Nietzschean terminology, the Übermensch (or "superman")—a concept with which both he and Marinetti were deeply familiar.[18]

Mussolini was directly familiar with Saint-Simon's theories, and Marinetti's practices directly aligned with them. Dutifully, both men embraced the power of art and the media in realizing their political agendas—with an apparent level of overlapping influence between them. Understanding this, it is now possible to analyze Mussolini's performed persona as a piece of Futurist art, and it is fruitful to unpack the iconography of that performance. Mussolini, in the role of Il Duce, is remembered by his dominating physical characteristics; as Marinetti paints in his *Portrait of Mussolini*: "Physiological patriotism, because physically he is built all'italiana, designed by inspired and brutal hands, forged, carved to the model of the mighty rocks of our peninsula. Square crushing jaws. Scornful jutting lips that spit with defiance and swagger on everything slow, pedantic, and finicking. Massive rock-like head, but the ultradynamic eyes dart with the speed of automobiles racing on the Lombard plains. To right and left flashes the gleaming cornea of a wolf."[19] Mussolini, according to Gigliola Gori, performed his character "by means of theatrical gestures, which were rough but effective. Hands on hips, legs wide apart, with set jaw and rolling eyes, the orator Mussolini spoke to the crowd in a virile, stentorian voice."[20] Moreover, Mussolini performed the paragon of the masculine body by engaging the contemporary cultural memory. He decorated himself, Alessandra Swan notes, as a "virile Roman" and ensured he was regularly pictured on horseback, as both motifs are laced with historical connotations of leadership and testosterone. Swan notes, too, that the modern Italian culture was "predicated on physical prowess, the powerful male physique was now disciplined publicly. Men exercised outdoors, on the beach, and displayed their physically fit bodies in still or moving images, in the sports tabloids or at the cinema."[21] Mussolini engaged this popular imagery. His performed image consciously referenced popular figures like the cinematic strongman Maciste and the frequently photographed boxer Primo Carnera, ensuring that his masculine reputation preceded him, leaving an effective imprint on the Italian populace—an imprint that Mussolini could then fill with definitions of "new Italian" citizenship.[22]

Mussolini curated his carefully constructed character much in the style of Erving Goffman's "front," Goffman's term for the external demonstration of our performed identity. Goffman defines the "front" as "that part of the individual's performance which regularly functions in a general and fixed fashion to define the situation for those who observe [a] performance."[23] Mussolini was careful to present only an idealized, "new Italian" side of himself when in the public eye. As such, his very image came to define the concept to the Italian populace, just as Goffman's concept suggests. Almost serendipitously, Mussolini curated his "front," his image of the "new Italian," during the newfound age of media (notably photography and radio), allowing for the proliferation of this paragon image throughout Italy. The population of Italy then embraced this image as their collective "front" in their performance of citizenship, a performance to which this essay will turn in a moment.

Beneficially, Mussolini's eager use of photography and radio leaves us with direct evidence of his performance. For the sake of this essay, I'm most interested in his photographs, as they allow for and welcome direct iconographic comparison and analysis. Specifically, I'm fascinated by the dual nature of postcards, the image-as-object. Postcards bear examination both as images and as objects—the images on them offer one revelation, the manner of their use another. In the case of these Mussolini postcards, the images printed on them demonstrate the sentiments of the memento (was it pro-Mussolini or anti-fascist?); the manner of their use evidences the level of import of these objects. Regarding the imagery of Mussolini's captured performance, the photographs available in the Library of Congress archive depict such images as Mussolini saluting with Hitler from a balcony, Mussolini standing on a stage surrounded by members of his regime, and an image,[24] reproduced here, of Mussolini orating in front of a crowd (figure 3.1).

We see Mussolini enthusiastically gesticulating in front of a large tapestry that reads "Arx Omnium Nationum" ("The center of all nations"), his arm powerfully stretched before him, his fingers seemingly reaching for something only he can grasp; his barrel chest adorned with regalia; his strong jaw casting a dark shadow underneath his face (naturally mirroring a common depiction of his face in isolation surrounded by smoke or shadow).[25] Notably, these images position Mussolini physically above the viewer, a trend confirmed by Gori—who notes that this was likely due to Mussolini's naturally stocky stature.[26] Mussolini meticulously managed his public image in order to present (i.e., to perform) the ideal "new Italian." Moreover, his use of photography also engaged cultural memory. Allesandra Swan writes that "before Fascism and the rise of Mussolini, photographs were used to create an emotional link between the powerful and the people, as later they were used to forge a relationship between the Fascist hierarchy and the Italians during the regime."[27] Ultimately, through public performances and photography, Mussolini charismatically exploited the Italian cultural memory in order to present (and perform) citizenship. The Italian response to Mussolini's political performance can be seen as its performed public opinion, and the evolution of this performance demonstrates Italy's conclusions concerning Mussolini and his personal brand of citizenship.

Initially, Italians performed their approbation of Mussolini's photographed "new Italian" through their collection and presentation of those photographs in the form of postcards. Enrico Sturani exhaustively details the postcard-keeping practices of Italy during the fascist era in his essay "Analyzing Mussolini Postcards," in which he estimates a total of roughly 100 million Mussolini postcards were produced during his reign—in a country with a 1945 population of only 45 million. Sturani confirms that many of the common images on these postcards depicted

Figure 3.1. Benito Mussolini, 1940. (Courtesy of Library of Congress Prints and Photographs Division)

a Mussolini who was powerful, popular, and paternal. One such post-card depicts Mussolini orating on a battlefield, standing in a pose almost identical to that he took in the earlier-analyzed image.[28] Others show Mussolini carrying a small boy on his shoulders or listening intently to a woman in a crowd. Others portray the repeating motif[29] of Musso-lini as Napoleon Bonaparte—demonstrating that, once again, Mussolini carefully engaged cultural memory in crafting his image. These post-cards, these mementos of Mussolini-defined "new Italian" citizenship, were produced overwhelmingly by private publishers and purchased in a completely capitalist manner—as Sturani notes, "They were easy to sell,"[30] people wanted to purchase mementos of Mussolini's image, and they did en masse. It wasn't until the 1930s and Italy's highly unpopular invasion of Ethiopia that official, propagandist postcards dominated the market.[31] For the majority of Mussolini's reign, these postcards prolifer-ated because of Mussolini's popularity and the populace's approbation of his character, not some enforced sycophancy. Additionally, Sturani notes that the vast majority of these postcards were unused, unhandled; rather, "[once] purchased, they were then religiously kept like holy images, stuck in the frame of a mirror alongside images of Christ and the pictures of family members living abroad, pinned on a bedroom wall or gathered in albums."[32] These postcards were not simply mailed, Italians showed them openly in their homes and flaunted them like Christ-like iconography.

I argue that the communal act of collecting and displaying these post-cards was a performative one: the commons performing its collectivity in the more public spaces of the home (the foyers, the living rooms, the hallways), per the theories of Elizabeth Dillon—also recalling the work of Jürgen Habermas. In her book, *New World Drama*, Dillon devel-ops the theory of a "performative commons,"[33] a populace's ability to publicly perform its opinions. Dillon writes that "[in] the space of the theatre . . . audience and actors together form an assemblage that both embodies and represents the collectivity of the people."[34] Any collective body in a performative space, Dillon writes, performs its collectivity, the public opinion. Expanding our mind somewhat, it is possible to see that the performative commons can, and does, exist outside the walls of the theatre, in any space in which an actor and audience exist. We see the per-formative commons in Italy during this period most obviously at the ral-lies and speeches of Mussolini. However, the manner in which the Italians collected and displayed Mussolini postcards is also an act of performance. Richard Schechner writes that the subject of performance is transforma-tion, "the startling ability of human beings to create themselves."[35] The act of hanging a photograph of Mussolini beside a portrait of Christ, or

arranging it neatly in a scrapbook to be shown, is an act of identity creation. To place these images in the public spaces of the home, to show
them off proudly, is to perform that identity. As such, we can consider
this communal act of postcard collection to be Italy performing its approbation of Mussolini's definition of citizenship, the "new Italian." In
this act, we also see the Italians promoting Mussolini's iconography of
citizenship through the proliferation of a specific paragon image.

Moreover, this performed presentation of postcards engages Mussolini's "front," as discussed earlier. In defining the concept, Goffman
writes first of "setting," or the "furniture, decor, physical lay-out, and
other background items which supply the scenery and stage props for the
spate of human action played out before, within, or upon it."[36] Goffman continues that the "setting" is filled with "sign-signifiers" that carry
meaning during the performance of self within that space. For the myriad
Italians who presented these postcards in the public spaces of their homes
or included them in photo albums to be shown to guests or family members, these postcards were pieces of the "setting" of their performed
identity, and they carried a tremendous amount of meaning through
their connection to Mussolini's defining image of the "new Italian."
In Goffman's terms, these postcards were a primary aspect of the Italian's performed identities whenever they welcomed another person into
their homes—friend, family, stranger, or otherwise—especially as the regime continued accumulating power and the societally and government-
enforced expectation to perform Mussolini's "new Italian" rose.

From Mussolini's rise to power in 1922 until the invasion of Ethiopia
in 1935, the Italians performed their approbation of Mussolini's "new Italian" through the capitalist proliferation of postcards, but also through
performances of gender and childhood, as explored in works by Gori[37]
and Foss.[38] In her book *Italian Fascism and the Female Body*, Gigliola Gori
exhaustively details the ways in which women were encouraged to fall
into supportive, often domestic and traditional, roles for the male soldiers
in their lives. Clive Foss's essay "Teaching Fascism" is a survey of fascist
Italian schoolbooks at several levels of basic education that analyzes the
rhetoric of the propaganda employed—again, these schoolbooks encouraged children to fall into roles expected of their sex.

After 1936, however, the Italian obsession with Mussolini began to
fade. As noted earlier, this is evidenced by the rise of officially produced,
propagandist postcards. Additionally, as Martin Clark notes in his biography of Mussolini, a "marked shift" was reported between 1936 and 1938
when a "wave of pessimism" swept the country.[39] Outside Italy, the rise
of anti-fascist postcards beginning in 1935 represented a similar global
distaste for Mussolini.[40] After ten years of growing dissatisfaction, fueled

by an increasingly anti-fascist public sentiment, Italy's bubbling performance against Mussolini's brand of "new Italian" citizenship reached a boil on the morning of April 29, 1945, in the Piazzale Loreto when the Milanese public desecrated Mussolini's corpse.

Before dawn, the recently executed bodies of Mussolini, his mistress, Clara Petacci, and fourteen other fascists were dumped onto the ground of the Piazzale Loreto, a square rife with cultural memory, where eight months earlier Hitler's Schutzstaffel (or SS) had publicly displayed the bodies of fifteen executed anti-fascists. This began a roughly twelve-hour period when the citizens of Milan, representatives of the Italian populace, defiled the corpses of Mussolini, his mistress, and the other fascists. Mussolini's body was kicked, spat on, and beaten before being hung upside down from the girders of a nearby gas station. His hanging corpse now more accessible, the crowd continued to beat, shoot, and hurl insults and projectiles at it. Notably, it is recorded that one woman emptied five shots into Mussolini's body in retribution for the execution of her five sons. By the time American troops were ordered to remove his body and place it in a nearby morgue, Mussolini's iconic semblance was mutilated beyond recognition. As a thematic bookend to the performed opinion of Mussolini, Sturani notes that postcards depicting Mussolini's bullet-ridden corpse proliferated immediately following his death.[41]

This ultimate, highly performative act of citizenship marked a Bakhtinian carnivalesque usurpation of Mussolini's "new Italian," and this final iconographic evolution demonstrated Italy's ultimate opinion of Mussolini and his brand of citizenship. In her introduction to Mikhail Bakhtin's *Rabelais and His World*, Helene Iswolsky writes that the carnivalesque celebrates "liberation from the prevailing truth and from the established order; it [marks] the suspension of all hierarchical rank, privileges, norms, and prohibitions. . . . [It is] the true feast of becoming, change, and renewal."[42] The carnivalesque champions the utter reversal of social foundations; and the desecration of Mussolini's corpse was arguably modern Italy's most carnivalesque political performance. In this performative act, the Italian populace also reversed Mussolini's performed iconography. After two decades of seeing Mussolini presenting himself from on high, standing tall and powerfully, the Italians hung him by his feet for all to see—mocking his loftiness by presenting him with similar visibility, but usurping his power by flipping his image upside-down. This inverted iconography recalls centuries of anti-Christian imagery, including that proliferated throughout avant-garde art by Alfred Jarry, who regularly portrayed his Caesar Antichrist upside-down, bathed in a black sun, sometimes labeled with backward lettering to create an exact opposite of Christ (figure 3.2).[43]

Figure 3.2. The frontispiece from the original, 206-piece print run of Alfred Jarry's *César antechrist* (1895), which depicts Saint Peter both upright and inverted. The inverted position of the saint's body bears resemblance to both Christlike iconography and the display of Mussolini's dangling corpse as infamously photographed.

So too did the Italians create their anti-Mussolini in that moment. In those twelve hours on April 29, 1945, Italy liberated itself from Mussolini's established order and definition of citizenship. In rendering Mussolini's corpse unrecognizable, the Italians also destroyed the image of the "new Italian," performing the populace's new definition of citizenship. In inverting his image, the Italians defined themselves as the anti-Mussolini, vowing to place their new definition of citizenship as far from fascism as possible.

This creation of a new definition of citizenship began what Sturani calls a "new, democratic political phase."[44] Just over thirteenth months after the desecration of Mussolini's corpse, the Kingdom of Italy was dissolved and replaced by the Republic of Italy. Umberto II, king of Italy, abdicated and was exiled. In just over a year, the Italian populace had forcibly removed any threat of individual rule, defining their new ideal citizenship. Continuing this definition, the first prime minister of the new republic, Alcide De Gasperi, was a renowned centrist who, as Aldo Agosti writes, was "guided by a conception of state that, superior to the parties, was to be based on a balance between the guarantee of freedom for its citizens and the assertion of its authority."[45] The Italians chose as their representative a man who would uphold their individual freedoms, firmly cementing the new popular definition of Italian citizenship in the public memory. Holding office for nearly eight years, De Gasperi was the second-longest-serving prime minister of the Italian Republic, evidencing his support among the Italian populace.

As we can see, Italy's performance of citizenship was immensely polarized during the final twenty years of the kingdom, swinging madly from rampant support of the "new Italian" as Mussolini defined (and performed) it, to a visceral denunciation of this brand of citizenship and the subsequent development of not only a new "new Italian," but an entirely new Italy. This performance was decidedly avant-garde, per Enzensberger's definition. First, these Italians, while many, served as representatives of a larger communal entity in their upright postcard-collecting and their upside-down usurpation of Mussolini and his performed brand of citizenship. Second, as repeatedly discussed, this performance was deeply political, as Mussolini's image (again in the form of postcards and an inverted corpse) was a political signifier, and any reaction to it was either imbued with or read to have political intent.

Interestingly, an examination of the photographs of Mussolini and the Italian populace's swooning collection of those photographs in the form of postcards allows for a telling iconographic analysis of the communal performance of citizenship in Italy throughout the Fascist regime. Exploring the evolution of this iconography allows us to isolate Italy's defi-

nition of ideal citizenship and demonstrates the weight of this definition. Ultimately, the carnivalesque usurpation of Mussolini's power and
stature during the public desecration of his corpse marked the beginning
of Italy's performance of contemporary citizenship, laying the foundation for the last seventy years of the Italian Republic.

Notes

1. Hans Magnus Enzensberger and Michael Roloff, *The Consciousness Industry: On Literature, Politics and the Media* (New York: Seabury Press, 1974), 28.

2. As quoted in Matei Călinescu, *Five Faces of Modernity: Modernism, Avant-
garde, Decadence, Kitsch, Postmodernism* (Durham, NC: Duke University Press,
1987), 102.

3. James B. Whisker, "Italian Fascism: An Interpretation," *Journal of Historical Review* 4, no. 1 (1983): 5–27.

4. As quoted in James Joll, *Intellectuals in Politics: Three Biographical Essays*
(London: Weidenfeld and Nicolson, 1960), 141.

5. F. T. Marinetti and R. W. Flint, *Let's Murder the Moonshine: Selected Writings* (Los Angeles: Sun & Moon Press, 1991), 50.

6. As quoted in Joll, *Intellectuals in Politics*, 158.

7. Marinetti, *Let's Murder the Moonshine*, 86.

8. Theda Shapiro, *Painters and Politics: The European Avant-Garde and Society: 1900–1925* (New York: Elsevier, 1976), 184.

9. Anne Bowler, "Politics as Art," *Theory and Society* 20, no. 6 (1991): 763–
94, quotation at 785.

10. Walter Adamson, "The Language of Opposition in Early Twentieth-
Century Italy: Rhetorical Continuities between Prewar Florentine Avant-
Gardism and Mussolini's Fascism," *Journal of Modern History* 64, no. 1 (1992):
22–51, quotation at 50.

11. Graziella Marchicelli, "Futurism and Fascism: The Politicization of Art
and the Aestheticization of Politics, 1909—1944" (PhD diss., University of Iowa,
1996), 60.

12. Bowler, "Politics as Art," 784.

13. Joll, *Intellectuals in Politics*, 168.

14. Bowler, "Politics as Art," 763, and Shapiro, *Painters and Politics*, 184.

15. Christine Poggi, "Folla/Follia: Futurism and the Crowd," *Critical Inquiry*
28, no. 3 (2002): 709–48, quotation at 712.

16. Berghaus Günter, *Italian Futurist Theatre, 1909–1944* (Oxford: Claren-
don Press, 2004), 88.

17. See Clive Foss, "Teaching Fascism: Schoolbooks of Mussolini's Italy," *Harvard Library Bulletin* 8, no. 1 (1997): 5–30.

18. See Günter Berghaus and Society for Italian Studies, *The Genesis of Futurism: Marinetti's Early Career and Writings 1899–1909*, Occasional Papers No. 1
(Leeds: Society for Italian Studies, 1995), 13–16; also Gigliola Gori, *Italian Fascism and the Female Body: Sport, Submissive Women and Strong Mothers* (Milton
Park, UK: Taylor and Francis, 2012), 16–17.

19. Marinetti, *Let's Murder the Moonshine*, 166.

20. Gori, *Italian Fascism and the Female Body*, 13–14.

21. Alessandra Antola Swan, "The Iconic Body: Mussolini Unclothed," *Modern Italy: Journal of the Association for the Study of Modern Italy* 21, no. 4 (2016): 361–81, quotation at 363.

22. Swan, "The Iconic Body: Mussolini Unclothed," 363.

23. Erving Goffman, "The Presentation of Self in Everyday Life," Monograph no. 2 (Edinburgh: University of Edinburgh Social Sciences Research Centre, 1956), 13, https://monoskop.org/images/1/19/Goffman_Erving_The_Presentation_of_Self_in_Everyday_Life.pdf.

24. *Benito Mussolini* (Washington, DC: Library of Congress Prints and Photographs Division, 1940), black-and-white film negative, under 5 × 7 inches, LC-USW33-000890-ZC.

25. Alessandra Antola, "Photographing Mussolini," in *The Cult of the Duce: Mussolini and the Italians*, edited by Gundle Stephen, Duggan Christopher, and Pieri Giuliana (Manchester: Manchester University Press, 2013), 178–92, at 183.

26. Gori, *Italian Fascism and the Female Body*, 17.

27. Antola, "Photographing Mussolini," 178.

28. See figure 7 in Enrico Sturani, "Analyzing Mussolini Postcards," *Modern Italy* 18, no. 2 (2013): 141–56, image at 147.

29. Sturani, "Analyzing Mussolini Postcards," 149–50.

30. Sturani, 143.

31. Sturani, 142.

32. Sturani, 143.

33. Elizabeth Maddock Dillon, *New World Drama: The Performative Commons in the Atlantic World, 1649–1849* (Durham, NC: Duke University Press, 2014), 2.

34. Dillon, 4.

35. Richard Schechner, "A Student's Guide to Performance Studies," Harvard Writing Project, Harvard University, http://hwpi.harvard.edu/files/hwp/files/peformance_studies.pdf.

36. Goffman, "The Presentation of Self in Everyday Life," 13.

37. See Gori, *Italian Fascism and the Female Body*.

38. See Foss, "Teaching Fascism."

39. Martin Clark, *Mussolini* (London: Routledge, 2016), 225.

40. Sturani, "Analyzing Mussolini Postcards," 152–53.

41. Sturani, 153.

42. Helene Iswolsky, introduction to *Rabelais and His World* (Bloomington: Indiana University Press, 1984), 10.

43. Alfred Jarry, *César antechrist* (Paris: Mercure de France, 1895), 39, https://gallica.bnf.fr/ark:/12148/bpt6k1054662z.

44. Sturani, "Analyzing Mussolini Postcards," 153.

45. Aldo Agosti, "Alcide De Gasperi and Palmiro Togliatti," in *The Oxford Handbook of Italian Politics*, edited by Erik Jones and Gianfranco Pasquino (Oxford: Oxford University Press, 2015), 351.

Performing "Digital Citizenship"

in the Era of the Blind Spot

Becky K. Becker

I n 1998, WHEN PRESIDENT Bill Clinton was on his way toward impeachment hearings following the Whitewater investigation and subsequent Starr Report, many of us shrugged off his affair with White House intern Monica Lewinsky as "none of our business" and "unrelated to his work as president." In retrospect, and particularly in light of the Me Too movement, the longer view on this moment in history has changed dramatically. For some, performances of citizenship at that time now appear myopic and unempathetic toward the one person who should have garnered the most compassionate response at the center of the scandal: Monica Lewinsky. Still, it is worth remembering that many Americans performed our citizenship prior to the turn of the twenty-first century by assuming that even the president of the United States should have a private life. Perhaps this was our blind spot.

More than twenty years later, everything has changed. While we still manage to have private lives in between our posts, vlogs, and tweets, our social media presence has become increasingly politicized. Whether we choose to engage in the political process or not, as individuals we seem to perform our citizenship in a very public way via social media. Given this shift toward "sharing," I am interested in examining the ways in which we perform our citizenship online. How do we choose to represent ourselves? With whom do we align? How do we perform those alignments? How willing are we to gather information in an unbiased manner, weigh facts, and make conclusions that blur the lines of party and politics? And how might this performance contribute to the current state of American politics, which is not really "politics" in the historic sense at all?

Although I have conducted traditional research regarding digital citizenship and its performance, this piece moves somewhat fluidly between theory and reflection. Most of my social media research was done on Facebook—or "mombook," as many of my students call it—conducted somewhat sporadically over the past several months. However, the ideas explored have been developed over the past several years while observing our country's descent into the divisiveness that currently characterizes our national dialogue. I do not think it is hyperbolic to note that now more than ever, the personal is political. In a time when the national stage has become fraught with more personal attacks than actual facts, it is difficult to refrain from taking our politics too personally. Another blind spot.

What does it mean to be a digital citizen? Do we engage in cyber citizenship simply by making posts or tweets that reference a particular political party? Or does "enacting ourselves in cyberspace"[1] involve more complicated representation than party alignments would suggest? According to Engin Isin and Evelyn Ruppert in *Being Digital Citizens*, "to understand what it means to be digital citizens requires theorizing between digital life (and its digital subjects) and political life (and its political subjects). Both are simultaneously undergoing transformation, and understanding the dynamics of these changes is a challenge."[2] Considering this description, if we can postulate that "political subjects" refers to individuals engaged in political acts and relationships, then we can also infer that digital citizenship is a dynamic, evolving state of being (or not being), dependent upon factors both digital and embodied.

In contrast, as theatre artists, our understanding of performance is likely to assume the embodied presence of the performer. Given the vitality of the physical body within live performance, Isin and Ruppert's appreciation of the interplay between digital life (think cyberspace) and political life (think embodied space) may be useful in describing digital performances of citizenship.[3] Equally valuable is Erving Goffman's *Presentation of the Self in Every Day Life*, in which he likens daily interactions to theatrical performance. For Goffman, such exchanges are face-to-face and involve the incorporation of a "front" or, as he describes it, "expressive equipment of a standard kind intentionally or unwittingly employed by the individual."[4] Interestingly, Goffman's discussion of "front" in the context of daily performances is reminiscent of cognitive scientists George Lakoff and Mark Johnson's theory of embodied cognition, which posits that concepts like "front" and "back" have emerged from the ways in which humans experience our physical bodies.[5] Also interesting to note is that our embodiment affords us a literal blind spot—our backs—that may serve as a physical manifestation of our tendency to miss details in otherwise plain view. As will become apparent later, a nuanced understanding of embodiment is necessary as we consider digital performances of citizenship and the incorporation of "front"—even in the absence of traditional corporeal embodiment.

In the dramaturgical sense, Goffman's concept of "front" can be linked to the traditional notion of "character." Characters behave in particular ways in order to influence the action of a play. Following this same logic, in life we perform particular characters or "fronts" in order to manage the presentation of self—and thereby influence our own stories. As an example, as the chair of a university department, I might refrain from sharing my opinion regarding Trump's presidency while courting potential performing arts donors whose political leanings I do not know. It goes without saying that a discussion of politics is not likely to be helpful in making a case for supporting the arts, and could even prove detrimental—unless I know what my audience wants to hear and can perform to that perspective. While we may not perceive our daily selves as playing characters in the Aristotelian sense, Goffman's assertion that we cultivate and maintain particular behaviors with the intent of presenting ourselves in a certain light to persuade an audience is akin to conventional explanations of character. Goffman describes the phenomenon at length—and it is his use of language that I find particularly useful: "Regardless of the particular objective which the individual has in mind and of his motive for having this objective, it will be in his interests to control the conduct of others, especially their responsive treatment of him. The control is achieved largely by influencing the definition of the situation which the others come to formulate, and he can influence this definition by expressing himself in such a way as to give them the kind of impression that will lead them to act voluntarily in accordance with his own plan."[6] In other words, according to Goffman, part of our embodiment involves filtering or masking our intentions or reactions in order to *control*, influence, and/or please others. Our bodies are the means through which we communicate—or embody—our "fronts." As performers in our daily lives, we work to create certain outcomes—be they small-scale and interpersonal or actions intended to affect a wider audience.

Goffman's astute observations on how we utilize "fronts" to influence daily interactions is helpful, particularly when paired with embodied cognition and the physiological fact of our embodiment, involving a front-back orientation. However, neither serves to fully bridge the gap between live performance (whether onstage or in life) and its digital counterparts. In the spirit of *Performance and Media: Taxonomies for a Changing Field* by Sarah Bay-Cheng, Jennifer Parker-Starbuck, and David Z. Saltz, I would like to suggest that if live performance and digital performance exist on opposite ends of a continuum, reflecting "some form of distortion and manipulation of a conceptual ideal," then that distortion is also particularly influenced by our embodiment.[7] Even when we engage in what may appear to be a solely digital performance—such as posting on Instagram, Twitter, or Facebook—there is an inherent "liveness" within that performance due to the embodied manner in which such a performance is achieved. Just as we project "fronts" in our daily lives and on-stage performances, it can be argued that we project "fronts" onto our Facebook and Twitter feeds, in an attempt to control the impact of our performance.

Similar to face-to-face interactions, then, digital performances appear to be for the benefit of an audience—a means of impacting others through our digital presence. As Aylin Yildirim Aykurt and Elif Sesen see it, "Social networks place the individuals in the center rather than the subject or the event when compared to other websites or traditional media."[8] It follows that when attention shifts from the event or subject to specific individuals, cyber interactions become performances of self, aimed at affecting the event or subject. For example, in response to the Democratic presidential candidate debate on July 30, 2019, President Trump tweeted the following: "Very low ratings for the Democratic Debate last night—they're desperate for Trump!"[9] By making himself the focus of the narrative, Trump attempted to shift audience attention away from the *event*—the Democratic debate—to himself. While the purpose of this first night of debates was to highlight the ten Democratic candidates' qualifications and positions on a variety of issues, Trump used his prolific Twitter performance of citizenship to shift attention to himself and away from the democratic process.

How do we characterize such digital performances? Have we come to view online presence as another form of embodiment? Do I see my social media presence as an extension of my physical self? Who am I in that virtual space? How do others see me? And what do my digitally embodied actions accomplish?

Perhaps I am getting a bit ahead of myself, shifting so quickly from establishing social media as a virtual performance space in which the individual is at the center, to the notion of digital embodiment. However, this leap is necessary in order to imagine social media as a potential location of action and interaction. Digital space offers a location where performances of self may serve as digital representations of our lived embodiment, placing us in an interactive space across the world (wide web), and connecting us to others we might otherwise never physically encounter. Digital space represents an active space that, for many scholars who study the internet, is a mechanism for enhancing social performances, rendering them more democratic. Social media—in the many ways that we embody it—can be empowering.[10] Except, of course, when it's not. Which points to our most crippling blind spot.

It can be argued that in a setting like Facebook, we see ourselves at the center of a "performance," using posts to garner attention, earning likes and comments, thereby employing our embodied selves to manipulate our "fronts" in order to attain power over the grander narrative. This characterization of Facebook as a performance space is particularly reminiscent of the months (many long months) leading up to the 2016 presidential election during which cyber performances of citizenship were (or at least appeared to be) at an all-time high. Russian bots and "fake news" aside, it was during the lead-up to the election that I noticed what many other Facebook users likely took note of as well. Individual users tended to make frequent posts declaring their political allegiances via memes or news stories about candidates, sharing online petitions, liking and commenting affirmatively when they agreed, and, in contrast, making snide comments or, perhaps worse, blocking and ignoring noncompliant "friends" whose views did not align with their own. During the course of the election, our digital performances of citizenship, or "fronts," became particularly rigid as we learned that we could not influence, let alone *control*, the wider narrative—to use Goffman's language. We pretended, in that digital performance space *and*, I would argue, in our embodied lives, that this was election politics as usual. In that digital space of our ever-increasing blind spots, the divide between liberal and conservative became a chasm. And yet we "felt" engaged in the process; we "felt" engaged in a dialogue. Never mind that the dialogue was largely with ourselves—and those with whom we happened to agree. Our blind spots multiplied.

Perhaps this was just my experience. Perhaps the proliferation of social media performances along political lines was also an indication of more highly engaged embodied performances of citizenship. After all, didn't I post a sign in my yard, make donations, and canvas (a little) for my candidate? Wasn't social media making us all more aware and involved? Weren't we better able to see the candidates for who they were and, in turn, make better choices? Interestingly, according to Goffman, "when the individual presents himself before others his performance will tend to incorporate and exemplify the officially accredited values of the society, more so, in fact, than does his behavior as a whole."[11] This embodied phenomenon appears to have played out somewhat differently as we have migrated more fully toward a kind of "digital embodiment." In 2006, two years prior to our first "Facebook Presidential Election" in 2008, when Barack Obama was elected president, the Pew Research Center reported, "Americans cannot be easily characterized as conservative or liberal on today's most pressing social questions," referring to such hotly contested issues as abortion, stem cell research, and marriage equality.[12] Nearly twelve years and three social media–influenced presidential elections later, Eugene Scott reported in the *Washington Post* in 2018 that "while Americans have always known they don't share the same politics, more of them are now questioning whether their political opponents even share the same values."[13]

What happened to a more nuanced understanding of complex social issues? How did we move from a tendency to "incorporate and exemplify the officially accredited values of the society" into our embodied performances to an inability to identify shared values across political lines—and across our shared humanity?[14] Have we slipped into a casual "slactivism," digitally embodied by posts and tweets?[15] Or have we come to care so much about maintaining distinctly partisan acts that we have migrated from "slactivism" into digital performances that aggressively enact a blind spot of unempathetic bluster?

To explore this notion of cyber-citizen performativity gone awry, I turn to a Facebook post from March 16, 2019, in response to an actual theatrical performance at a theatre in a midsized city in the state of Georgia.[16] According to the individual's lengthy post, a specific performance during an evening of No Shame Theatre became a hurtful and offensive attack against the poster's religious beliefs. For those unacquainted with No Shame Theatre, it was named as such by Todd Ristau and Stan Ruth in 1986 when they first performed it "from the cargo bed of [Ristau's] pickup truck"[17] (figure 4.1). Since that time, dozens of No Shame venues have popped up across the country, some flourishing for a period and dying out, with others holding steady over many years.

According to the unnamed Georgia theatre company's website, there are only three rules associated with No Shame Theatre: "All acts have to be original material. All acts have to be five minutes or less." It goes on to read, "You can't break anything, including yourself, the space, or the law." As a former audience member and performer at No Shame Theatre, which has been hosted by the unnamed theatre for ten years, I can attest to the no-holds-barred, uncensored, and ultimately supportive atmosphere fostered in the spirit of No Shame. When I encountered the Facebook post citing an offensive performance, the only surprising factor was that an audience member knowingly attended No Shame and went away offended (figure 4.2). As the post acknowledged, the individual had been to No Shame Theatre several times before without incident, but the religious nature of a particular performance on the evening of March 15 crossed the line for this patron.

Despite not having witnessed the offending performance myself, I am

The first performance of No Shame Theatre was given on October 3, 1986 from the back of this truck.

Really.

Figure 4.1. The original pickup. (Courtesy of No Shame Digital Archive)

Figure 4.2. Reenactment of original No Shame. (Courtesy of No Shame Digital Archive)

aware of the basic content of this recurring improvisation, titled "Sex with Me." (Readers who are interested in learning more about this sexually suggestive improv game can refer to the endnote.)[18] This particular night's "Sex with me" performance involved a reference to Jesus, which is why the patron was offended. However, this element of the interaction is less interesting to me than the individual audience member's digital performance in response to the live one. After leaving the theatre, the patron returned to complain, noting in the post that "I went back in afterward to tell the employee that while I knew the organization had the right to say those things, I was disappointed that . . . [they] . . . chose to exercise that right."[19] According to the post, the employee encouraged patrons not to return if they did not appreciate what was presented.

Whether we find the theatre employee's response reasonable or not, what transpired following this embodied, in-the-moment interaction is a digital performance involving 660 Facebook reactions of all kinds, including 106 "likes," 464 shares, upward of 2,400 comments, several newspaper articles, and eventually an open forum hosted by the theatre to discuss No Shame's place within the community—arguably the most positive outcome of the entire incident. On the morning after the performance, the offended audience member made a lengthy post, part of which I quoted earlier, noting that although the theatre had the "right" to say what it said, the patron was disappointed that the theatre "chose to exercise that right." Not surprisingly, after a digital performance simultaneously acknowledging and discouraging one of our most prized rights as Americans, freedom of speech, commenters hungrily embodied the digital divide one might expect from such a spectacle. Here is just a smattering of such remarks:

"I would make it my business to close it down. Im [*sic*] sure that is ART."

"That is disgusting. Will make me have second thoughts on attending the [name redacted] again. Yes, they need to apologize."

"I'll bet if he yelled 'I love Jesus' they'd have run him out of the building."

"I find that very offensive for so many reasons. I wish you had identified the 'person.'"

"Many shameless things said and done all in the 'name of free speech.' Thanks for sharing. If we don't stand for what's right, we will fall for anything."

"Freedom of speech worked well in the old days when you had freedom to kick ass in retaliation."

"Wow, the demons have really taken over that building."

"No shame is an outlet so people can go express themselves without people like you whining about it."

"It is no ones [*sic*] job to define an artists [*sic*] art except the artist. Someone making a joke about your religion, political views, etc. is not a personal attack. Get over it."

"So much for liberals being the snowflakes."

"Getting offended that they said something 'vulgar' at a show that is literally called NO SHAME is like going to an ice cream shop and getting mad that they serve dairy products."

"WWJD?" [What Would Jesus Do?]

The above comments are all quite tame—particularly when compared with those posted once the online discussion became heated. In wading through the hundreds of comments, what is abundantly clear is how divided the commenters are in their digital embodiment of citizenship. For many, a raunchy joke told in poor taste at an event evocatively titled "No Shame" is evidence of hate speech. For others, commenting was a gleeful opportunity to repeat the original offending joke—along with decidedly more offensive comments—over and over again. For most commenters, the irony of acknowledging an individual's right to free speech, while simultaneously discouraging that right, was completely lost. Reading many of the comments, it felt as if the person who made the initial post was merely reporting a crime to the community, and the fallout could only be the justified removal of the offending source of that crime: No Shame Theatre and all of the deplorable people who support it.

Deplorable. That is a charged word in our political theatre. When Hillary Clinton used it to describe Donald Trump's supporters during a campaign speech prior to the 2016 election, at first I thought she was using it intentionally.[20] It felt to me like someone needed to call out the despicable behavior of Americans who would presume to vote a notoriously sexist, racist, abusive bully into office. In retrospect, I wonder if her use of the word may have been less intentional and more symptomatic of the ways in which we embody the political divide represented in our country—and most particularly, in and *through* social media.

Returning to the notion of "front," it seems important to note that according to Goffman, aspects of our embodiment must be concealed in order for us to maintain a particular "front."[21] "The line dividing front and back regions is everywhere in our society,"[22] meaning that the messy details of being human are removed from view. In keeping with the notion of a continuum stretching between live and digital performance, perhaps these hidden aspects of our embodiment represent a particular kind of distortion, allowing us to "radically reorganize space," as Bay-Cheng and her coauthors suggest in *Performance and Media*.[23] For example, Facebook is a digital platform that allows individual users to curate their own image—or "front"—in ways that may profoundly limit perceived flaws or inconsistencies. We make every effort to mask our private selves in order to be more appealing, more together, more in control of the impression we leave on our audience. Yet, in face-to-face performances, it is impossible to mask all inconsistencies. We remain human, even if we do maintain a "front" that is suited to our intentions. In our digital performances, we can disconnect ourselves from our embodied stutters, mistakes, contradictory beliefs, and behaviors—in part by correcting our online presence, and in full by monitoring it. Perhaps the blind spot—the distortion—in our digitally embodied performances is in our ability to erase our own bodies and thereby erase the very human bodies of those with whom we disagree. If empathy is a defining factor in embodied performances by actors who share human stories with live audiences on a stage in real time, a lack of embodied empathy may define digital performances of citizenship in the era of social media.

Arguably, as social media has become central to our lives, we have transferred primarily face-to-face, embodied interactions to increasingly (dis)embodied digital interactions. While it may seem like a natural consequence that empathy is diminished when interactions are conducted primarily via digital embodiment rather than face to face, what can we understand about the ways in which our digital embodiment influences our corporeal embodiment—the lived, fleshy, messy experience that is often hidden from view? In "The End of Empathy," Hanna Rosin points to a troubling trend toward "selective empathy," observed since 2000 by researchers who study empathy: "There's . . . a point at which empathy doesn't even look like the kind of universal empathy I was taught in school. There is a natural way that empathy gets triggered in the brain— your pain centers light up when you see another person suffering. But out in the world it starts to look more like tribalism, a way to keep reinforcing your own point of view and blocking out any others."[24]

As our engagement with social media has increased over the past two decades, is it possible that elements of our embodiment have transformed along with it? In performing our lives, and in turn, our citizenship, via digital interactions, have we begun to migrate a distinctly compartmentalized, (dis)embodied approach to the world (wide web) into our corporeal lives? How might these performances affect our tendency toward tribalism and selective empathy?

Reflecting upon this distortion of empathy—an "empathy" nurtured by our digital and embodied distrust of difference—I am brought back to the Clinton-Lewinsky scandal. In the past, many of us may have had a blind spot where Bill Clinton was concerned. Whether this was motivated by political leanings, by Clinton's charm, by Lewinsky's unfairly "trashy" portrayal in the media, or by a combination of these factors, it is understandable to harbor regret and perhaps even shame about one's performance as a citizen in that moment. The very human fallout was the radical disruption of a young woman's life. While she willingly engaged in a relationship with the president of the United States, over time many have come to see her for what she was in that moment: a very young woman, who was used not just by Bill Clinton but also by the fervent team who sought to bring him down. Today I wonder, where is my blind spot? How can I perform my own citizenship responsibly without an awareness of it? And has a lack of empathy—or worse, a disembodying shift toward selective empathy—been our collective blind spot all along?

Notes

1. Engin Isin and Evelyn Ruppert, *Being Digital Citizens* (London: Rowman & Littlefield, 2015), 43.

2. Isin and Ruppert.

3. In *Being Digital Citizens*, Isin and Ruppert describe internet actions using J. L. Austin's "speech act" as lens, along with other theorists who serve to unpack the concept. While this lens is useful, I am not convinced that it adequately incorporates the fact of our embodiment into the discussion, particularly when we consider how embodied actions are transformed via "digital embodiment."

4. Erving Goffman, *Presentation of the Self in Every Day Life* (Edinburgh: University of Edinburgh Social Sciences Research Center, 1959), 13.

5. George Lakoff and Mark Johnson, *Metaphors We Live By* (Chicago: University of Chicago Press, 2003).

6. Goffman, *Presentation of the Self in Every Day Life*, 2–3.

7. Sarah Bay-Cheng, Jennifer Parker-Starbuck, and David Z. Saltz, *Performance and Media: Taxonomies for a Changing Field* (Ann Arbor: University of Michigan Press, 2015), 46.

8. Aylin Yildirim Aykurt and Elif Sesen, "Social Media in Social Organization," *European Scientific Journal* 13.20 (July 2017), 9.

9. Donald Trump, Twitter post, July 31, 2019, 7:06 p.m.

10. Hintz, Arne, Lina Dencik, and Karin Wahl-Jorgensen. "Digital Citizenship and Surveillance Society," *International Journal of Communication* 11 (2017), 731–39.
Hintz, Dencik, and Wahl-Jorgensen, "Digital Citizenship," 731–39.

11. Goffman, *Presentation of the Self*, 23.

12. "Pragmatic Americans Liberal and Conservative on Social Issues," *Pew Research Center*, August 3, 2006.

13. Eugene Scott, "The 'Value Divide' between Democrats and Republicans Is Getting Bigger and Bigger," *Washington Post*, March 18, 2018.

14. Goffman, *Presentation of the Self*, 23.

15. A term coined by Evgeny Morozov in 2009 to refer to "an easy and comfortable way of pretending to care about political and social matters," as referenced by Aykurt and Sesen in "Social Media in Social Organization," 16.

16. I have chosen not to name the theatre company described in this example because this particular situation is not characteristic of it or the community in which it functions. Rather, the unnamed theatre company maintains a generosity of spirit and artistic engagement with the community that is highly valued and central to the city's artistic environment.

17. "A Short HISTORY of No Shame Theatre," No Shame Theatre, http://www.noshame.org/iowacity/history.htm, accessed April 6, 2019.

18. According to numerous commenters on the original post, the complainant misrepresents the performance in question, which involved the No Shame host improvising using a favorite comic theme called "Sex with me." In the course of the improv, which is shared between host and audience, many similes are made to describe what "sex with me" is like. The basic structure of this imagery-filled improvisation is as follows: The host begins by saying "Sex with me is like . . ." and then he or she elicits a theme from the audience. For example, an audience member might say "peanut butter," to which the host might then say "Sex with me is like peanut butter. It sticks to the roof of your mouth." On the night in question, someone brought Jesus into the improv, creating a simile something along the lines of "Sex with me is like Jesus . . . he doesn't rise until the third day." Etc.

19. Name redacted, Facebook post, March 16, 2019, accessed April 6, 2019.

20. Clinton's use of the word "deplorable," in which she referred to Trump supporters as a "basket of deplorables," occurred on September 9, 2016, at a campaign fundraising event. A transcript of the speech can be found at https://time.com/4486502/hillary-clinton-basket-of-deplorables-transcript/?amp=true.

21. Goffman, *Presentation of the Self*, 75.

22. Goffman, 75.

23. Bay-Cheng, Parker-Starbuck, and Saltz, *Performance and Media: Taxonomies for a Changing Field*, 46.

24. Hanna Rosin, "The End of Empathy," Special Series: Civility Wars, npr.org, April 15, 2019, accessed May 18, 2019.

Awarding America

Multiple Views of Citizenship in the Pulitzer Prize for Drama

David S. Thompson

In 1903 JOSEPH PULITZER signed the first version of the agreement to establish the noted prizes that would bear his name. Regarding the Pulitzer Prize for Drama, it should come as no surprise that the original document essentially serves as the powerful publisher's personal vision of dramatic theory, given that he was creating not only a bequest for the funding the accolade but also a description to serve in guiding its presentation. What might prove a bit more surprising is the realization that the concept behind the drama prize (and, one could argue, all of the Pulitzer Prizes) additionally serves to define the qualities valued in American citizenship. This essay explores the circumstances surrounding the creation of the prize, including key elements of Joseph Pulitzer's life and interpretations of the text created to describe the prize, as well as examples of unusual or unexpected moments in the administration of the drama prize. Each area of consideration carries the potential for seeing a range of definitions of American citizenship. Like the citizens of the country it celebrates, the decisions of those associated with granting the Pulitzer Prize reflect a range of attitudes from stubborn intransigence to agreeable flexibility, from originalism to pragmatism.

The Immigrant Experience

Given his reputation as a self-made man, we often assume that the life of Joseph Pulitzer provides a prime example of a rags-to-riches immigrant success story. However, aspects of his early life and family influences paint a more complicated picture.

Pulitzer was born in 1847 in Makó, a small town in southeast Hungary near the western tip of Romania. There his father, Philip, owned a successful grain business—so successful, in fact, that in 1853, shortly after Joseph reached age six, he had accumulated sufficient means to retire.[1] Upon taking account of his holdings and realizing that his wealth would allow for a grand level of comfort and style, he moved the family to Budapest. There they took advantage of the cultural offerings of the city. Young Joseph quickly became a fine student who excelled in languages and literature but also displayed a love of classical music and theatre.[2]

In addition to the comfort that he found, Joseph Pulitzer also found his early life marked by social and political turmoil. The revolutions of 1848, also known as the Year of Revolution, traumatized over a dozen nations, including Hungary. Pulitzer's uncles became active in the struggles and continued to support factions fighting for better working conditions, free speech, and a free press. As in many locations, the revolutionaries did not fare well in Hungary. Authorities suppressed the revolution leading to many deaths and exiles. Numerous Hungarians sought refuge in the United States. Although scarcely past infancy at the time of these uprisings, Pulitzer's association with relatives, and others immersed in the conflict, gave him an understanding of recent history and instilled in him a passion for democratic ideals.[3]

In 1858, Pulitzer's father died after a lengthy illness, leaving the family in debt. Pulitzer's mother would remarry, and the future publisher frequently clashed with his stepfather. In 1864, having reached age seventeen, Pulitzer wished for more adventure than his home provided, so he left his family to forge a new life. He sought a commission in the Austrian army and then the French Foreign Legion, only to have both applications summarily rejected. Using funds provided by recruiters for the Union army, Pulitzer traveled to America where he served in a German-speaking regiment during the latter months of the Civil War. Although Pulitzer possessed prodigious language skills, speaking German, Hungarian, and French, his isolation with German speakers made knowledge of English unnecessary; indeed, he did not study English seriously until after the war.[4]

Following his military service, Pulitzer embarked on a series of Midas-touch endeavors, each one leading to ever more lucrative opportunities. Such menial jobs as shoveling coal on a steamboat and burying the corpses of cholera victims eventually took him to St. Louis. Reporting on life on the river and inserting himself into the local German-speaking community afforded him entrée to an intellectual cadre interested in politics, social reform, and journalism. Such connections resulted in an election to the Missouri state legislature, an appointment as St. Louis police commissioner, and the opportunity to invest in a small newspaper, the *Westliche Post*. By age thirty, Pulitzer had turned a profit on his first investment and used the experience to buy the *St. Louis Post* and the *St. Louis Dispatch* and merge them into the *St. Louis Post-Dispatch*. He proceeded to make the paper legendary through the lessons he had learned from his family and brought with him as an immigrant—working hard (often torturously long hours) and providing a voice for the people. These attributes would provide Pulitzer with financial independence and lead him to gamble on his abilities by moving to New York and purchasing *The World*, the newspaper that would secure his fortune and his legacy.[5]

The Drama Prize

Many who hear about the annual awarding of the Pulitzer Prizes may assume that Joseph Pulitzer intended them as his chief legacy. Initially, the concept involved the creation of the journalism school at Columbia University. However, Pulitzer became interested in bestowing awards in journalism and other fields. Such an interest made sense in the wake of the creation of the Nobel Prizes, first presented on December 10, 1901, the fifth anniversary of Alfred Nobel's death. Additionally, like many wealthy citizens of the era, Pulitzer could not escape Andrew Carnegie's ideas, particularly those included in his 1889 article "Wealth" (often referred to as "The Gospel of Wealth"), which is "considered a foundational document in the field of philanthropy."[6] Within his essay, Carnegie's most prominent assertion rests upon the notion that surplus wealth is a sacred trust that its possessor is bound to administer during his lifetime for the good of the community.[7] Within a year or so of those first Nobel Prizes, Pulitzer had discovered that a rival publisher, James Gordon Bennett of the *New York Herald*, had begun discussions that would lead to the creation of a school of journalism and that the plan involved placing the *Herald* in a trust in order to endow the operation. Pulitzer wanted to create that sort of legacy, promoting his good citizenship through the judicious use of wealth in a manner consistent with the views of Carnegie.

Pulitzer did not specifically say that any individuals or concepts cited above provided the inspiration for his decision. However, in the first years of the twentieth century, working with colleagues and advisors, including Nicholas Murray Butler, president of Columbia University, he developed a plan to use his wealth for the public good by endowing both a journalism school and the prizes that bear his name. After several revisions he formalized the final version of his plan in his will, drafted in April 1904.[8]

Among the prizes in the arts, the drama prize carries a particularly haughty characterization among its qualifications: "Annually, for the original play, performed in New York, which shall best represent the educational value and power of the stage in raising the standards of good morals, good taste, and good manners, One thousand dollars ($1,000)."[9]

One's mind might easily drift toward questions of who has the right to judge—à la the *Le Cid* controversy. Pulitzer's drama prize qualification also echoes the Uniform Rule of Naturalization of 1790, which describes the background appropriate to a new United States citizen by requiring that "he has behaved as a man of good moral character."[10] Since Pulitzer composed these words at the beginning of the twentieth century, they appear guided by the transition from the Gilded Age to the Progressive Era. The prize description suggests an elite interest in, and understanding of, morals, taste, and manners, tacitly implying that the right people would know how to interpret the concepts. The statement also suggests the progressive notions of educational power and the raising of standards associated with what would come to be called "uplift" in future Pulitzer Prize controversies. Another interpretation of the prize description might also reveal some of the duality (perhaps multiplicity is more accurate) of the American character, a desire to see oneself as reaching a pinnacle of success coupled with the desire to lend a hand to fellow citizens.

An interesting contrast exists in a comparison with some of the other Pulitzer Prizes. Consider the original wording for the novel category (subsequently termed the fiction category): "Annually, for the American novel published during the year which shall best present the whole atmosphere of American life, and the highest standard of American manners and manhood, One thousand dollars ($1,000)."[11]

Whether referring to drama or fiction, both prizes suggest their own sort of gatekeeping, a "know-it-when-I-see-it" form of elitism in which those in power choose those they wish to admit to their number. In that way, the Pulitzer Prize for Fiction, with its reference to an undefined notion of "manhood," might also find resonance within the Uniform Rule of Naturalization that initially limited citizenship to a "free white man."[12]

Whatever the reaction to the wording of the prizes, the implication is clear. The Pulitzer Prize definitions provide us with Joseph Pulitzer's view of dramatic and literary theory. As such, the descriptions also suggest what one should strive for in the creation of an artistic work and the standards by which we should judge such works. But beyond the litcrit triad of theory, practice, and criticism in which each concept touches the other two like sides of a triangle, Pulitzer has also provided excerpts from his personal guide to American citizenship. This particular vision of citizenship suggests something akin to gatekeeping at an exclusive club at which entrance standards are known only by the existing members. Curiously, it also emerges from the position of wealth and influence that Pulitzer attained and not necessarily the role of voice of the people that served as a catalyst for his ascent.

Setting aside the notion of a perspective born of privilege, what might have prompted Pulitzer to place such emphasis and responsibility on American drama? The original journalism prizes in public service, editorial writing, and reporting feature some of the same ideas but not to the same extent. Their language favors technique, "clearness of style," and "strict accuracy," for example. Only the public service prize uses the adjective "American"; the others seem to assume location.[13] Was the great publisher moved by the theatre of the day?

Since the original text of the drama prize specifically mentions New York, a consideration of productions of the era might prove instructive. During the five seasons prior to the finalization of Pulitzer's will, New York theatres saw nearly 750 productions. Only 11 percent of them ran for more than 100 performances; less than 2 percent ran for more than 200 performances.[14] Here I should note the obvious differences in production standards and practices, not to mention associated economic factors in the American theatre of 120 years ago. Productions running 100 performances would have been profitable well into the 1930s, and undoubtedly some productions with shorter runs may well have proved profitable.[15] However, in 1900 New York was a city of 3.5 million people.[16] A modest run would have reached a tiny fraction of the local citizenry, much less have an influence on the larger American scene.

If production statistics do not necessarily suggest influential dramatic models, what artists and productions might have provided models for American citizenship? The large number of productions staged during the era suggests an opportunity for quite a range of styles, and indeed such a range did exist. As one might assume, Shakespeare was a mainstay, often with companies performing works in repertory. Revues and light musical entertainments appeared frequently. The vaudeville team of Weber and Fields offered a variety of idiosyncratic titles, including *Hoity Toity*, *Twirly Whirly*, *Whirl-i-gig*, *Fiddle-Dee-Dee*, and *Whoop-Dee-Do*. Each of these works appeared in a different year, with each running more than 250 performances. Popular and entertaining, perhaps, but one wonders if these represent the educational power of the American stage.

The longest-running production of the era, *Florodora*, recorded 505 performances, but it was a London import. The era saw repeated visits by the Henry Irving–Ellen Terry Company and a repertory of the most famous productions of Sarah Bernhardt, all international artists.

Of course, many of the most notable names in American theatre history plied their trade during this era. Minnie Maddern Fiske presented several of her most noted roles, while William Gillette was a hit as Sherlock Holmes. We also saw the work of Augustin Daly, David Belasco, Clyde Fitch, Flo Ziegfeld, and Sam Shubert. During the years immediately prior to the preparation of his will and his namesake prizes, Pulitzer might well have seen the work of these noted titans, but most of their productions that straddled the beginning of the twentieth century had far shorter runs than those cited above. As such, the ability of a single title or single production to exert considerable influence upon the general population—or other theatrical artists, for that matter—seems unlikely.

Is it possible that Pulitzer was thinking of theatre in New York collectively or cumulatively rather than as an incubator for individual great works representing the ideals he sought to promote? Or was this actually an instance of Pulitzer using his father's desire to offer the benefits of culture, including exposure to the performing arts, to his family? Was he actually combining childhood memories of cultural opportunities in his native Hungary with adult aspirations as an artistic tastemaker, merging the past of an immigrant with the present of a prominent citizen? Such a construct suggests that "the power of the [American] stage" represents citizenship derived from different generations, from different times, representing various cultures, hailing from a range of lands. Rather than the gatekeeping elitism suggested by a strict reading of the criteria for Pulitzer Prizes in arts and letters, adding the personal viewpoint of the early years of Pulitzer's life evokes a more egalitarian enterprise, one consistent with the notion of the diversity of heritages among the American citizenry.

The Prize in Practice

As with many prizes and awards, administered by individuals with their own opinions and human limitations, the Pulitzer Prize has, at times, appeared inconsistent in naming recipients. Some moments in Pulitzer Prize history suggest something less than celebratory and less that a full embrace of the citizenship it would otherwise seem to purport. What follows are a few snapshots suggesting some curiosities and an attendant range of possible interpretations.

For all the hullaballoo associated with the Pulitzer Prize, particularly the anticipation surrounding its inaugural administration in 1917, it seems odd that the drama prize was not awarded along with the other citations bestowed in the year of the program's inception. With attention focused upon the power of the American stage, one might assume that, rather than declining to recommend a play, the jury could have found some suitable candidate. Given the range of possible subjects, tones, and styles, one might expect the same thing about any theatrical season. Yet the Pulitzer board has declined to bestow its prize for drama fifteen times. The inability to declare any play one that shall "best represent" (in the original language) the desired qualities, or even "a distinguished play" (the current language), could mean a strict upholding of standards or a staid unwillingness to offer recognition.[17]

Certainly more egregious is the fact that for most of its history the years without a drama prize outnumbered the years when a prize went to a female playwright. Not until Lynn Nottage's award for *Ruined* in 2009 did the total number of Pulitzers awarded to women outpace the years without an award. Since Nottage's original citation (her first of two, as of 2017), plays by women as Pulitzer winners have outpaced those by men.[18] One could easily read such a record as a marker of gender bias in dramatic criticism. It may also posit members of the drama jury or Pulitzer board as placing themselves in a position to serve as arbiters of citizenship, gatekeepers for who is allowed full participation.

The Pulitzer organization might have followed the example of the New York Drama Critics' Circle, founded in 1935 as a result of "widespread dissatisfaction, in the critical community, with the annual winners of the Pulitzer Prize for drama" as well as the overall administration, and the ultimate selection, of the several drama prizes. The Critics' Circle proposed a clear mission: offer an award to the best play of each theatre season and get it right. Perhaps as a result, the Critics' Circle has seen fewer years in which their award was not bestowed than in the history of the Pulitzer Prize for Drama. The Circle also recognized women overlooked for the Pulitzer, including noted twentieth-century writers Carson McCullers, Lorraine Hansberry, and Lillian Hellman.[19]

Additionally, women fared arguably worse in the early years of the Pulitzer Prize, specifically in the cases of Zona Gale's *Miss Lulu Bett* (1921), Susan Glaspell's *Alison's House* (1931), and Zoë Akins's *The Old Maid* (1935). Each of these plays earned a Pulitzer Prize for its playwright and should have cemented the reputations of both the dramas and their authors. However, overwhelming public controversies associated with these selections may have produced a negative perception.[20]

Arguably the most famous, and perhaps most shocking, example of declining to name a drama prize recipient occurred in 1963, when the Pulitzer board judged Edward Albee's *Who's Afraid of Virginia Woolf?*, the recipient of nearly unanimous praise as the best play of the season, not sufficiently "uplifting," referring to "a complaint that related to arguments over sexual permissiveness and rough dialogue," an obvious reference to the script's strong language and sexual references. The Pulitzer Prize website lists this event among the controversies throughout its history. By comparison, the Pulitzer organization cites the award for Tony Kushner's *Angels in America: Millennium Approaches* in 1993: "Kushner doesn't shy from strong language, a change from earlier playwrights whose cursing could have cost them an award."[21] The Pulitzer board has even awarded the drama prize to works other than those listed as finalists by the drama jury, making one wonder why the organization would enlist expert jurors only to ignore their recommendations. In 2007 Quiara Alegría Hudes, a finalist for the first play in her *Eliot* trilogy, saw that year's award go to a play not mentioned by the jury, *Rabbit Hole* by David Lindsay-Abaire. (Hudes eventually received the 2012 Pulitzer Prize for another play in the *Eliot* trilogy, *Water by the Spoonful.*) In 2010 the Pulitzer board ignored the nominations of plays by Kristoffer Diaz, Rajiv Joseph, and Sarah Ruhl in favor of the Tom Kitt and Brian Yorkey musical *Next to Normal.*[22] Such moments may produce doubt regarding the overall structure of the organization or the willingness to follow the rules and procedures agreed upon. Such issues provide analogs to citizenship, where fairness, openness, and representation prevail, at least in a common view of democratic societies.

Conclusion

Whether one agrees or disagrees with the structure put in place by Joseph Pulitzer or the methods by which the Pulitzer organization confers its prizes, its history may bring to mind current political debates. Calls for consistency and return to normal order seem based on expectations of fairness in representation. Such expectations may well lead to disagreements based upon perspective. Did the great publisher mean his heralded prizes to celebrate immigrant perspectives or the ways in which peoples navigate America as a home? Should they serve as aspirational guidelines or celebrations of accomplishment? Must consistency remain a part of the citizenship equation or should we rightfully expect human imperfections? As Yale professor William Lyon Phelps, himself a drama juror, expressed, "For my part, I am very glad that every year the award of the Pulitzer Prize stirs up so much argument and controversy; the sharper, the better. Surely it is a good thing for the American public to become excited over a question of art."[23] Here, the artistic debate mirrors those regarding citizenship as both benefit from basic concepts—access, inclusion, and equity.

Notes

1. Don C. Seitz, *Joseph Pulitzer, His Life and Letters* (New York: Simon and Schuster, 1924), 40–41.

2. Marty Gitlin, *Joseph Pulitzer: Historic Newspaper Publisher* (Edina, MN: Abdo Publishing, 2010), 17.

3. *American Masters*, "Joseph Pulitzer: Voice of the People," season 33, episode 5, directed by Oren Rudavsky, written by Oren Rudavsky and Robert Seidman, PBS, March 1, 2019.

4. *American Masters*, Seitz, 41–42. Seitz suggests that Philip Pulitzer's illness and death "reduced" the family's wealth, but he does not provide details regarding the nature of the reduction. It appears that Joseph Pulitzer, unhappy with his new stepfather and eager to find adventure, probably would have left home regardless of his family's specific financial circumstances.

5. *American Masters*.

6. Carnegie Corporation of New York, "The Gospel of Wealth," accessed September 7, 2019, https://www.carnegie.org/about/our-history/gospelofwealth/.

7. Andrew Carnegie, "Wealth," *North American Review*, no. 391 (June 1889, https://www.swarthmore.edu/SocSci/rbannis1/AIH19th/Carnegie.html), accessed May 20, 2019.

8. John Hohenberg, *The Pulitzer Prizes: A History of the Awards in Books, Drama, Music, and Journalism, Based on the Private Files over Six Decades* (New York: Columbia University Press, 1974), 9–15.

9. Hohenberg, 19.

10. U.S. Immigration Legislation Online, "1790 Naturalization Act: An Act to Establish a uniform Rule of Naturalization" (March 26, 1790, http://www.indiana.edu/~kdhist/H105-documents-web/week08/naturalization1790.html), accessed May 20, 2019. I am indebted to my colleague Charlotte Canning for the timely reminder of the wording of this document.

11. Hohenberg, 19.

12. "1790 Naturalization Act."

13. Hohenberg, 20.

14. Internet Broadway Database, "1899–1900," https://www.ibdb.com/seasons ?id=1001, accessed March 7, 2019; Internet Broadway Database, "1900–1901," https://www.ibdb.com/season/1002, accessed March 7, 2019; Internet Broadway Database, "1901–1902," https://www.ibdb.com/season/1003, accessed March 7, 2019; Internet Broadway Database, "1902–1903," https://www.ibdb.com/season /1004, accessed March 7, 2019; Internet Broadway Database, "1903–1904," https://www.ibdb.com/season/1005, accessed March 7, 2019. Subsequent data regarding productions and performance histories are also drawn from these database pages.

15. David Scott Thompson, "Merit and Mythos: A Study of Major Dramatic Prizes Awarded Plays by Women Playwrights" (PhD diss., University of Texas at Austin, 1997), 68; Alfred L. Bernheim, *The Business of the Theatre: An Economic History of the American Theatre, 1750–1932* (New York: Benjamin Blom, 1932), 167–69, 176–77.

16. World Population Review, http://worldpopulationreview.com/us-cities /new-york-city-population/, accessed April 8, 2019.

17. The Pulizer Prizes, "*Fairview*, by Jackie Sibblies Drury," https://www .pulitzer.org/winners/jackie-sibblies-drury, accessed July 14, 2019; The Pulit-

zer Prizes, "*The Subject Was Roses,* by Frank D. Gilroy," https://www.pulitzer .org/winners/frank-d-gilroy, accessed July 14, 2019. The Pulitzer Prize Board has altered the phrasing of the citation associated with the drama prize several times. Since 1965, over half of Pulitzer Prize history, the award has carried the description, "For a distinguished play by an American author, preferably original in its source and dealing with American life, One thousand dollars ($1,000)." The monetary award has increased with inflation, rising to the current level of $15,000 in 2017.

18. The Pulitzer Prizes, "Drama," https://www.pulitzer.org/prize-winners -by-category/218, accessed April 2, 2019. In the years immediately preceding 2009, there was a bit of back and forth with the tallies for prizes to women playwrights and years without an award, but women are now recognized far more often.

19. New York Drama Critics' Circle, "History," https://www.dramacritics .org/dc_history.html, accessed July 16, 2019; New York Drama Critics' Circle, "Past Awards," https://www.dramacritics.org/dc_pastawards.html, accessed July 16, 2019. In comparing the history of the Pulitzer Prize for Drama and the New York Drama Critics' Circle Award for Best Play, I am not suggesting simply replacing one recipient with another. Given that each organization featured (and continues to feature) its own agenda, operating procedures, and collection of personalities, diverging opinions remain possible, even likely. However, variance in the selection of prize winners paints quite distinct pictures of the nature of the drama in the United States.

20. Elsewhere I argue in favor of the possibility of such a circumstance, stressing an acknowledgment that the reputation of a creative work remains difficult to gauge. Thompson, "Merit and Mythos," 81–83.

21. The Pulitzer Prizes, "History of the Pulitzer Prizes," https://www.pulitzer .org/page/history-pulitzer-prizes, accessed July 14, 2019.

22. The Pulitzer Prizes, "Drama."

23. Hohenberg, 150.

Citizenship in a Space, on a Stage, at a School, in the South

Xanti Schawinsky's Stage Studies at Black Mountain College

Alex Ates

Here were students who search something [*sic*] they would not find in the glamorous universities with their impressive diplomas—Harvard, Yale, Princeton, etc.—opening the doors to "success." Instead of success, here there was the search for the truth.

—Xanti Schawinsky, "My Two Years at Black Mountain College"

From the Bauhaus to Black Mountain

JOHN RICE'S INVITATION FOUND Alexander "Xanti" Schawinsky in Italy. It was 1936, and the newly married master teacher of Bauhaus fame was jobless and without a nest. Though the Bauhaus community had gotten considerably nimbler in their nomadism, the rising Nazi regime permanently shuttered the brutalist campuses of Germany's most famous art and design school in 1933. As a refugee-artist, Schawinsky, a Swiss Jew of Polish descent, fled to Italy and slipped into circles of the young intelligentsia who were resisting the rising fascist movement there.[1] With totalitarianism seemingly tailing Schawinsky wherever he fled, an invitation from a renegade American professor arrived as a well-timed opportunity. The offer? Come to America and set up shop in rural North Carolina. Mountain country.

A new experimental school was opening, Black Mountain College. Select Bauhaus teachers had claim to faculty positions. No English? No problem. World-famous Bauhaus teachers like the weaver Anni Albers and her husband, color theorist Josef Albers, had already arrived stateside and testified to the school's legitimacy. For teaching, only a small salary could be ensured with modest housing and some square meals a day. The offer would have been insulting to an artist of Schawinsky's eminence only a few years prior, but now, with the world's order upending, Schawinsky needed only two things: space and freedom. And Black Mountain College, this new little school, had both to offer in America. As a location, the village of Black Mountain, North Carolina, revealed an unsuspected economic and social promise of the American South: land, distance, and affordability made for a vital hideout for social and political outlier artists.

At the Bauhaus, theatre was a visual method for bewitching physical space with the intervention of unconventional line, form, and mass.[2] The Bauhaus' theory of artistic alchemy would define Xanti Schawinsky's citizenship in America, introducing a new form of theatre pedagogy. For Schawinsky, artistic and academic truth was defined by the exploration of his new American space on stage and in exile. In this paper, the unacknowledged presence of Schawinsky's tools and innovations in the contemporary theatre will be defined and termed as "Schawinskian Space."

Because the American imagination historically distinguishes the South as a politically, socially, and artistically alien region, experimental expressions of citizenship conducted there can expand our understanding of theatre.[3] Such contributions are compounded when a refugee's expressions are formalized by an educational institution and multiplied through the regenerative platform of progressive pedagogy. Schawinsky was not only innovating but sharing. The theatrical innovations Xanti Schawinsky contributed at Black Mountain College are vital to acknowledge, as they reveal a blind spot in American academe. In popular discourse on citizenship and immigration, theatre in the southern United States often gets left out. I aim to provide a brief corrective to this historical oversight and contribute analysis of Schawinsky's innovations to the discourse on American performance and pedagogy. This essay acknowledges the vital significance of how a European refugee in the rural South reshaped performance and citizenship.

At the Bauhaus in Germany, Schawinsky was a jack-of-all-trades. His artistic dexterity typified the persevering spirit of the institution, particularly in its last years on the run, traveling between satellite campuses in Dessau and Berlin to avoid the Nazis' strengthening grip. Schawinsky was a living mascot of the Bauhaus. As a student, he joined the Bauhaus theatre workshop led by Oskar Schlemmer and fostered by school founder Walter Gropius (who would make his American academic debut at Harvard in the same decade).[4] Schawinsky was also a member of the Bauhaus Band, an experimental ragtime-Dixieland cabaret that enchanted Bauhauslers with mutated instruments at weekend socials.[5] At the Bauhaus, theatre and performance were engineered to deconstruct the mechanisms of pedestrian life with a machine or circus-like aesthetic that emulated the popular physical antics of Buster Keaton and Charlie Chaplin.

The highly stylized performances of the Bauhaus, be they theatrical or musical, were derivative of the school's mission of enacting the German principle of Total Art—altering how the world's visual order is perceived and sensed.[6] The Bauhaus's pedagogy was pithily summarized in the de facto classroom catchphrase of Bauhaus-to-Black Mountain faculty member Josef Albers: "I will not make you artists; I will teach you to see."[7]

At Black Mountain College, Schawinsky conjoined the principles of aesthetic totality with an academic totality designed to alter how *knowledge* is perceived.

The Circumstances of Black Mountain College's Founding and Schawinsky's Arrival

In 1933, when John Rice lost his job at Florida's Rollins College after refusing to take a loyalty oath to the school's president, he instigated an exodus.[8] Eight students and four teachers followed the Rice cult of personality out the door with wild plans to start a new, freer, school. Their unaccredited college would be run by a board of students and faculty members—no administration. This board would dedicate most of the school's funds to financial aid.[9] At Black Mountain, the arts would be a pedagogical tool for emphasizing continuous learning through kinesthetic projects. Pedagogue John Dewey, a champion of experiential learning, was in correspondence with Black Mountain College's cofounder Theodore Dreier and eventually joined the school's advisory board.[10] During a visit to the college, Dewey even served as a substitute teacher for Rice.[11]

The students Rice sought to charter the college needed to be as independent as they were curious; as adventurously minded as they were academically so. Rice understood the only way he could magnetize the caliber of students he desired would be to open the school with rockstar professors who could fast attract attention and legitimacy to the ramshackle school.

After Rice secured a YMCA retreat hall in the agrarian Blue Ridge Mountains thirty minutes outside of Asheville, he sent letters to some of the nation's most prestigious professors at the wealthiest and most selective institutions.[12] Rice was a classicist of some note and had many distinguished colleagues cataloged in his address book. Professors from Harvard, Yale, Columbia, Princeton, the University of Wyoming, the

University of Oklahoma, and the University of Chicago all got invitations to join Rice in inaugurating the school. While many professors were fascinated by Rice's experiment, they declined or delayed the offer. After all, Robert E. Lee Hall (the name of the woodsy retreat center Rice had rented from the YMCA) was not a comparable campus to the hallowed halls of elite American academe. Black Mountain, North Carolina, was no Cambridge, Massachusetts. Though certainly scenic, the new school was isolated, destitute, and Southern—something that elite professors enjoyed more from a distance at a *romantic* level than a practical one. For the academy's crème de la crème, Black Mountain College would be an expedition to monitor, maybe visit, but not to join.

In a pinch, and with few Americans on board besides his Rollins conspirators, Rice got creative and decided to outsource. Knowing Bauhaus teachers were in exile for having refused to take an oath to Hitler, Rice shaped a wild, transatlantic offer.[13] If he could get German Jewish Bauhauslers to staff his school, Black Mountain College would have immediate international validity—and the refugees would have safety and space.

Initially, Black Mountain College's international influx elicited suspicion locally in the politically homogeneous Blue Ridge Mountains. Being dubbed "the red college" by European onlookers gave the school a fashionable mystique and a reality of free-range danger for anyone bound to Black Mountain College.[14] Federal law enforcement saw the arrival of the mysterious Bauhaus artists as a radical leftist infection, not a boon.[15] After a thorough (and hard-nosed) grilling by US immigration agents— which nearly provoked Schawinsky to call the whole move off—Black Mountain's newest Bauhausler arrived with his wife, Irene von Debschitz, to, as Schawinsky reflected, "live in freedom—to an extent at least."[16] Before arriving on American soil, Schawinsky was disturbed by the governmental inhibitors that qualify a refugee's belonging and citizenship in America with suspicion. Despite the geographic isolation of the Blue Ridge South, Washington, DC's eyes were on Black Mountain College from its founding in 1933 to its closure in 1957. Though the South offered the perception of freedom because of its ruralness, and the school offered the same perception because of its educational methods, as a Bauhausler, Schawinsky viewed the United States in totality by skeptically critiquing the limitations.

Stage Studies at Black Mountain

Schawinsky utilized the academic mission of the new school (and its purposeful lack of structure) to devise a new form of study that built upon the work he had done in Germany on the Bauhaus stage. Irene, a designer and origami master of note, installed a popular costume and fashion design course that supplemented her partner's vision.[17] Together, the couple expanded their transatlantic artistic heritage to the infant American college, where the school's contribution to performance had yet to be determined.

In addition to teaching drawing, painting, color theory, and playing in the college's ragtag chamber orchestra, Schawinsky created a Stage Studies course that he saw as the evolutionary culmination of his work at the Bauhaus. In the 1936–37 course catalog for Black Mountain College, Schawinsky distinguished the thrust of his teaching from standardized performance pedagogy: "This course is not intended as training for any particular branch of the contemporary theatre but rather as a general study of fundamental phenomena: space, form, color, light, sound, music, movement, time, etc. The studies take place on the stage for several reasons: it is by nature a place of illusion; it is well suited for representation of the sensibilities of today and for training in the recognition of conscious and visual order; and it is an excellent laboratory for the investigation and illustration of all these elements."[18] Stage Studies continued the Bauhaus exploration of perspective through visual categorization, but the course applied a new Schawinskian lens—a performative approach to the understanding of physical space. Schawinsky termed this experimental process "Space Play."[19] Inherent in the concept of play is the principle of experimentation. Because Black Mountain College gave Schawinsky the flexibility to experiment, the school became a big American test: could a refugee artist not only import a heritage of foreign performance to the South, but advance an avant-garde practice there?

In Schawinsky's Stage Studies program, Black Mountain students went through a progression that started with tutoring in basic geometric principles. Schawinsky was shocked by the degree of incompetency the students exhibited regarding the concept (he blamed this on anti-math bias in liberal American education). Students defined dimensional relationships between geometric objects to stimulate creative talents lurking in the subterranean levels of their minds.

Once students understood geometric principles and could creatively relate shapes to each other, Schawinsky guided the class through his procedure of Space Play. Using props and materials that would change a subject's height or direction, Schawinsky had the students improvise chaos on stage as Schawinsky improvised his citizenship as a refugee through the chaos of the world's stage.

As an educator, Schawinsky was adamant that neither speech nor written words should be the only assessment of one's prismatic intellectual potential. This approach aligned with the Black Mountain style, which only used grades as a formality for transcripts.[20] Thus, Schawinsky proposed that, as the students released their inhibitions regarding the performance of improvised instincts, a kinesthetic and performative logic would be elicited, revealing capital-T Truth.

Space Play guided students to embrace a primitive spatial logic and create an experimental narrative with their bodies enhanced with the improvised music of Black Mountain instructor John Evarts. The next step was for students to devise a *structured* Space Play with props, masks, and lighting.

Stage Studies was fundamentally pictorial and deeply interdisciplinary. Schawinsky invited professors and experts to lecture to his Stage Studies class on abstract or humanistic subjects such as time, death, personhood, or theology. Students would then respond to the lecture with the Space Play process. In a 1973 letter to the North Carolina Museum of Art's Benjamin F. Williams, Schawinsky wrote about "form, composition in space, color, color composition, optics, sound, language, noise, music, rhythm, poetry, space-time, numbers, the dream building, architecture, building materials, and illusion. As the class was composed of members of all disciplines, opinions on the above subjects differed according to scientific, artistic or sociological and other considerations, and complex solutions had to be worked out in order to illuminate and to express on the stage theatrical deconstruction of validity."[21] The jewels of Space Play devising would be mined to produce community performances known to students as "Spectodrama." This form of performance was conceptually inspired by Schawinsky's academic interpretations of medieval allegories and iconography like Hans Holbein the Younger's 1538 print "The Dance of Death," or the Latin hymn "Day of Wrath" of the thirteenth century. Performances took place either in the Lee dining hall, where there was a stage, or in a campus gymnasium.[22]

The dramatic structure of Schawinsky's Spectodrama had a continuous flow ascending through four poetics. The first was *optics* or *seeing*—the second, *acoustics* or *hearing*. Third, the term "*building*," Schawinsky thought of as architecture or symphony. The fourth term was *illusion*, which defined a production's metaphysical aspects.[23]

Obsessed with the mechanics and manipulations of the human form, Schawinsky often utilized masks to remove the language of facial expression and encourage only gestural communication. His proposal for a weekly "Silent Day" on the Black Mountain campus where all were to wear neutral masks for the day's entirety was emphatically rejected when

pitched during a faculty meeting.[24] Schawinsky's ideas for how to interact with space were sometimes seen as too radical or conceptual even on
the Black Mountain campus.

In her essay "Bauhaus Theatre at Black Mountain College," Eva Díaz
highlights how at Black Mountain, the Bauhausian intentions would shift
away from a model of theatre-making in a circus clown, machine-like aesthetic of sculptural brutalist costumes and instead root performance in
something more historical and sociological, and thus more wholly human. Dìaz notes that Schawinsky used his laboratory at Black Mountain
to "push [the Bauhaus'] notions of spatial totality further."[25] In this assessment, there is an opportunity to emphasize two points: the totality
of Schawinsky's fascination with all academic subjects and the specificity
of a rural South location. As Schawinsky was innovating at Black Mountain College, regionalism was an increasingly utilized mode for artists
to define national art of an American character; from the Dallas Nine
to the Little Theatre Movement in the 1930s, artists were emphasizing
self-reliance and independence by pushing ruralized representations of
American citizenship in regional locations.[26] Philosophically, regionalism
encouraged artists to assume the vantage of an immigrant, critically investigating authentic distinctions of the country with a tabula rasa eye.
Schawinsky's lens was regional by default as Black Mountain was the foyer
into the United States.

In her comprehensive book, *The Experimenters: Chance and Design at
Black Mountain College*, Díaz emphasizes that Schawinsky was expanding the Bauhaus concept of totality into academic fields.[27] Indeed, Stage
Studies was a one-class college made of many different departments: an-
thropology, psychology, theology, architecture, English, music—the list
is long. Thus, Spectodrama and Stage Studies were not only an artistic response to the Bauhaus theory of totality, they were an artistic response to many academic studies inspired by the Black Mountain's theory
of educational totality. Schawinsky was hybridizing two school missions
equally in Stage Studies—not just *recreating* Bauhaus performance, but
rather *manifesting* Black Mountain College performance. The performative pedagogy Schawinsky contributed to the college's global body of
students defined the refugee's citizenship in America. As former student
Suzanne Noble quipped, "Everybody was a refugee from somewhere at
Black Mountain College."[28] Noble's remark implies that even American-
born students—many of whom, class records and interviews indicate,
were from the North—felt disconnected to their own national identity;
it was the artistic contributions of Black Mountain College that redefined
their sense of citizenship in America.[29]

Schawinskian Space

Díaz passes over this key emphasis: the lone American outpost of Bauhaus theatre was in the *South*. This detail matters because the American South is a region that is popularly othered as a space that squelches cutting-edge culture.[30] For an analysis to truly contextualize Schawinsky's work, the rural specificity of where his innovations were fostered needs to be underlined. The record needs to pay attention not only to how Schawinsky, an immigrant, was perceived as a refugee artist in America but to also assess how the region where Schawinsky innovated was perceived by the country's cultural gatekeepers at large. If the regional context is categorized as a superfluous detail, the foundational nature of immigrant innovations that were fostered in the American South go unacknowledged, allowing incomplete perceptions of the region to persist. In concert with the region-specific art movements of the time, Schawinksy contributed a new theatrical process as a mechanism for determining citizenship and belonging in unconventional space.

Because theatre is an interdisciplinary and interactive medium, Schawinsky utilized it as a tool for discovering validity, or truth, in his new American home. The theatre, Schawinsky realized, was the closest medium to the Holy Grail of Total Experience—the kinesthetic offshoot of the Bauhaus Total Art principle. Thus, we can use Schawinsky's theatre process as a rubric for defining the artist's interpretation of American space—not only his sense of belonging within it but also his contributions to it: his citizenship. This particular artist-teacher's citizenship is notable because it established the avant-garde identity for performance at Black Mountain College—which incubated the globally renowned performance methods of Merce Cunningham and John Cage at the school in the 1940s and 1950s.[31]

The concept of American freedom, despite its political limitations, was integral to Schawinsky's innovations. As a refugee, Schawinsky evolved the Bauhaus theatrical model to explore the institution of American liberal arts pedagogy that was "traditionally unknown in Europe."[32] Thus, Stage Studies, Space Play, and Spectodrama, though German-inspired, are American-born. Though in the American South, freedom is a contradictory and highly contextualized term, within the liberal Black Mountain College, the artist-in-exile was given pedagogical, artistic, and logistical liberty to blend mediums and innovate his learnings and lessons from Germany.

Stage Studies, Space Play, and Spectodrama can all be grouped under the term "Schawinskian Space," which is categorized by Schawinsky's pedagogical intentions and artistic poetics. Schawinskian Space is physical space functionalized for *total experience* through a visual intervention that interdisciplinarily coordinates with sound, shape, and liberal arts academic theory or cultural iconography in the venue of immersive theatrical presentation through unconventional narrative expressions.

Entangled in the aesthetics is a refugee's aim of uncovering total truth in the exploration of human form in the frame of American space and academic rebellion. The style was catapulted by this space that made itself most *easily available* at the time when its presence was most critical. Because the Great Depression (and the school's unstable endowment) limited access to traditional art-making supplies and materials, Bauhaus artists utilized the Blue Ridge ecosystem to instruct and make art. "We use materials to satisfy our practical needs and our spiritual ones as well," Anni Albers wrote in a 1938 college newsletter. "We have useful things and beautiful things—equipment and works of art."[33] The Black Mountain aesthetic was literally made of Southern land. When compared with metropolitan culture hubs, the commonsensical agrarian style of art-making embraced a Southern aesthetic of social contrarianism. This dynamic was epitomized when Schawinsky once invited mountain villagers and farmers to wear neutral masks and robes (becoming "a unified wall of individuals without identity") to watch the Spectodrama *Danse Macabre* in the candlelit round.[34] Schawinsky's presence as a refugee typified a sociopolitical dissonance in a space that culturally validated rebellions of citizenship as part of its "regional consciousness and special history," as historian Sheldon Hackney phrased it.[35] This "special history" distinguishes the South from other regions in the United States. Despite the school's pedagogical uniqueness, Black Mountain College is inseparable from, and distinguished by, Black Mountain, North Carolina. The location defined the school because it had the land accessible to host Black Mountain College, absorb its growth, feed its students, and provoke its artists. Black Mountain College is part of the South's "special history." Thus, Schawinskian Space is not simply American—it's *Southern* American.

Schawinsky's Impact and Legacy

Schawinsky didn't stay long at Black Mountain—few did. As most participants in progressive ventures eventually discover, truly utopian institutions are a fiction, and utopianistic egos have a toxic way of polluting academic tranquility. Additionally, Schawinsky's auteur demeanor, coupled with his habit of angrily throwing ashtrays at students out of frustration, did not make him the most revered professor on campus.[36] After Rice was ousted in scandal and Schawinsky was denied a bonus to his satisfaction, the Bauhaus master left North Carolina for America's cosmopolitan artistic epicenters to install Stage Studies–like curricula in other schools and seek exhibitions in contemporary art museums.[37]

For the time he was at Black Mountain, Schawinsky's relationship to Southern space defined his citizenship in America. In search of academic and artistic veritas, he formulated a distinct definition of belonging in new space by creating Schawinskian Space through Stage Studies, Space Play, and Spectodrama.

Schawinsky's work was not only an evolution of the Bauhaus style but also the flag-planting of a new theatre in a new land and the launch of a non-narrative visual performance style that affected the Black Mountain approach for the remainder of the school's existence. Xanti Schawinsky's performative canon in America signifies an extraordinary cultural interchange between a refugee and a region where innovative contributions are too often diminished.

Notes

1. Curiously, despite later reflecting on the fear of Mussolini's rise in a 1973 letter, Schawinsky was commissioned while in Italy to design propaganda for the tyrant that appeared in the magazine *Il Rivista Illustrata del Popolo* in April 1934.

2. I have utilized the word "bewitching" because it adopts a term used by Schlemmer at the Bauhaus to describe the stage as "space bewitched." Oskar Schlemmer, László Moholy-Nagy, Farkas Molnár, Walter Gropius, and Arthur S. Wensinger, *The Theater Bauhaus* (Middleton, CT: Wesleyan University Press, 1961).

3. Shawn Chandler Bingham, "Bohemian Groves in Southern Soil," *The Bohemian South: Creating Countercultures from Poe to Punk* (Chapel Hill: University of North Carolina Press, 2017).

4. "Xanti Schawinsky," Bauhaus 100, www.bauhaus100.com/the-bauhaus /people/masters-and-teachers/xanti-schawinsky/, accessed July 16, 2019.

5. Xanti Schawinsky, "From the Bauhaus to Black Mountain," *Tulane Drama Review* 15, no. 3 (1971): 31.

6. Richard Wagner, "Outlines of the Artwork of the Future" (1850, in German; Lincoln: University of Nebraska Press, 1993). Wagner redefined K. F. E. Trahndorff's theory of a "total work of art" in 1849.

7. Anne Chapin Weston, interview by Mary E. Harris, 1971, North Carolina Western Regional Archives.

8. Mary Seymour, "Ghosts of Rollins (and Other Skeletons in the Closet)," *Rollins Magazine*, Fall 2011.

9. Emile Willmetz and Suzanne Noble, interview by Mary E. Harris, 1971, North Carolina Western Regional Archives.

10. Jonathan Fisher, "The Life and Work of an Institution of Progressive

Higher Education: Towards a History of Black Mountain College, 1933–1949," *Journal of Black Mountain Studies*, vol. 6 (2013).

11. Weston interview.

12. Elvin Hatch, "Delivering the Goods: Cash, Subsistence Farms, and Identity in a Blue Ridge County in the 1930s," *Journal of Appalachian Studies* 9, no. 1 (2003): 6–48.

13. Nicholas Fox Weber, *The Bauhaus Group; Six Masters of Modernism* (New York: Random House, 2009), 481.

14. Schawinsky, "My Two Years."

15. Jon Elliston, "FBI Investigation of Black Mountain College Revealed in Newly Released File," *Carolina Public Press*, August 5, 2015, https://carolinapublicpress .org/23088/fbi-investigation-of-black-mountain-college-revealed-in-newly-released -file/.

16. Schawinsky had an impression of America gleaned through movies and media. From the letter "My Two Years at Black Mountain College": "the grilling [by US immigration agents] has been such that I almost decided to say: 'keep your America for yourself, who wants to go there and get murdered on a fire escape ladder like in your movies, or to live in misery as depicted in them!'"

17. Irene Schawinsky grew up with an artistically supportive family. Her mother, Wanda von Debschitz-Kunowski, was a German portrait photographer of note. Beate Ziegert, "The Debschitz School, Munich: 1902–1914," *Design Issues* 3, no. 1 (1986): 28–42.

18. Black Mountain College, *1936–1937 Course Catalog* (np, nd), North Carolina Western Regional Archives.

19. Schawinsky, "My Two Years," 4.

20. Roderick Louis Mulholland, interview by Mary E. Harris, 1971, North Carolina Western Regional Archives.

21. Schawinsky, "My Two Years," 4.

22. Schawinsky, "My Two Years," 7.

23. Schawinsky, "My Two Years," 5.

24. Schawinsky, "My Two Years," 5.

25. Eva Díaz, "Bauhaus Theater at Black Mountain College," *Migros Museum für Gegenwartskunst: Xanti Schawinsky*, exhibition catalogue (Zurich, JPR|Ringier 2015), 57–65.

26. "Lone Star Regionalism: The Dallas Nine and Their Circle, 1928–1945," Dallas Museum of Art, https://files.dma.org/multimedia/document/145321711007971 _original.pdf; Dorothy Chansky, "Composing Ourselves: The Little Theatre Movement and the American Audience" (Carbondale: Southern Illinois University Press, 2004); Elizabeth Osborne, "Staging the People: Community and Identity in the Federal Theatre Project" (New York: St. Martin's Press, 2011).

27. Eva Díaz, *The Experimenters: Chance and Design at Black Mountain College* (Chicago: University of Chicago Press, 2015).

28. Willmetz and Noble interview.

29. Don Page, interview by Mary E. Harris, 1970, North Carolina Western Regional Archives.

30. Jon H. Carter, "A Community Far Afield: Black Mountain College and the Southern Estrangement of the Avant-Garde," in *The Bohemian South: Creating Countercultures, from Poe to Punk*, edited by Shawn Chandler Bingham and Lindsey E. Freeman (Chapel Hill: University of North Carolina Press, 2017), 55–69.

31. Arabella Stranger, "Merce Cunningham's Ensemble Space," *Journal of Black Mountain Studies* 3 (2011).

32. Schawinsky, "My Two Years," 2.

33. Anni Albers, "Work with Material," *Black Mountain College Bulletin 5* (Black Mountain, 1938).

34. The faulty rural electricity infrastructure resulted in sporadic electrical stage lighting. Schawinsky, "My Two Years," 8.

35. Sheldon Hackney, "The Contradictory South," *Southern Cultures* 7, no. 4 (2001): 68.

36. Don Page interview.

37. Xanti Schawinsky to Board of Fellows, The Corporation of Black Mountain College, April 12, 1938, North Carolina Western Regional Archives.

A Theatre's Responsibility

to Its Community

Jennifer Toutant

Regional theatre companies in the last decade have become more focused on how to better serve their communities. As a result, our education departments have become less marginalized and more central to the theatre's programming and ethos. Furthermore, new community engagement departments have formed at our theatres across the nation. Additionally, equity, diversity, and inclusion efforts have increased as we have been called out for wanting to serve our diverse communities despite the fact that many theatres are primarily white institutions.

Theatre has long been an art form that examines humanity's role as citizens of the world. Theatre has the potential to challenge society and tell stories that evoke empathy and understanding. In *Theatre and Citizenship: The History of a Practice*, David Wiles claims, "Theatre was for centuries a place of public encounter where opinion was shaped and relations of power were negotiated. Today we must ask ourselves whether that space of interaction has devolved to the internet, or whether face-to-face encounter of theatre is indeed still of relevance in the making of an active citizenship."[1] I assert that it is still relevant, but only if theatre exists for all rather than an elite subset of our population. By definition, citizenship means "membership in a community" and "the quality of an individual's response to membership in a community."[2] Theatre can be a gathering place for individuals to explore their community membership through storytelling. Additionally, a theatre as an institution can be thought of as a citizen of its own community. A theatre not only creates a space of collective experience for its audiences within its own walls but is also a member of its larger community, and it must exist with and for that community. Given the American theatre's history of exclusionary practices, it is imperative today that the work of a theatre extends beyond its own building. To realize our potential to be a communal place for all, we must build relationships with those outside our subscriber base.

I am interested in exploring the changing role of community engagement and education in professional theatre, its function in theatre's responsibility to citizenship (though I challenge the use of that word in this context), and the need to better prepare future theatre practitioners in the art of engagement. How are we to truly engage with the communities in which we are located if they are far more diverse than the practitioners we employ, and programming we produce, at our theatres? How do we expect diverse populations to attend our productions if the narratives we share on our stages are chosen primarily for their ability to appease aging white subscribers? How are we building meaningful relationships with our surrounding communities, and responding to their needs?

In exploration of this topic, I solicited peers, colleagues, and young adults at professional theatres and academic institutions to answer the following questions: How do professional theatres define and value citizenship in our work? How are mission and vision statements of theatres changing and why? How has the role of community engagement and education changed in professional theatre in the last five years? How has community engagement and education programming been used in a theatre's desire to become more inclusive? How are we preparing college students for the rapidly changing landscape of professional theatre, both as artists and as engagement practitioners? In answering these questions, I draw from my own experiences as the director of education for over thirteen years at Milwaukee Repertory Theater as well as the professional relationships I have developed in my career.

Before I explore this litany of questions, I would like to scrutinize the word "citizenship." As a field, we need to interrogate the usage of that word if we are to uphold it as a value. Theatres have a responsibility to examine our role as citizens of their broader communities. But in 2019, citizenship can be seen as a volatile word. As Milwaukee Repertory Theater's director of community engagement Leah Harris describes: "Today, we have a news cycle that is constantly reminding us of who does and doesn't belong in this country. I personally hold the belief that the culture of theater belongs to everyone."[3]

Challenging the use of "citizenship" has been a hot topic at Milwaukee Repertory Theater (Milwaukee Rep) as we undergo our next iteration of strategic planning. Citizenship was identified as a core value in our 2015 strategic plan, but that has changed this year. "We made the decision to get rid of the word 'citizenship,'" says executive director Chad Bauman.

"Since we did this plan in 2015 to where we are in 2019 the word 'citizenship' has become loaded, mostly because of talks about a border wall, and tracking down illegal citizens." Responding to the concerns expressed by some key community members and with the support of key staff members including myself, Milwaukee Rep replaced the word "citizenship" with "relevance": "Because if you are going to be part of the civic dialogue of your region" and help to create a better region, "then it all comes back to relevance."[4] As we continually seek to create inclusive environments in our theatre companies, how we utilize the word "citizenship" must be considered when there are people in our country for whom that word is loaded with exclusivity. One possible synonym for "citizenship" could be "social responsibility."

Some theatres view social responsibility as an essential component of their work. Director of education Johamy Morales of Seattle Children's Theatre expresses, "I don't think that all theatres necessarily look at their season or programming as a form of citizenship, but how amazing it would be if all theatre implemented citizenship in their mission and [it] was part of their core values."[5] Some theatres do this and go so far as to change their mission statements to better reflect their responsibility to the community.

Milwaukee Rep is one such example, and we changed our mission statement in 2015. Not many theatres actually change their mission, though they may change their vision statements to better reflect the changing nature of theatre in our country. Bauman explained, "It's not easy to change your mission statement, particularly if you are a really mature organization. I think a lot of people change internal messaging and they leave their mission the same."[6] Milwaukee Rep decided to focus its mission around positive change because we wanted that to be a significant driving factor in our work both onstage and in the community.

That same year, Milwaukee Rep added a community engagement department. This is aligned with a nationwide trend toward a heightened focus on community engagement. The executive director of the Theatre Communications Group, Teresa Eyring, comments, "It is sometimes the case that a theatre's community engagement work is considered secondary to the work onstage. More and more, though, I am observing it become part of the urgent core. And when you come into contact with the people doing the work, you recognize instantly the churning of a new American theatre movement—one that is not slowing down any time soon."[7] There is no one model adopted by all theatres, as this work varies according to each theatre's community and the history of how engagement has been implemented, if at all, in other departments. Some theatres increased community engagement activity under the umbrella of their education department. Some designed their community engagement department to oversee or even replace the education department. And others, like Milwaukee Rep, have added a new community engagement department in addition to the education department. When asked about the growth trend of engagement programming, Bauman said, "I think theatres are handling this one of two ways—they are either doing ultra-popular work and they aren't as interested in engagement and other theatres are viewing it not only as the right thing to do, but also critically important to business. I think there are theatres that have completely had their head in the ground and then they close."[8]

Along with the rise in community engagement, we are also seeing an increased effort towards equity, diversity, and inclusion (ED&I) work; however, the converse might be true. It is difficult to distinguish which came first, as the need for community engagement might arise through increased work in ED&I. If a theatre is genuinely working to be more relevant to the full population of their communities, they are learning the need to make sincere programmatic shifts. At the same time, we are often also seeing community engagement or education departments taking the lead on ED&I initiatives and, in many cases, they are the impetus for the effort.

Theatres need to know what they are getting into when they design initiatives in community engagement and ED&I in order to ethically and responsibly approach the work without causing harm to the communities they wish to serve. Too often theatres begin these efforts in order to follow national trends, or at the bequest of grant funders. This work needs to be done as our world is changing rapidly—to the point of having to reevaluate the language used merely five years ago thanks to today's political climate around citizenship. It needs to be done with the right intentions, with a clear understanding of the theatre's goals for ED&I work, and with a thoughtful and inclusive plan for achieving those goals.

Efforts in ED&I often begin or live primarily in education and community engagement, but it is crucial that the entire institution be involved if we are to make positive change in our communities. In her March 2018 keynote address to the Intersections Summit, artEquity's Carmen Morgan entreated, "I'm asking you to make sure that the work you are doing around community engagement is not transactional—that you're not inviting people into your spaces trying to connect them to the things that you are doing, but instead centering them and their lives, their needs, and their issues at the core."[9] If a theatre is changing its mission to be more community-minded, it is imperative that its leadership consider the people they want to reach, and to redefine what they mean by audience. "We do ourselves a disservice in assuming the community we want to engage is sitting [in] our audiences," says Harris. "In my experience, the 'why' behind doing the work ultimately came from a place of the institution wanting to activate its mission in the fullest way and be in direct dialogue with people who make up our city, not just those who wrote checks for our theater or are subscribers in our audience."[10]

Community engagement and education is often on the frontlines in the inclusivity efforts of a theatre due to the community relationships our departments develop. It is also then our responsibility to bring that learning back into the overall operations of the theatre. Artistic directors need to be aware of what we are learning from residents and community organizations to better understand the community that their theatre serves beyond the current subscriber base. This is especially true when most theatres are experiencing a downward trend in subscriptions. Harris provides a great perspective on how the work begins to infiltrate throughout an institution:

> The minute you start being in authentic dialogue with [the] community, you start taking [an] audit of your institution and the ways it caters towards a specific demographic/audience. You start looking closer at marketing materials and messaging, you lean into artistic programming and ask which stories are being centered and by whom, and you start questioning the homogenous board leadership who is proud of the work happening in the community. Eventually, you start looking at your audience, front of house staff, and the physical and financial barriers that keep people out of your theater and wonder how the work can be done in earnest. I fundamentally believe that community engagement has to be two-way learning, meaning, what you learn from the community is taken back to your institution and applied.[11]

This work then has to be fully embraced on every level of the institution, including leadership and the more grassroots-level departments.

Consider the season planning process at most theatres. The artistic team or a planning committee puts forth a slate of plays. The artistic director then ultimately decides on a season for the board of directors to approve, and "then it is the marketing department's job to convince the public to come and see the selected plays."[12] The education and community engagement departments then have the challenging task to center community after the main programming has already been decided.

As director of education, I often refer to my job as "the dot connector." I strive to connect the art we do on our stages to work I do in the schools and community. However, the methodologies applied to implementation in the classroom are informed by the schools, the teachers, and youth we serve. Through an understanding of each school environment, we adapt the pedagogical approach to our curriculum to meet the needs of the students.

Approaching work with the community lens begins to permeate throughout all operations of the theatre. Theatres are now asking themselves the big questions around shifting institutional culture, relevance, accessibility, and inclusivity. Harris calls for theatres to build cultural competency if we are going to truly move this work forward. "Institutions have to work on building internal cultural competency when engaging with communities of color. Cultural competency will have direct impact on many aspects of internal practices and the idea of two-way learning is only going to be fruitful if a shared understanding of different cultures is being built between both community partners and the theater."[13] I have found cultural competency critical in my own work to ensure that programmatic design and delivery is aligned with the cultural needs of the people we are serving. We often have to adapt curriculum based on the youth we are serving. We cannot expect every community to conform to our own cultures if we want to engage them in our art. It is not enough to only adjust the season selection and casting decisions.

Statistics in casting are often used to measure diversity efforts in theatres. Yes, representation on stage is critical, as is programming non-white-centric narratives on our stages. However, that does not mean that non-white communities are attending the productions. The "if you build it, they will come" mentality is not applicable to the diversification of our audiences.

Lonnae Hickman, a student at DePaul University and former Milwaukee Rep teen council president, offered, "I believe that theaters should listen to the demands, concerns, [and] positives . . . of its communities that are right next to them. These citizens and their concerns are important, but often neglected by the theatre world as a whole. . . . Its responsibility can branch through its season selections, its education, its other programming, and even its visibility and proactiveness in the community."[14] The cost of seeing theatre, intimidation, and reputation are all topics that come up in my conversations with community residents. If we are hoping a specific neighborhood will attend our productions, for example, I build that into the grant proposal after a conversation with that community about whether or not they even want to see the shows. Accessibility takes many forms, and we should be examining that on every programmatic level.

I recently hosted a neighborhood night at Milwaukee Rep for a neighborhood we have not yet engaged, aside from a few school programs. I asked the participants, many of whom had never stepped foot in our theatre before, what role they felt the arts played in their community. One resident expressed how many folks in lower income neighborhoods have never heard of Milwaukee Rep and, if they have, they certainly do not feel like the theatre is a place for them. Milwaukee Rep is historically a white institution in one of the most segregated cities in America, so it isn't surprising that communities of color often do not feel welcome there. Milwaukee Rep has been making strides in programming a season of plays that better represent Milwaukee's rich diversity, but, like most large regional theatres, it still has a long way to go with staff, volunteers, board, and audiences. It is vital that we spend abundant time in the community listening and learning without imposing our own agenda. We should be attending neighborhood events, town halls, and celebrations, which we have begun to do at Milwaukee Rep. Our presence at their events have opened up the possibility of two-way learning, and residents are much more interested in learning how to engage with us more deeply. How can we expect people to participate in our work, even as audiences, if we do not make an effort to build a relationship with them?

Milwaukee Rep's education department conducted community engagement programming before the addition of the dedicated department. One programmatic example was a resident-led intergenerational program that was devised because young people expressed their need for more adult-positive interactions. This program is still run by education and provides an example of how listening to residents can influence programmatic decisions. Currently, our neighborhood program includes youth storytelling classes, facilitating and organizing entertainment during neighborhood events, and exploring how to use theatre and storytelling to raise awareness of prevalent community issues, such as lead poisoning in water and paint (figure 7.1).

Some background information on the neighborhood is essential in order to understand the relevance of Milwaukee Rep's involvement. On March 20, 2017, the *Milwaukee Journal Sentinel* published an article that described the current conditions of the neighborhood: "Today, more than half of Amani lives below the poverty line, making it one of the most extreme enclaves in one of America's poorest cities. More than one in three residents is unemployed, nearly five times the rate in 1970. Nearly every block has boarded up and abandoned homes. The ZIP code it lands in—53206—led the city in homicides six of the past nine years of available data. Even after ten years of effort, researchers at the University of Wisconsin–Milwaukee failed to locate any other ZIP code in the nation with a matching per-capita share of residents who are or were incarcer-

Figure 7.1. Youth storytelling program's showcase performance at Milwaukee Repertory Theater. (Courtesy of author)

ated."[15] We have been active in Amani for over five years with youth and community programming as the only performing arts group in a collective impact model. The goals of this coalition are to address some major and complex problems, such as community violence, housing, and Milwaukee's lead crisis in its water and older homes. Since this work began, the neighborhood has seen a reduction in crime each year. "Crime in the Amani neighborhood of Milwaukee continued to decrease another 12.08% in 2017, while at the same time City of Milwaukee crime increased 1.94%."[16] Milwaukee Rep cannot lay claim to the success in ameliorating living conditions in the neighborhood, but we are at the table.

In 2015 I hosted Milwaukee Rep's first Amani neighborhood event and was barraged with a series of questions by a resident. She asked if I had been to the newly renovated Moody Park in the Amani neighborhood, and whether I had been to an Amani United meeting, which is a group of residents and community partners that gather monthly to discuss neighborhood concerns and future planning. Moody Park is a central gathering place in Amani, and it is an expectation that if you want to engage with the residents, it is important to attend events there (figure 7.2). This resident was essentially testing me on whether or not I was genuinely interested in knowing the neighborhood. I was, thankfully,

Figure 7.2. Community Fun Night event in the Amani neighborhood in Milwaukee, Wisconsin. (Courtesy of author)

able to answer in the affirmative to each of her questions. If I had not been able to, the dialogue on how a theatre might be involved with the neighborhood would have been essentially shut down.

In initial listening sessions when we first started to engage the neighborhood, resident leaders identified collective experiences to bring people together as one strategy in which theatre is a natural fit. Theatre can also take an active role in pushing beyond performance and into relevance through meaningful dialogue, hopefully resulting in action. Milwaukee Rep has done this both during facilitated dialogues following performances on our stages, as well as with conversations in the neighborhood. At community meetings, residents now consider how the arts can assist with various tactics in their neighborhood revitalization plan, which entered the strategic conversation partially as a result of the work we have done in the neighborhood.

One example of how the neighborhood has turned to the theatre in hopes of collaboration is to raise awareness of Milwaukee's lead crisis, which strongly affects the Amani neighborhood. According to the City of Milwaukee's Health Department, 53206 is one of the neighborhoods in Milwaukee most negatively affected by the crisis. The zip code was identified as one of the densest neighborhoods for the elevated blood lead levels for children under the age of six.[17] One of the anchor organi-

Figure 7.3. Thanksgiving storytelling potluck event in Milwaukee's 53206 neighborhood. (Courtesy of author)

zations in Amani, the Dominican Center, is working to raise awareness among residents of the lead crisis so that families can take necessary precautions. They reached out to Milwaukee Rep for help. Given the theatre's expertise in storytelling, they are hoping that Milwaukee Rep can create an ensemble of artists and residents to devise a theatrical piece to tell the story of the lead crisis in a way that actually gets folks to listen and receive the message. If they truly understand what is at stake, then maybe they will be moved to action. This project is currently in development and we look forward to learning how it will make an impact (figure 7.3).

This is an instance of how a theatre company can truly listen to the needs of one community, focus on depth rather than breadth, and collaborate with non-arts groups to make some serious change. Residents in this neighborhood have expressed more interest and willingness to experience our productions as a byproduct of the intentional work we have done in their neighborhood. And they now know who we are. If we want to survive as a theatre in a world with ever-increasing diversity, we must examine our relevance and focus on the community in which we serve.

As illustrated in the previous example, the work of education and engagement programming can be influential in building relevance in the community. Developing community engagement programming in our theatres is vital to remaining relevant.

As citizens of our theaters and our communities, the work we do in engagement and education is personal and is influenced by our own life experience. In an effort to seek additional insights, I asked a few peers for their input. Seattle Children's Theatre's Johamy Morales offers her perspective on the influence of theatre education on her own life: "Growing up as a young Mexican-American girl in Southern California I struggled not to become another statistic. . . . Theatre opened a door of artistic possibilities and more importantly it led me to my personal mission of educating, exposing and mentoring others less privileged."[18] Morales's personal experience influenced and inspired the work she does in professional theatre, opening doors for the youth of today. Leah Harris speaks similarly about her career in community engagement: "First, I think the biggest lesson I've learned and been reminded of time and again in this work is that theater does NOT change lives. We, as artists and administrations, are so quick to place our art on a pedestal and position it as the thing that will save humanity and it actually won't. If anything, theater, or any art form, is simply the vehicle that has the potential to unlock something in the human spirit that can lead to change."[19]

Growth of community engagement and education is rapidly occurring at theatres across the country. So how do we prepare the next generation of theatre artists to engage in this work? Current community engagement staff came to this work from very different paths; few have actually had the opportunity to study this work in higher education. Many come to the career through backgrounds in teaching, social justice, or the arts. There is no manual to consult about how to be a Director of Community Engagement or a Director of Education for a professional theatre. Personally, in my short time with a community engagement department, I have been a part of two job searches for the director position. The candidates have all brought an incredibly wide variety of experiences to the table and, if hired, would ultimately shift the direction of the department one way or another. When asked about the hiring process, executive director Chad Bauman said:

> It's hard to hire this position because you either find people that are really good at community organizing and civically engaged, but they have a lack of knowledge of the theatre. Or you find people that are very knowledgeable about the theatre, but they have less of a knowledge of community organizing. It's really rare to find both. And then when you find both, a lot of the times they are very, very young people and then they struggle with being senior leaders. And that's because the field is so new. So, that combination of having to have the experience and the wisdom and the maturity to be able to see things globally from more of a senior leader, mashed with community organizing, mashed with theatre knowledge is very difficult to find. You usually get, if you're lucky, two of the three.[20]

It is essential that education director positions and their support staffs have multiple and diverse skillsets.

I asked Leah Harris and Johamy Morales what they look for when hiring staff. For community engagement, Harris expects staff to have "a fundamental knowledge of cultural competency and how that manifests in the work . . . and ultimately, someone who sees the gift that every human has to offer our world."[21] In hiring education staff, Morales states: "I am always looking for candidates who have a diverse experience in the industry. I wish educators had more opportunities to work in the field. There are less and less programs that offer these opportunities that are accessible to more students of marginalized communities. Generally, internships don't pay as well or at all, and only those who can afford to do the internships get that experience."[22] It is difficult to hire these positions when there are so many specialized skills required, especially due to the fact that most community engagement and education departments comprise two or three employees. Before some recent growth in my department that allowed for the hiring of an education administrator, we had a position that was responsible for administration, teaching in-school and after-school programs, writing play and teacher guides, and more. There are a multitude of job skills needed, and we must better prepare people to enter this field.

Looking at the needs that theatres have in hiring engagement and education staff, the academic field should be taking a deep dive into what courses they offer to prepare students for this work. Based on conversations with professors and an internet search, I question how well colleges are preparing students for this work. It appears that even those colleges with robust coursework in community engagement and education do not require all their theatre students to take these classes, but rather offer them as electives.

To be prepared for theatre's current direction, it is becoming more important for students to take required courses in community engagement and education, even if they have no intention of working full-time in those departments. There are two good reasons for this. First, if theatres are changing their missions and core values to be more civically minded and aware of their responsibility to the community in which they serve, every hired employee—from contracted actors, directors, and designers to full-time staff—should understand how to embody these values in their work. This should extend to volunteers and part-time employees as well. As the field is making the art form more inclusive and relevant to all, it is vital that everyone is embodying that vision and approaches patrons with a lens of cultural competency. Second, as engagement and education programs continue to flourish and grow, theatre practitioners on all levels are asked to participate in the work beyond the production.

Milwaukee Rep, for example, pays actors to lead audience engagement programs, teach pre- and post-show workshops in school environments across a very segregated city, and participate in community engagement programs. It will only help actors, directors, and designers to have this skill set as a part of their formal education and training.

Thanks to the rise of community engagement, we have also learned there is a vast spectrum of understanding about the definition and purpose of community engagement. It would behoove academic programs to create an understanding of the differences between community engagement, education, audience engagement, and audience development. Each theatre is currently defining those terms for themselves, and hopefully as the work continues to be better delineated and understood throughout the field, we won't have to take so much time talking about what the work is and we will be better at actionizing the work with the community.

There are some wonderful examples of coursework happening at academic institutions that are worth highlighting. The University of Texas at Austin has a full MFA in Drama and Theatre for Youth and Communities as well as a Performance as Public Practice curriculum that offers coursework in community and social justice. Additionally, the professors will often engage the students in their work in professional theatre. One of the professors there, K. J. Sanchez, describes their focus as "primarily on coursework, so we don't do things like internships with professional companies, but all of the faculty is working in the field and we bring our students with us wherever we go."[23] This provides exposure to the work of engagement for students that elect to participate.

Some colleges may not have the capacity to implement a full program track but find ways to engage their students in community engagement. This is another great method to prepare students for contemporary professional theatre. Marquette University does not offer a full track in education or community engagement but finds opportunities for students to participate through presenting a social justice–themed play each year with community programming, thus giving students the chance to see implementation and relevance at both the production level and in community dialogue.[24] And other colleges have a full program for students such as the University of Wisconsin–Milwaukee, which offers a theatre practices program for undergraduates. "Focused on community engagement and social justice, [the] Theatre Practices program encourages students to create, innovate, and collaborate through explorative and diverse theatre making and scholarship."[25] There are many more examples of universities offering coursework that aligns with theatre for social justice or social change.

In the words of Sojourn Theatre's founding artistic director Michael

Rohd, "Theatre allows us to converse with our souls, to passionately pursue and discover ways of living with ourselves and with others. We have no better way to work together, to learn about each other, to heal, and to grow."[26] I encourage us all to reconsider how we are preparing the next generation of theatre artists to be prepared for today's world of theatre. Students must enter the workplace with an understanding of inclusion, cultural competency, the work of community engagement, and education. All theatre practitioners must be prepared to understand how their work, no matter their focus area, aligns with the mission, vision, and core values of the theatres that employ them. With this knowledge, the next generation of our theatre makers will be well equipped to engage with diverse communities through relationships. Understanding and engaging community provides the pathway for theatre to be inclusive, relevant, and socially responsible.

Notes

1. David Wiles, *Theatre and Citizenship* (New York: Cambridge University Press, 2011), 208.

2. *Merriam-Webster Collegiate Dictionary*, "citizenship," https://www.merriam-webster.com/dictionary/citizenship, accessed March 15, 2019.

3. Leah Harris, email to author, March 2, 2019.

4. Chad Bauman (executive director, Milwaukee Repertory Theater), interview with the author, March 21, 2019.

5. Johamy Morales, email to author, February 24, 2019.

6. Bauman interview.

7. Teresa Eyring, "Theatre, Community, and Justice," *American Theatre*, April 23, 2018, https://www.americantheatre.org/2018/04/23/theatre-community-and-justice/.

8. Bauman interview.

9. Quoted in Allison Considine, "At the Intersections," *American Theatre*, April 23, 2018, https://www.americantheatre.org/2018/04/23/at-the-intersections/.

10. Harris, email to author.

11. Harris, email to author.

12. David Diamond, *Theatre for Living* (Victoria: Trafford Publishing, 2007), 51.

13. Harris, email to author.

14. Lonnae Hickman, email to author, March 28, 2019.

15. John Schmid, "The Unlikeliest Neighborhood: A 19th Century Concept Finds a New Home, as Amani Becomes a Test Case Watched Nationwide," *Milwaukee Journal Sentinel*, March 29, 2017, https://projects.jsonline.com/news/2017/3/29/the-unlikeliest-neighborhood.html.

16. COA Youth and Family Centers, "Major Crime Decrease in Milwaukee's

Amani Neighborhood," *Milwaukee Neighborhood News Service*, January 22, 2018, https://milwaukeenns.org/2018/01/22/major-crime-decrease-in-milwaukees -amani-neighborhood/.

17. City of Milwaukee Health Department, *Childhood Lead Poisoning Prevention Program: Assessment of Operations and Recommendations for Corrective Actions*, January 29, 2018, https://localtvwiti.files.wordpress.com/2018/01/mhd -lead-report-1-29-18.pdf.

18. Morales, email to author.

19. Harris, email to author.

20. Bauman, interview.

21. Harris, email to author.

22. Morales, email to author.

23. K. J. Sanchez, email to author, February 9, 2019.

24. Stephen Hudson-Mairet, email to author, February 13, 2019.

25. "Theatre Practices," University of Wisconsin–Milwaukee, https://uwm.edu /arts/theatre/ba/, accessed February 27, 2019.

26. Michael Rohd, *Theatre for Community, Conflict & Dialogue: The Hope is Vital Training Manual* (Portsmouth: Heinemann, 1998), 140.

It's Not Easy Being Orange

Animatronic Presidents, Patriotic Muppets, and the Configuration of Citizenship in Disney's Liberty Square

Chase Bringardner

The AFTERMATH OF THE 2016 election resonated widely into almost every nook and cranny of society, nationally and globally. What once had seemed an impossibility to so many now suddenly stared the nation directly in the face as a stark reality. Uncertainty and disbelief permeated pages and screens and media of all sorts struggled to make sense of what had happened. As norms faltered and new nationalisms emerged, the very ideas or constructs of citizen and citizenry were turned on their head. The previously established scripts no longer held together. The fragile threads that sought to hold together the citizenry unraveled. As the new administration sought to actively restrict and redefine what it meant to be American under the auspices of renewed greatness, the future for many suddenly seemed to have a whole lot less hope. At Walt Disney World's Magic Kingdom, the self-proclaimed happiest place on earth, "imagineers" (those tasked within the Disney corporation with implementing new, innovative, and imaginative concepts and technology) faced a particular challenge. As polls had consistently shown former Secretary of State Hillary Clinton a clear favorite to win, imagineers had (allegedly) already begun construction on a Clinton animatronic figure to join the forty-three men who had served as president of the United States in Walt Disney's Hall of Presidents, an animatronic enhanced show celebrating the institution of the presidency that opened with the Magic Kingdom in 1971.[1]

As imagineers behind the scenes struggled to (literally) shift gears and refashion latex and paint to reflect this new reality in this classic theme park attraction, for park guests and Disney employees alike, the area surrounding the attraction, known as Liberty Square, offered a possible framework to understand the rapidly shifting terrain. For just a month before the election, a roaming band of felted, vaudevillian performers took residency in the building next door, entertaining crowds with two different retellings of American history. These performances offer an opportunity to provide a new script on how to *engage* with the presence of the new animatronic figure in that theatre next door. Moreover, they also *perform* a certain kind of disruptive and unruly citizenship to respond to this new administration. Through the Muppets' raucous performance of "Great Moments in History"—delivered with gusto by a frog, a pig, a bear, an eagle, chickens, and Gonzo—audiences get to experience ruptures in the historical narrative and potentially ascertain strategies for performing and perhaps creating alternative citizenries.

Walt Disney World's Magic Kingdom theme park consists of six different "lands," each located on a spoke that emanates from the central wheel's hub (which is immediately in front of Cinderella's castle). Liberty Square, nestled between Frontierland and Fantasy Land, recreates an idealized Colonial American town square complete with replicas of the Liberty Tree and the Liberty Bell. The land is the primary launch point for the Liberty Bell river boat and home to the Hall of Presidents attraction as well as one of Disney World's most beloved (albeit perhaps oddly placed) attractions—The Haunted Mansion—which is neither particularly Colonial nor American. The center of Liberty Square contains a replica of Philadelphia's Independence Hall, which houses the Hall of Presidents attraction (figure 8.1). Surrounding that central building are a number of other smaller Colonial structures that give the sense of a bristling Colonial town. In theory, and in Walt Disney's original conception, these buildings recreate a historical civic space. In practice, these buildings primarily serve to offer theme park guests opportunities to buy products ranging from ornaments from Ye Olde Christmas Shoppe to funnel cakes and foot-long corn dogs from the Sleepy Hollow snack shop.[2]

The central attraction in Liberty Square, the Hall of Presidents holds a revered place in Disney history as one of Walt Disney's legacy projects, a project he himself shepherded through the design process until his death in 1966. Originally intended as part of an early expansion to Disneyland titled "Liberty Street," the Hall of Presidents eventually opened along with Walt Disney World in 1971. The animatronic advances Disney had made with the "Conversations with Lincoln" attraction were now expanded to include a state-of-the-art theatre with five movie screens that at the climax of the performance revealed animatronic likenesses of every single president in a dramatic and moving tableau. The accompanying film tells a sweeping, deeply respectful, and solemn narrative of American exceptionalism that, while it has changed and been updated

Figure 8.1. The Hall of Presidents at Walt Disney World's Magic Kingdom. (Courtesy of Jordan Lunstead)

over the years, chiefly champions the presidency, the Constitution, and American democracy within a narrative of struggles overcome and compromises achieved, all accompanied by soaring, patriotic music. While initially, from 1971 to 1992, only Abraham Lincoln's animatronic figure spoke in the climactic presidential reveal, Bill Clinton's presidency saw a new precedent established in which the sitting president would record a brief address to include within the show. This particular precedent faced its greatest challenge with the advent of a President Trump and led many within the company to seek alternatives. Yet tradition won out, and the animatronic Trump took up residency in January 2018 after a year-long period of reflection and refurbishment. Animatronic Trump framed within the tableau of the other forty-three presidents and enjoying all the symbolic weight of the office cemented a solid position for theme park audiences within the traditional historical narrative. It would take a disruption outside the space of the hall itself to properly place and contextualize this animatronic performance and provide a means of disrupting that narrative.[3]

Up until the arrival of the Muppets in the town square, the reverence required of the experience inside the Hall of Presidents translated to a certain formality within Liberty Square itself. The space maintained a certain kind of seriousness and solemnity, an attempt at a mostly faithful historical recreation of Colonial America complete with cast members outfitted in historical costuming and the occasional appearance of a fife and drum band. This historical "accuracy" stands in stark contrast to the fantastical, German–inspired architecture of Fantasyland that directly backs up to Liberty Square. However, the presence of the Muppets, who literally burst through a series of windows above one of the seemingly innocuous historical buildings, radically disrupts the visual and oral narratives of the "land" and indicates from their very presence a change in positionality. Their presence forces a productive juxtaposition between the authentic historical creations and the more modern, shtick-laden commentary of the Muppets' performance style. Though not the original intention, perhaps, this juxtaposition prepares audiences for an arguably greater juxtaposition once they enter the Hall of President's attraction and see the sea of presidents framing the animatronic Trump.

Liberty Square is not the first time Trump and Muppet met. While Trump himself or iterations of Trump never appeared on *The Muppet Show* proper, *Sesame Street* has a somewhat surprisingly long history of engagement with him and his larger-than-life persona. In 1988, for example, *Sesame Street* introduced the character of Ronald Grump, a scheming landlord Muppet that takes over Oscar the Grouch's trash can home with a structure of receptacles called "Grump Tower." Grump then attempts to evict Oscar from his own home in a nod to Trump's reputation as a ruthless real estate villain. This segment, while certainly gesturing toward important basic lessons on honesty and ethical behavior, appears to comment directly on reporting at the time of the questionable practices of the Trump real estate company toward its many tenants.[4]

In 1994, Ronald Grump returned not in Muppet but in human form for *Sesame Street All-Star 25th Birthday: Stars and Street Forever!*—played by actor Joe Pesci in a lookalike wig. This segment mirrors themes from the 1980s but significantly ups the stakes: Grump announces plans to build his new theme park, Grump World, on Sesame Street, displacing all the Muppets who live there—mirroring Trump's real-life real estate practices. In one particularly strange and prophetic moment—especially in light of Trump's persistent attempts to defund the Public Broadcasting System—a reporter, played by Julia Louis-Dreyfus, says, "It looks like Sesame Street may be no more due to one man: Ronald Grump," to which Elmo responds, "If we don't do something about Mr. Grump, Elmo thinks we will be history!"[5] Videos of the actual skit are only intermittently available on the internet (they seem to be removed regularly)—

but there is outtake footage of Pesci in costume interacting with the Elmo and other Muppets.

Finally, in 2005, at the height of *The Apprentice*'s popularity, Grump returned yet again—this time with the first name "Donald" instead of "Ronald." Complete with a new orange wig, Donald Grump travels to Sesame Street to audition Grouches (in an *Apprentice* parody), putting them through a series of trials to determine his new Helper. Over the course of the skit he even fires a character named Omagrossa, a nod to frequent *Apprentice* contestant and former White House staffer Omarossa Manigault Newman.[6] In each of these examples, taken from three different decades, Ronald Grump/Donald Grump/Donald Trump represents negative, undesirable attributes—greed, selfishness, lack of empathy— and the show uses his Muppet visage to educate children to choose a different path.

While Grump/Trump does not make his way into the "Great Moments in History" performances, his previous relationship with the Muppets' *Sesame Street* brethren makes Kermit, Miss Piggy, and the rest the ideal mouthpieces to provide audiences with means to disrupt the dominant historical narratives and conventional understandings of American history espoused in the Hall of Presidents. Moreover, the Muppets' unique place within popular culture and particularly within Generation X's shared nostalgia (Generation X roughly comprises those born between the late 1960s and early 1980s) make them a particularly strong force to combat the forces of Trumpism embodied in the president's animatronic representation.

In her 2014 article for *Salon*, Elizabeth Hyde Stevens makes a strong case for why this particular generation—Generation X—cares so much about the Muppets. Stevens argues that more than simply making people nostalgic for their youth in the 1970s and 1980s, the Muppets "gave us a worldview" that many carried into adulthood—a trajectory that began with *Sesame Street*, its curriculum created by Harvard psychologists at the Children's Television Workshop, and progressed through *The Muppet Show* and various other Henson-related projects, including *Fraggle Rock*, *Emmet Otter's Jug Band Christmas*, *The Dark Crystal*, *Labyrinth*, and *Muppet Babies*, to name a few.[7] Stevens contends that this worldview taught viewers to value "education, inclusion (witnessed in the diversity of casting choices both human and Muppet), global citizenship (embracing cross-cultural understanding and cultural difference), collaboration (both in terms of stated or sung values and in the performance of the puppets themselves which required a collaboration of two or more people), environmentalism (through focus on nature and sustainability), creativity, and technological innovation" (remember Kermit riding that bicycle in *The Muppets Take Manhattan?*).[8] These values, according to Stevens, became the "core values" for a generation and, among other things, influenced a generation of comedians, including Jason Segel, Ricky Gervais, Tina Fey, and Bret McKenzie (creator of *Flight of the Conchords*). When Stevens asked her fellow *Salon* author Alexander Chee "what exactly did the Muppets teach us," his answer really distilled the essence of that worldview: "I have the sense that it's about a sensibility—a way of finding humor in things, in loving the ridiculous you find in the ordinary. And it's also the love of fairness and justice—karma is a big part of that show's humor."[9] Stevens makes the argument that now that many of this generation have become parents, they bring this worldview forward in their own parenting. I would expand her assertion to say that many members of Generation X, whether parents or not, bring this worldview with them as they confront the current moment. They bring with them what Stevens summarizes as "the idea that life is about making a difference, a positive change."[10]

Within the "Great Moments in History" performances, this fundamental belief in "making a difference, a positive change" exists in the constructs of two different skits that very much rely on humor and ridiculousness as well as a profound sense of fairness and justice. In fact both skits, in many ways, reflect the Muppet values Stevens outlines above, combining within an educational story lessons of inclusion, global citizenship, collaboration, and creativity. When taken together, these values stand in stark contrast to the values and ideas represented in and performed by the animatronic Trump in the Hall of Presidents. The Muppets afford audiences the opportunity to choose an alternative script, one aligned with those "Muppet values," to cultivate an alternative understanding of themselves as citizens, and a different approach that challenges the dominant narrative through humor while directly poking holes in the kinds of toxic masculinity embodied by Trump and those of his similar ilk.

The "Great Moments in History" performances each tell the tale of a classic moment in the history of the United States—"The Declaration of Independence" and "The Midnight Ride of Paul Revere"—both set squarely in the Colonial Period in accordance with the performance's location in Liberty Square. The selection of these specific moments, more than simply matching the historical time of the themed land, perhaps comes from an impulse to avoid more controversial subjects or engage in war or violence. I am intrigued, however, that both these moments are anticipating conflict, at the precipice of war—the Declaration spelling out the justification for war and Revere's ride occurring the day before the first battles of the Revolution at Lexington and Concord. These moments also highlight revolutionary action, resisting and fighting back against oppressive and unfair, unjust ruling systems. They also mark moments of creating a citizenry. These are moments when a citizenry defined themselves through rebellion; through disruptive and unruly action they challenged the system and fought for a different way. While there is no explicit call from these performances necessarily to start a revolution, the spirit of revolution, especially when taken together with the Muppets' belief in fairness, justice, and karma and their calls to make a difference, certainly permeates the square.

Both these performances share some basic elements that frame the narrative. They both contain an initial appearance by Sam the Eagle (figure 8.2) reprising his traditional function of attempting to establish decorum, wholesomeness, and a serious tone only to be thwarted by the antics of Kermit, Miss Piggy, Fozzie Bear, and Gonzo. Sam also embodies a heightened, overstated patriotism—bloviating about American exceptionalism and reminding the audiences that while this is "Great Moments in History"—it's "only the American parts."[11] In "The Declaration of Independence," he even appears from his own window in the Hall of Presidents building itself, speaking to the other Muppets in the building next door. Sam is thus closely identified with the more traditional narrative occurring inside the Hall and is positioned in juxtaposition or opposition to the other Muppets. Both performances also initially incorporate a song, "Great Moments in History," that introduces the general concept of the performance in a similar way to how the Muppet Show always began with its theme song. This framing device serves to hail the audience, which consists of those wandering through Liberty Square around show time. These times are published each day in the park guide map. Importantly, these performances occur outdoors in the square itself and audiences simply stop and watch while standing or sitting directly on the pavement—there is no formal theatrical seating (as in the Hall of Presidents attraction). The length of these performances—"The Declaration of Independence" is roughly ten minutes while "The Midnight Ride of Paul Revere" is roughly seven—supports the looseness and flexibility of this performance setup and also seems to highlight and foster its rough and raucous nature. These performances seem sanctioned but also push on established boundaries; they seem somewhat radical both in the audacity of their irreverence and in their embrace of total ridiculousness (figure 8.3).

"The Declaration of Independence," the longer of the two performances, contrasts primarily with the other one in that it incorporates a live, human actor. A town crier emerges from the ground level of the

Figure 8.2. Sam the Eagle perched above the Hall of Presidents at Walt Disney World's Magic Kingdom. (Courtesy of Jordan Lunstead)

neighboring Hall of Presidents and proceeds to "Hear Ye, Hear Ye" everyone into listening to his introduction before ceding the spotlight to Sam the Eagle emerging from above the Hall of Presidents. The crier then starts to sing the "Great Moments in History" song along with Sam and eventually the rest of the Muppet performers. Throughout the subsequent performance the human actor engages the audience as an in-

Figure 8.3. The Muppets' Stage in Liberty Square at Walt Disney World's Magic Kingdom. (Courtesy of Jordan Lunstead)

termediary between them and the Muppets, encouraging audience responses at designated times and even at one moment staging a "vote." I employ quotation marks here because with this "vote" the audience is offered only one choice in the constructed narrative—to say "Aye" and thus leave English rule. The presence of this human intermediary works to move the narrative forward and to encourage direct audience partici-

Figure 8.4. The Town Crier in front of the Muppets' Stage in Liberty Square at Walt Disney World's Magic Kingdom. (Courtesy of Jordan Lunstead)

pation while also serving as a sort of referee between Sam and the rest of the Muppets (figure 8.4).[12]

Equally striking within "The Declaration of Independence," and most certainly connected to how these performances rewrite traditional historical narratives and offer alternative models of American citizenship, is the presence of Miss Piggy (figure 8.5). Created by Jim Henson and Frank Oz in 1976, Miss Piggy looms large in the Muppet universe as one of the very few female-identified Muppets. From her inception, Miss Piggy has consistently and forcefully argued and fought for her place in the show, continuing in the strong comedic lineage of other women like Lucille Ball of *I Love Lucy*. Like Lucy, Miss Piggy often finds herself in a relationship with the show leader, Kermit, and the drama that ensues spills over from backstage to onstage. Yet Miss Piggy's excessive persona reaches well beyond her relation to Kermit; she exerts a strength of will and performance of confidence that has led many to consider her a symbol of female power and self-acceptance. As scholar activist Lesley Kinzel argues, "Miss Piggy is not a positive figure for self-acceptance because she demands and receives respect from her colleagues and the public at large; she is a positive figure because she doesn't. She is a character who has to fight

Figure 8.5. Miss Piggy and the company of "The Declaration of Independence" on the Muppets' Stage in Liberty Square at Walt Disney World's Magic Kingdom. (Courtesy of Jordan Lunstead)

against the pressure to internalize the negativity that surrounds her; she refuses to allow the assumptions and aspersions of other people to influence her opinion of herself. Nor does Piggy contain her rage; she resists, sometimes with violence."[13] Some contemporary cultural commentators even call her a feminist icon, a title Miss Piggy herself confirmed in a series of interviews surrounding the launch of the 2015 show *The Muppets* that culminated in her acceptance of the Sackler First Award presented to her by Elizabeth Sackler and Gloria Steinem in which she proclaimed, "Starting today, moi IS a feminist!"[14]

While her violent tendencies, often unchecked narcissism, and frequent complicity with regressive standards of beauty and representation certainly complicate her status as a feminist icon, her presence directly challenges the status quo. Alyssa Rosenberg, in a 2015 article in the *Washington Post*, goes so far as to compare Miss Piggy to none other than Donald Trump: "And she, like Donald Trump, has provided a career for a generation of reality stars whose deluded confidence has an entertainment and business value entirely separate from their actual, often modest, talents."[15] Perhaps this parallel of Trump to Miss Piggy makes her the perfect foil for his animatronic visage in the neighboring building. For as Rosenberg remarks, in her "immense appetites and conviction that she should get whatever she wants exactly when she wants it, Miss Piggy represents a wild, voracious sort of freedom."[16] Miss Piggy's "embrace of the sort of entitlement normally reserved for men is an unruly, defiantly unrespectable feminist act"[17]—a freedom that defies and deflates the kinds of toxic masculinity and strict conceptions of citizenry modeled by the animatronic (and real-life) Trump.

From the very beginning, both performances establish Miss Piggy's outsider status: as a female-identified pig, she does not fit within the traditional tellings of the story. So she must, as she does on *The Muppet Show* and in the Muppet movies, insert herself into the narrative, providing a model for audience members who might not see themselves in dominant national narratives. She also repeatedly calls out the performance as a performance: "You have a bear playing Benjamin Franklin!"[18] She constantly reminds the audience of the constructed nature of history and the narrative they are witnessing. Miss Piggy demonstrates a remarkable fluidity of identity in her performance, morphing from one character to another to improve her position in the story. Miss Piggy as Georgette Washington, alongside Kermit as Thomas Jefferson, Gonzo as John Adams, and Fozzie as Benjamin Franklin fashion an alternative depiction of that historical moment that embraces humor and ridiculousness while also illustrating fairness and justice—the audience believes Miss Piggy should be in the show and thus in the history. Her presence ruptures any sense of historical convention left after the broad jokes and irreverence of the opening moments of the skit.[19]

Her presence alongside the other Muppets encourages audience members to be active participants in the telling of history and, in the case of the Hall of Presidents, actively resist narratives that ring unfair, untrue, or unjust. In fact, this particular skit ends with a more sincere moment where Kermit reminds his fellow Muppets that "when Jefferson wrote the Declaration it was more than a list of demands . . . it was about things we all believe in . . . things worth fighting for . . . things that inspired the birth of a new Nation."[20] He then starts to recite the beginning of the Declaration accompanied by a chicken chorus and is then joined by the fellow Muppets and then, at the urging of the town crier, the entire audience. This collective act moves Sam the Eagle to tears, leading the town crier to remark that he is the real Town Crier (wacka wacka, right?). Confetti then explodes from the buildings and sparkly patriotic banners emerge from the windows. The performance ends with a reprise of the "Great Moments in History" song, a raucous and ridiculous call to action that reminds the audience of the collective nature of their citizenry and of their active participation in it. The crier even goes as far as encouraging audiences to then enter the Hall of Presidents, armed with a healthy dose of irreverence and knowledge of the constructed nature of historical narrative.[21]

In many ways, while "The Midnight Ride of Paul Revere" embraces most of the same messages as "The Declaration of Independence," "Revere" is really a more traditionally structured Muppet skit—with Sam the Eagle repeatedly trying to recite Henry Wadsworth Longfellow's Paul Revere poem while battling constant interruptions by various Muppet shenanigans. There is no human actor to mediate. Notably, Miss Piggy again in this skit repeatedly tries to insert herself in the historical narrative despite Kermit telling her "there is no part for you." At one point she even tries to sing "by the light of the silvery moon" in a completely anachronistic moment that infuriates Sam. She subsequently appears as a redcoat flanked by Gonzo's chicken friends. She refuses the narrative as written and continually alters the story through the sheer force of her presence. Unlike "The Declaration of Independence," this one ends in utter chaos with no sentimental summary or conclusion. Their disparate antics are only resolved through the loud reprise of the initial "Great Moments" song accompanied by an explosion of confetti and sparkly banners similar to the first performance. The chaos interestingly stages historiographical processes and the messiness and chaos often contained within them. Furthermore, this active messiness also speaks to the constructions of citizenship itself. As opposed to a fixed, predetermined "vote" with one scripted way to perform citizen, this second performance embraces the chaos and emphasizes the multifaceted nature and performativity of citizenship itself.[22]

Aside from the humor and the revelry, the takeaway message of both performances is that narratives are flexible, stories can be altered, and your presence makes a difference. These messages provide a critical frame for audiences' engagement with a more traditionally rendered experience like the Hall of Presidents through encouraging a kind of irreverence, urging audiences not to take things too seriously. There is a certain kind of revolutionary spirit in irreverent humor—a positioning that suggests a different conception of "American" and of citizenship. They offer a humor that is not cruel, that is instead steeped in fairness and justice and karma. The Muppets embody this celebration of the revolutionary spirit and encourage their audience's possible alternative citizenships. They offer up a role of citizen that resists dominant narratives and platitudes, champions the underdog, and embraces the collaborative all while singing songs, telling jokes, and embracing the power of a not-so-carefully placed pun—Making America Green Again.

Notes

1. Kristyn Pomranz, "Twitter Is Freaking Out Because the New Trump Robot in Disney's Hall of Presidents Looks Like Hillary Clinton," Bravotv, December 19, 2017, https://www.bravotv.com/jetset/trump-hall-of-presidents-robot-disney-world-looks-like-hillary-clinton, accessed March 29, 2019.

2. Mark Eades, "A Former Disney Imagineer's Guide to Walt Disney World's Liberty Square," *Orange County Register*, May 10, 2017, https://www.ocregister.com/2017/05/10/a-former-disney-imagineers-guide-to-walt-disney-worlds-liberty-square/, accessed April 1, 2019.

3. "The Hall of Presidents Story," *D23: The Official Disney Fan Club*, https://d23.com/the-hall-of-presidents-story/, accessed March 15, 2019.

4. Maeve McDermott, "'Sesame Street' v. Trump: The Show's Long History of Mocking 'Donald Grump,'" *USA Today*, March 22, 2017, https://www.usatoday.com/story/life/entertainthis/2017/03/21/sesame-street-v-trump-shows-long-history-mocking-donald-grump/99445290/, accessed March 25, 2019.

5. Carey Purcell, "'Sesame Street' Trump Video Clips: 4 Times the PBS Children's Show Mocked the President," Mic, March 22, 2017, https://www.mic.com/articles/171813/sesame-street-trump-video-clips-4-times-the-pbs-children-s-show-mocked-the-president, accessed March 25, 2019.

6. McDermott, "'Sesame Street' v. Trump."

7. Elizabeth Hyde Stevens, "Millennials Just Don't Get It! How the Muppets Created Generation X," Salon, April 6, 2014, https://www.salon.com/2014/04/06/millennials_just_dont_get_it_how_the_muppets_created_generation_x/, accessed March 25, 2019.

8. Stevens, "Millennials Just Don't Get It."

9. Stevens, "Millennials Just Don't Get It."

10. Stevens, "Millennials Just Don't Get It."

11. "The Muppets Present Great Moments in American History—Full Declaration Show at Magic Kingdom," YouTube, October 2, 2016, https://www.youtube.com/watch?v=dZONJvKEtvY, accessed March 15, 2019.

12. "The Muppets Present Great Moments in American History."

13. Lesley Kinzel, "The Passion of Miss Piggy: We Need More Multi-Dimensional Fat Women Characters in Film and TV," *Lesley Was Here* (blog), March 3, 2016, http://www.lesleykinzel.com/the-passion-of-miss-piggy-we-need-more-multi-dimensional-fat-women-characters-in-film-and-tv/, accessed March 26, 2019.

14. Harris, Aisha, "An Interview with Miss Piggy about How She Decided to Call Herself a 'Feminist,'" Slate, June 5, 2015, https://slate.com/culture/2015/06/miss-piggy-declares-herself-a-feminist-while-accepting-sackler-center-first-award-video.html, accessed March 26, 2019.

15. Alyssa Rosenberg, "Why Miss Piggy Is an Unruly Feminist Hero," *Washington Post* Blogs, August 5, 2015, https://advance.lexis.com/api/document?collection=news&id=urn:contentItem:5GM1-8Y01-JB4M-V4MV-00000-00&context=1516831.

16. Rosenberg, "Why Miss Piggy Is an Unruly Feminist Hero."

17. Rosenberg, "Why Miss Piggy Is an Unruly Feminist Hero."

18. "The Muppets Present Great Moments in American History."

19. "The Muppets Present Great Moments in American History."

20. "The Muppets Present Great Moments in American History."

21. "The Muppets Present Great Moments in American History."

22. "The Muppets Present Great Moments in American History—Full Paul Revere Show at Magic Kingdom," YouTube, October 2, 2016, https://www.youtube.com/watch?v=Aef8wiPzMLc, accessed March 15, 2019.

Contributors

Alex Ates is an actor, writer, director, and educator from New Orleans. His writing has appeared in *American Theatre, Backstage, Howlround,* and *Scalawag.* Alex has directed new works in New Orleans, Boston, and Off-Broadway. He is a board member of the American Alliance for Theatre and Education (AATE), editing their publication of practice, *Incite/Insight.* Alex has worked as an artist-educator at Agnes Scott College, Emerson College, Tulane University, and Teachers College, Columbia University. As a graduate student, his teaching methods were featured twice by the University of Alabama's Teaching Hub. In 2019, he was the recipient of SETC's Young Graduate Scholars Award. His website is iAmAlexAtes.com.

Becky K. Becker is the chair of the Department of Performing Arts and a professor of theatre at Clemson University. A director, dramaturg, and playwright, Becky has directed a wide range of established and new works, such as *Compañeras, The Old Ship of Zion,* and *Eddie's Stone Song: Odyssey of the First Pasaquoyan.* She has conceived, written, and directed several documentary plays, including *Westville: Collected Lives* and *Bibb City: Collected Lives from a Mill Town.* Becky is the chair of the National Playwriting Program for Region 4 of the Kennedy Center American College Theatre Festival, serves on the Publications Committee for the Southeastern Theatre Conference (SETC), and was the editor for *Theatre Symposium: A Journal of the Southeastern Theatre Conference,* volumes 24 and 25. Her research interests include new plays, cross-cultural theatre, hidden histories, social justice, and embodied cognition. She has been published in various edited volumes and journals, including *The-*

atre Journal, Feminist Teacher, Review: The Journal of Dramaturgy, and *Theatre Symposium*.

Chase Bringardner, associate editor, is an associate professor of theatre at Auburn University and the chair of Auburn's Department of Theatre. His research interests include regional identity construction and intersections of race, gender, and class in popular performance. He has contributed articles and reviews to publications such as *Theatre Topics, Theatre Journal, Studies in Musical Theatre, Theatre Symposium*, and *Southern Theatre*. He has also published chapters in volumes including *The Oxford Handbook of the American Musical* and, most recently, *Performing Dream Homes: Theater and the Spatial Politics of the Domestic Sphere*. He is the president-elect of the Association for Theatre in Higher Education (ATHE) and has served that organization as a two-term vice president of membership and marketing; in addition, he has been the book review editor for *Theatre Topics*, the vice president of Conference Orlando 2013, and a member of multiple conference committees. He was program chair for the 2018 conference of the American Society for Theatre Research. At Auburn, he works extensively as a director and dramaturg, recently directing *Mr. Burns: A Post Electric Play* and dramaturging, adapting, and directing Hannah Cowley's *The Belle's Stratagem*.

Charlotte M. Canning, keynote speaker, is the Frank C. Erwin Jr. Centennial Professor in Drama at the University of Texas at Austin, where she also serves as the director of the Oscar G. Brockett Center for Theatre History and Criticism. Her books include *On the Performance Front: US Theatre and Internationalism* (winner of the Joe A. Calloway Prize), *Representing the Past: Essays in Performance Historiography, The Most American Thing in America: Circuit Chautauqua as Performance* (recipient of the Barnard Hewitt Award for Outstanding Research in Theatre History), and *Feminist Theaters in the USA: Staging Women's Experience*. She has published in many journals, including *Theatre Topics, Theatre Research International, Theatre Survey, Theatre Journal, Theatre Annual*, and *Theatre and LIT: Literature Interpretation Theory*. Her work has also been included in such anthologies as *Staging International Feminisms, Restaging the Sixties: Radical Theatres and Their Legacies, Women Writing Plays: The New Historiographies*, and *Twentieth Century American Drama and Virtual Gender: Fantasies of Embodied Space and Subjectivity*. Currently, Dr. Canning is coediting an anthology on global feminist performance. Additionally, Dr. Canning is writing a book on the history of theatre in Texas for the University of Texas Press. Her op-eds have appeared in *The Conversation*, the *Washington Post*, *Truthout* and *American Theatre Magazine*.

Andrew Gibb, editor, is Head of History, Theory, and Criticism in the School of Theatre and Dance at Texas Tech University. He is the author of *Californios, Anglos, and the Performance of Oligarchy in the U.S. West*. He has published work in *Theatre Symposium*, *Theatre History Studies*, the *Latin American Theatre Review*, and the *Texas Theatre Journal*.

Sarah McCarroll is an associate professor of theatre at Georgia Southern University, where she is also the resident costume designer and costume shop manager. She is a member of the faculty of the Center for Irish Research and Teaching at GSU. Her published scholarship appears in *Theatre Symposium* and in the anthology *Theatre, Performance and Cognition: Languages, Bodies and Ecologies*, and she is currently at work on a manuscript theorizing the relationship between stage costume and the body. She is the immediate past editor of *Theatre Symposium* and is the chair of SETC's History, Theory, Criticism, and Literature committee. Sarah's professional home for more than a decade has been the Utah Shakespeare Festival, where she has been a dramaturg, draper, first hand, and wardrobe supervisor.

David S. Thompson is the Annie Louise Harrison Waterman Professor of Theatre at Agnes Scott College. He is a past president of the Southeastern Theatre Conference as well as a former editor of *Theatre Symposium*. In addition to his contributions to SETC publications, his commentaries have been carried by leading newspapers, including the *Wall Street Journal*, *Atlanta Journal-Constitution*, *Baltimore Sun*, and *The Chronicle of Higher Education*; major news services including the New York Times News Service, Knight Ridder, and Scripps Howard; and websites including TheaterMania and the American Council on Education Online Resource Center.

Jennifer Toutant is the Director of Education at Milwaukee Repertory Theater. She began her employment there as the Education Assistant in the 2005–2006 season, and took on the leadership of the department in June of 2006. As the facilitator for the outreach and training programs for the Rep, she designs programming for all ages. Rep Education serves over 20,000 students each year with student matinee programming, in-school arts-integrated residencies, and student-driven community engagement programming. Jennifer is also an associate lecturer at the University of Wisconsin–Milwaukee. She has also taught for the University of Wisconsin–Parkside, Virginia Commonwealth University, First Stage Children's Theater, and School of Performing Arts in the Richmond Community.

Shadow Zimmerman is a doctoral student at the University of Washington School of Drama. He has a BA in Theater and Ancient Studies from St. Olaf College and an MA in Theater Arts from UC Santa Cruz. His publication, a teaching exercise for *Hedda Gabler* in the collection *How to Teach a Play* (edited by Miriam Chirico and Kelly Younger), was released in 2020.